The Family Made of Dust

LAINE CUNNINGHAM

The Family Made of Dust

Published by Sun Dogs Creations
Changing the World One Book at a Time
ISBN: 9781946732576

Cover by: Angel Leya

Winner of the

JAMES JONES LITERARY SOCIETY FELLOWSHIP

and the

HACKNEY LITERARY AWARD

Supported by:

Cornucopia Arts Center Residency
New York Mills Regional Cultural Center Arts Residency
Jerome Foundation Fellowships

From the very beginning, we are in the hands of an exceptional writer as well as a master storyteller...and it is a rare treat to find both of those things in one place. A seamless package that explores not just the soul of her main character but the soul of a nation and its people. A truly special book.

—Edmund R. Schubert, award-winning author of *Dreaming Creek* and Editor of Tor anthologies

Written by a master storyteller, this fast-paced novel initiates Cunningham into the ranks of respected authors such as Michael Ondaatje and Sarah Gruen. A deeply felt work sure to please.

—Dena Harris, award-winning author

This is not an uptown homicide but one inked with shamanic intrigue and a spiritual battle of the souls.

—Dale Stacy, author, *Diamond in the Rough*

...Characters so real and memorable you won't put this book down. This book will leave its mark as one of the best stories ever to lie in our laps.

—Pamela King Cable, author, ALA's 2012 Top Fiction Pick *Televenge*

Ranking alongside Pulitzer-Prize winning authors like
William Styron *(Sophie's Choice)*
and Horton Foote *(To Kill a Mockingbird)*

1 The Precious Dead

When a man dies in the desert, he is completely alone. At thirty-nine, Ian McCabe knew this simple fact. He had spent most of his life working the demanding seasonal jobs that kept Australia's rural towns alive. He had seen a flat tire turn deadly, and knew that beauty and danger were the sisters who bore the land.

Ian was not a tall man but a shock of blond hair added inches to his height. Quick blue eyes and a steady aim were useful in his career as a kangaroo culler. Every night the slim .22 found its target between the shine of an animal's eyes. On cattle stations hundreds of kilometers wide, engine trouble and the bite of the brown snake posed constant threats.

Ian's white Land Rover was nearly twenty years old and it still ran like a lizard drinking—non-stop and practically unstoppable. In the rear a skillet, bedroll and a case of green beans were strapped onto narrow shelves. A bottle of port nestled in its own padded compartment, and a few golf clubs were tied to the wall. Sleep, slurp and sport, he called the collection, everything a man could want in one mobile space.

He eased the truck down the track. The spur was rough, really a strip of earth scraped clean of boulders, but it saved nearly half an hour. Besides, the less traveled a road was, the happier Ian felt. Cities, he knew, were for suckers. Why squeeze into a rabbit hutch when the outback was right next door?

This area, so close to the Davenport Ranges, was typical of the Northern Territory. Wide plains of twisted mulga trees reached southwest to Alice Springs. A network of creeks and rivers that ran only during the Wet sustained gum trees taller than most buildings. Cockatoos raised their young in the hollow trunks, and after a rain lorikeets gorged on the nectar in the blossoms.

Grass was sparse, edged out by the ubiquitous spinifex that cut flesh as cruelly as broken glass. Only the toughest creatures survived and half-feral Brahma cattle were the breed of choice. To a rancher beleaguered by drought and debt, every blade eaten by native animals robbed them of beef. Roo shooters were always welcome. And judging by the sun, Ian would arrive at the station house in time for dinner.

A flash of metal caught his eye. Through binoculars, he watched a red SUV beetle across the property. The truck stayed behind the ridges and moved slowly enough to keep its dust cloud low. The same stealth kept Ian from sight as he followed.

Eventually the trespassers parked beside a hill topped by a stone pinnacle. Ian stuffed the Land Rover under a mulga tree and watched as a pair of men hiked up the slope. The first, a sturdy white fellow about thirty years old, clutched a rifle. His legs were bowed so severely he rocked as he mounted the boulders.

The other man, an Aborigine who might have been in his sixties, moved steadily upward. He was wiry yet had the grace of a predator. The outback was filled with men like them, drifters who found the bush far removed from the law.

At the top, the elder found a cleft in the rock. From this cache he retrieved a board nearly as long as his arm. Ian had seen dancers perform with similar objects and knew they were supposed to be magical. The cubby surrendered perhaps a dozen other artifacts. All would fetch a small fortune on the black market.

While the older man worked steadily, the bowlegged bloke couldn't keep a proper watch. First he rubbed his nose with the back of his arm. Then he adjusted his shorts. He scanned the landscape, rifle at ready. Then he swatted a fly. Rubbed sweat through his hair. Tugged at his crotch. Abruptly he was alert again, scowling while the gun grew hot in the sun.

As they retreated, the Aborigine erased his footprints with a leafy branch. Ian let the SUV jangle out of sight before picking up the trail. They traveled faster now and corkscrewed across their original path. Where the spur intersected a paved road dusty tread marks headed toward the Stuart Highway, the only paved north-south road through the Territory. The pair could pick from dozens of unmarked byways. The artifacts would disappear.

Ian pushed the Land Rover to its limit. Although the old truck handled beautifully in the bush, it was as sluggish as a fly in winter. The needle was still climbing when Ian saw the red SUV parked beside the highway. If he pulled over, the men would surely notice when he followed them later.

The Toyota, a new model free of dents or scrapes, faced the road. The younger man smirked and the lines around his mouth twisted. Again Ian was struck by the elder's expression. White pipe clay severed his forehead and chin, and his face was a jigsaw of violence.

"So you've seen me," Ian murmured, "and I've seen you." He adjusted the rearview mirror but couldn't make out the tag number.

A roadhouse a quarter-hour away was a convenient place to watch for the men but they never appeared. It was possible they had turned east toward the coast. More likely they had dodged off into the bush. As night covered the sky, Ian had plenty of time to consider his next action.

He didn't need a fraction of it. The kangaroos could wait.

Thousands of kilometers to the east, Gabriel Branch loaded the last of his bags into the hatchback. At six feet tall, Gabe barely fit behind the wheel even with the seat pushed all the way back. But the rear compartment was roomy enough to hold all his diving gear, and the hatch was easier to use than a station wagon. He squeezed in and steered for the coastal highway out of Townsville.

The next few days would be spent an hour or so south on the Whitsunday Islands. In the forty-five years Gabe had lived in Queensland, he rarely traveled more than a hundred kilometers inland. The neighbors never quite understood why his vacations didn't take advantage of the expansive desert at their back doors.

They didn't understand the...complications of Gabe's life. Oh, they knew about the Aboriginal land rights issues that had consumed the media for decades, and had heard about the children adopted by white families in a long-defunct effort to assimilate the race. But they didn't know what it was like to be caught by those issues against their will. Only a biracial Aborigine who had been assimilated at the age of three could tell them that. And Gabe wasn't talking.

Nor was he interested in drawing attention. Black faces were scarce in Australia, so he stuck close to the coastal cities that hosted international travelers in all their rainbow colors. He blended in better there and no one asked many questions about his background. Even when they did, they were met with silence.

Silence had kept his life on the smooth, orderly track he worked so hard to create. Last week he had hit a bump—a big bump—in his relationship with a Jamaican woman. Chance hadn't been in the country more than a few years. But she had some definite ideas about how much Gabe should say about his experiences and how loudly his voice should sound.

They had fought about it more of late. He supposed it was the same with all couples, as if money or household chores or work schedules were the cause of their problems instead of a symptom. Whatever the real reason, Gabe and Chance had split up last week. The separation was supposedly temporary, just a little breathing and thinking room, but Gabe knew where that would lead.

If Ian had been available, Gabe would have talked things over with him. In fifteen years of friendship, the men had seen each other through a number of breakups. None had been as serious as this one, though, and Gabe wished Ian would call. He already missed Chance's rapid-fire commentary and her odd machinegun laugh. Before the split, Gabe had been thinking of proposing. But courage in one person required courage in the other. And that, he knew, was the real reason their separation would be permanent.

When Ian did call, Gabe was already out of range. He heard only the clack of sugar cane as he sped past the coastal farms.

Ian tracked the men for days without coming within twenty kilometers of the truck. The outback was so big and its population so small, a little luck and a few calls let him keep tabs on the thieves as they passed through different roadhouses. At a tourist site called Devil's Marbles, a vendor remembered the odd pair and pointed to a faint track heading west.

When he located the Toyota, he parked some distance away and hiked in for a better look. Perhaps a dozen coffins had been removed from crevices in a wadi. The thieves were stealing bodies. Ian trotted back to the Land Rover and gunned the engine, all but honking to make sure they heard as he rattled toward the ridge.

The thieves took the hint. After the Toyota disappeared, Ian walked into the gully to inspect the damage. The coffins, each a cradle for the precious dead, were lined up in the center. Tarps and coils of rope had been left behind, along with cigarette butts and candy wrappers. The urine drying on the cliff face still smelled sharp.

Then Ian spotted the truck tucked under a ledge. It was the same one he had seen leave, he was sure of it. The guano he had noticed days earlier was still smeared on the side window. Yet the culvert had no other entrance except the one he had just walked through.

A bullet spun him off his feet. He heard nothing, not even the echo of the shot, as his shirt soaked in a red tide. The blood was brilliant at first, like the eyes of the metallic starlings that congregated around his boyhood home. He saw the Aborigine kneel beside him as his breath fled past his tongue.

The man was older than he had thought, much older, and carried with him the aura of ancient things. He wore only a string belt, a pair of shorts, and bands on his arms and legs. Tufts of cockatoo feathers framed a radiant face. On his chest a swirl of dots and circles, made hypnotic by his breath, pulled Ian into a galaxy of red.

He was terribly confused. He tried to separate the ringing in his head from his memories. *They ran away,* he thought. He had *seen* them drive across the plateau that drained west of the escarpment, had watched them until they were out of sight. The tire tracks he had crossed floated in his mind. Only one set of tracks, he realized. The truck had never left. How could he have been so wrong?

As if to offer comfort, the elder caressed Ian's forehead. The man's hair, shot with gray, looked nutmeg. It was as if his great age had worn the shine off the strands and leached away the pigment. His eyes were luminous, though, beyond the touch of time. Ian thought of the dingoes that gazed into his spotlight. The dogs always waited, knowing he would leave the kangaroo's heart and liver and kidneys for their feast.

Suddenly he understood. This man was a shaman. Ian had been lured into the culvert just as he had been tricked into speeding down the highway. He smiled and reached up.

"There, now," the man soothed, and flicked his blade across Ian's throat.

2 Aussie Luck

As the earth gathered the blood, Dana Pukatja watched the life force drain from the body like sparks off a candle. He thought of the wattle blossoms that lit the desert every spring, of how the brightest parts of nature were always the shortest lived.

The *piṟanpa,* the Europeans, were a foolish race. They had no concept of the energy that pooled in every rock and stone, every raindrop and river. The force was so strong, men became sick or died when they entered areas like this burial ground.

Dana used ochre and crystals for protection. The dying man had only a wide-brimmed hat and that fabled Aussie luck. His patchwork tan proved that he worked outdoors, and his eyes had the same texture as the two-cent pieces the wind occasionally unearthed. Otherwise he was like all the other *piṟanpa,* sticking their beaks in where they didn't belong.

Shale clattered over the ledge as Dana's partner slid down the hill. Kevin was as useful as a mule and about as bright. But he had lasted four years now, longer than any other drudge. He was strong enough to do the lifting and greedy enough to keep their secrets. He was also white, without kin, and could be disposed of easily.

"I had to finish him." Dana cleaned his knife, a wedge of flint mounted on an ironwood handle. "I told you that gun's not good for much."

"I've taken full-grown roos with a single heart shot. He don't weigh much more."

"You didn't make a heart shot."

Kevin cleared his throat and spat. It was less a dirty habit, Dana knew, than a comment. He ignored the gesture and pulled a tarp from the pile.

"Load the truck," he said. "Then we'll find a place for our visitor."

The Townsville row house was a small but efficient two bedrooms with picture windows that overlooked the ocean. Although the second room had been converted into an office, Gabe spent most of his days on the balcony. From there he could take care of the paperwork generated by his dive boat business and still hear the chatter of palm fronds.

As evening seeped down from the nearby mountains, Gabe set his life in order. Clothes and beach towels had to be washed, voice messages had to be cleared, and the townhouse wanted air after barren days of waiting. He retrieved the mail from a neighbor and sat on the couch. Amid the usual assortment of bills and ads was a box listing Ian's parents in the return address.

The most Ian had ever sent before was a postcard from this or that town. Presents were stored in the truck or at a friend's home until they could be given in person. A box, Gabe knew, was a serious breach of protocol. Ian's normally metronomic handwriting wavered across the front and the plastic leader from a new role of tape was entombed beneath rumpled layers.

He nearly slit his finger in his haste to open the box. Inside lay a stick as long as his hand. Notches were carved along its length and time had worn the edges smooth. Clearly it was a piece of Aboriginal history with a story of its own. But without a note, he had no way to know what it might mean.

Gabe replayed the messages on the answering machine. Ian hadn't called but there was one hang-up. The tape had recorded the usual background rumble of a pub. He wondered if Ian had started to leave a message about the package and had been interrupted.

He emptied the box. Wads of paper from *The Darwin Register* had been used as packing material, and the date on the paper matched the post date. He scanned every sheet to see if Ian had circled some obscure article. He found nothing, and questions haunted him like the call of an owl.

<hr>

Dana marveled at how well the caskets had been preserved. The sides had been rubbed with emu fat and decorated with red ochre and charcoal. Blotches showed where mourners had spilled their own blood, a gesture beyond any value. The stains doubled Dana's fees.

Spirit warriors stirred the earth. If Dana cocked his head, he could hear them chittering among the boulders. Their curses sent shards of wood and quartz into a victim's body, and no doctor could ease the agony. The shaman sang to keep them at bay, and flies beat the taste of death into his mouth.

When everything was packed, the truck's rear door refused to shut. The handle hadn't worked right since the SUV came off the lot. Now the latch plate was bent so badly the gate jammed every time it was used.

As Kevin struggled with the door, Dana covered the corpse's face with its hat. If the ghost couldn't identify the murderer, it couldn't seek revenge. The living person had been trouble enough. Righteous young men always were.

Damn *piranpa,* he thought, always meddling. The *Tjukurpa,* the collection of Aboriginal law and lore they called the Dreamtime, had predicted their arrival. It also said the invaders would one day return to the place of ghosts. Dana hoped to see the vanishing.

Yet he knew that times changed. He, too, had adapted, and thought of the continent as a vast warehouse catalogued by clan lines. Spears, grinding rocks and mummies converted easily to cash, the modern measure of power.

Only Pitjantjatjara sites were safe. Dana would not steal from his own people. Artifacts from other tribes—the Pintupi of the Western Desert, the Yirrkala along the north coast, the Koori in the south—were fair game. By moving between different states and avoiding looted areas for years after a theft, he had eluded serious trouble.

He watched as Kevin stumped over to the corpse. The rifle, a slim .22 that weighed mere pounds, looked as harmless as a lacrosse racket in his massive hand. The excitement of murder without a beating to savor clearly left him dissatisfied. He would drink heavily the rest of the day.

Appetite, Dana mused, without discipline. He turned west and examined the landscape beyond the gap. The tombs were listed with the Aboriginal Heritage Preservation Board and would be examined annually. While the police rarely pursued a relic thief, murder would rank high on their list. The body had to be hidden.

Not far from the ridge stood a cluster of snappy gums. A large snag at the center of the trees sported a perfect hollow. The cavity was high enough to discourage dingoes and as the body decayed, the bones would fall deeper into the trunk.

He led the mule down the slope. Only pituri, a native tobacco, flourished here. Its ivory buds indicated that rain had fallen recently. The spinifex was still dormant so the shower had been brief. *Just enough,* Dana thought. The land and its people had fared well on just enough.

He stepped into the shade that wept from the trees. A flock of galahs, pink cockatoos with gray wings, muttered in the branches. The shaman wasn't surprised that the birds waited. It was their job to escort dead souls to the next world. The buzz of flies grew louder as Kevin arrived, and Dana turned his face from the breeze stirred by their wings.

The young man's hat was gone and his eyes were filmed with dust. In a few hours or a few days the wind would erase the drag marks, just as it rubbed away gullies drawn by snake bellies and mounds pushed up by dingo paws.

When Dana plucked an ant from the man's tongue, he hoped the ghost would remember a small kindness.

The galahs broke through the canopy. Their cries were tin and stone, and their flight scattered the clouds.

Christ, Kevin thought, *what makes a bloke weigh more dead than alive?* The body was a full three stones heavier than it looked. He hoisted the corpse and pinned it against the snag.

"Damn this heat," he grumbled. The flies drank his sweat and left specks of blood on his skin. He wondered when they'd get back to the truck. All this undertaker crap had given him a thirst, and a six-pack waited in the cooler.

He folded the legs and stuffed the body headfirst into the tree. The boots were in good shape, just too damn small to steal. The man's pockets had yielded a few coins and a penknife, so it wasn't a total wash. He snuffed up a gob of snot and spat. Nothing like a hard day's work to make a bloke feel good.

The old man cut a few small branches and sharpened the ends. Kevin feigned interest but he didn't give a dingo's dick. Damn gins were always up to some strange trick or another. So long as Kevin didn't have to sing those fucking songs, the old pantywaist could jerk off with roadkill. He perked up when Dana punched the sticks into the stiff's belly.

"Well, if that don't fuck all," Kevin said. "What're the sticks for?"

"Killing."

"But he's already dead!"

As usual, he laughed alone. He belched and tugged at his hat while Dana tied the corpse's feet to the trunk.

"Why'd you tie him up?" Kevin asked.

"So he can't come after us later."

Should know better than to ask about some black mumbo-jumbo, he thought. All the talk about A-bo-riginal culture was a load of shit. It irritated the hell out of him to work for a darkie but it was good business to keep his mouth shut. Good enough to keep him in beer and whores. And after today's haul, he could buy better beer and prettier whores.

He dragged his boots as he lagged behind. The old man always erased his own footprints so the ghosts couldn't follow them. How such an ignorant Abo could knock down piles of money was beyond him. Probably sells to morons who think the darkies should get back all their land to go along with Parliament's apology.

He hitched up his pants and wriggled around. The jeans had been cut so short his testicles got pinched between the crotch and his thigh. Maybe he'd buy another pair in Katherine. Maybe he'd keep this pair and buy a little speed instead. He broke into a trot and caught up with Dana at the truck.

The shaman drove the Land Rover deeper into the bush and parked it beneath a mulga. The shrub was infested with lerp, insects that excreted a sticky honeydew. As a boy Dana had soaked the branches in water to make a sweet broth or sucked it straight off the twigs. It was one of few pleasant memories.

As Dana circled the Land Rover, he noted how a faded pink golf ball on the antenna had attracted a few lerp nymphs. Flies struggled in the honeydew sprinkled across the hood, and the fenders wore gaiters of dust. Otherwise the truck was clean. The intruder must have picked up their trail soon after leaving a place where he could wash the vehicle.

A driver's license tucked over the visor gave the man a name. A dram of his spirit hung in the photo like the heat of sunlight lingering on skin. When Dana checked the glove box, culling tags announced the man's job. Katherine was the closest place to turn in kangaroo carcasses but the tags had been issued in Darwin. Had they really lost McCabe that day, he wondered, or had Ian followed them north?

Dana found a wad of bills under the dash and shucked off half for the mule. The rear compartment held a wooden box full of ammunition cans, a gun-cleaning kit and a semicircular blade. He recognized it as an *ulu*, a knife used by North American Inuit to slice whale and seal skin. An uncommon tool for a roo shooter. But then, most roo shooters couldn't track anything less obvious than a blood trail.

They torched the truck and drove to a cairn nearly hidden beneath a hummock of grass. The artifact was nothing more than a few stones stacked in a particular way and was meant to warn people away from the burial ground. It was the perfect addition to the haul. The buyer Dana had in mind would nail tripe to his wall if he thought it was sacred.

His smirk disappeared as the latch plate gashed his finger. The song wavered. Launching from a nearby tree, a single galah gathered light under its wings. Dana reeled as ghosts welled up from the ground and his palms filled with lush, silken air.

Leaning on the bumper, the shaman began the chant again. The galah spiraled up to a pinpoint, red and gray, fire and wind. When the spirit warriors sank back under the earth, Dana climbed into the cab.

"You Abos got a chant for everything," Kevin smirked.

Only when the mule was drunk did he dare to stare. Otherwise he caught a peculiar light in the sorcerer's eyes. It was the light of his nightmares, worse than the nip of cockroach feet when the DTs arrived. He shied and slammed the truck into gear.

The return trip would take longer as they looped back over their trail to confuse any ghosts or men who might follow. Near the highway, Dana would bury the headband and feathers. Sandals and a vest would replace the ochre and pipe clay, and the sorcerer would take his first meal in three days. Among the city's anonymous black faces, he would be invisible.

In the side mirror, the wadi seemed like a nice place for a cup of tea, maybe even a picnic with the kids. Kevin had no idea how close they had come to joining the dead man. One day Dana would leave the mule to the spirits, perhaps one day soon.

He smiled. The song never wavered.

3 The Healing

Parents don't expect to bury their children. Gabe drove north along the Bruce Highway with that single thought weighing the back of his skull. He barely noticed the mountains to his left or the clarity of the air over the ocean.

It was one of those rare days when the water was the iridescent blue of reef sharks. The air was drenched with the smell of kelp and scrubbed sand, and sunlight shattered on the waves. The country was beautiful, as always, and it nearly blinded him.

He brushed away tears. In the weeks since Ian had disappeared, Gabe had been unable to read the sea. The beacons that preceded sun and storm, usually so transparent, were garbled. All he knew for certain was that a change stole further up the shore every day. And like tides that left curious gifts, the change brought an arcane knowledge he could not yet grasp.

For long evenings he had watched the rollers, deciding at every moment to look for his friend then sitting on the balcony until dawn found him still in town. It wasn't that he couldn't make such a difficult trip. So far, he had avoided the fallow spread that plagued most men his age. But some terrible thread had cinched up his spine until he was as rigid as the wicker chair. And so he sat, hours heaping up unnoticed beside him, counting the tides and keeping a lid on his emotions.

Dob, Ian's father, called every day. The phone always rang at two minutes past seven, two minutes past the last chance to hear from the missing persons unit. The news was always the same—no news—yet the men drew strength from sharing the silence. When Dob finally asked him to go into the outback, Gabe stayed up half the night preparing for the trip.

He remembered meeting Ian, who had not yet turned thirty, at a wildlife park. The young man fed bloody beef to dingoes, tempted crocodiles with dead chickens, and kept up a patter that was part history, part bull, and all easy charm. He made adults laugh and schoolgirls swoon while standing a skip away from predators. Now Gabe had to find him in a vast desert among those same animals.

He slowed as he approached Cairns. Even this close to the city, fields of sugarcane originally planted with forced labor covered the coast. Chance had told him about the Pacific Islander slaves. She had told him a lot of things, sprinkling their dinners with history and recounting myths on their strolls. He had never gotten around to asking how she knew so much about a country that wasn't her own.

She had left messages offering her prayers for Ian and his family, along with invitations for Gabe to call. They could still be friends, he knew; she was strong enough to care for him even though they weren't lovers. He wouldn't call her just yet. There would be time enough for that while he was on the road. Besides, he'd probably need an encouraging voice to help him through this journey.

He wound through the suburbs to a cottage framed by freestanding trellises. Fuchsia knotted every inch of lattice, and pansies corralled by driftwood splashed across the lawn. Against this background, Dob seemed gray and drained. He waited on the sidewalk with both hands squeezed over a cane and made no move as Gabe parked on the street.

Once taller than his son, pushing barrels of salted fish around a warehouse had compressed Dob's spine. Early retirement had turned into a second career carving birds and bush animals. He had always been able to make a go of whatever life dealt him. But recently he had lost a lot of weight.

"Chances are slim that you'll find him," Dob said as Gabe got out. "Search planes have flown over but a pilot won't find piss in a bright orange pot. We just need to know, is all. We need to know *something*."

They walked up the drive and met Rosie at the front door. She was a tiny woman with bones that caught the edges of the wind. He held her, bent under the shadows of the fuchsia, until she could take a breath without crying. They passed through a living room animated by Dob's carvings and sat in the kitchen.

He ate what they put before him. The soup, Rosie's own recipe of garden vegetables, basil and heavy cream, had been thawed out to go with the sandwiches. The meal was far different than the meat pies and cakes she usually prepared.

Rosie was giving up on the things that brought her pleasure. Suddenly Gabe wasn't sure he could do what they wanted. He chatted about the news and the weather and every other trifle that had no bearing on the emptiness brushing against their knees. As they got up from the table, Gabe saw that neither of the McCabes had touched their food.

Even after forty-odd years in the same city, Gabe's life had been parceled out in chores and favors in a matter of hours. A neighbor to watch the house, a hold on the newspaper, a trusted employee to run the dive boat had freed him for an undetermined time. *How quickly we fade,* he thought. Maybe that's why people raised families, so they would leave something behind.

He wrangled the tan Land Rover along the Gulf Development Road. The SUV had carried Ian into the outback when he was three days old. Dob had kept the vehicle in perfect condition in case his son needed it. If only the need hadn't been so dire.

The truck and everything in it were grim reminders of Gabe's goal. When he had left Cairns, Rosie had covered his hand with her own. Her fingers trembled like paper in the heat rising from his palm. She started to speak then sighed.

"Call us, won't you?" she said as her smile squeezed out more tears.

The McCabes wanted so much for him to find their son. And the words Rosie had not been able to say were hidden in Dob's final command. *Call us, no matter what.*

And so Gabe turned down every detour and climbed every hill along Ian's known path. After a short stint on the Burke Highway, he wandered along spurs made of earth and tread marks. Explorers and cattlemen had branded places with names like Blackbull, Donner's Hill, Warren Vale and Highland Plains. Ragged paths led to Mittagong and Kaileroi and Undilla, sounds heavy with Aboriginal history.

The region was a transition zone between the coastal estuaries and the interior. Past the Carrarra Range, the eucalyptus forests faded into plains dominated by mouse and hawk. Ian had taken him camping there once. Gabe had felt nervous with the sky shy of trees and the grass, heavy with seed, that tapped his belly.

He smoothed his scalp. The severe clip he favored had grown out enough to curl. According to his female friends, the soft tousle had made him fetching in his younger years. The style didn't seem appropriate on a man leaving middle age.

As tiresome as propriety could be, Gabe was a stickler for following the rules—even the unspoken rules—that governed society. *Especially* the unspoken rules. There was a benefit, he knew, in blending in. It let him live a quiet life where the bumps were not so savage.

Around the next curve, a roadhouse had staggered into a clearing. The walls bulged under the weight of the roof and flattened petrol drums had been nailed over the windows. Candy wrappers tangled in a thin line of scrub around the parking lot, and beer bottles fossilized in the earth. Hardly Gabe's first choice for a rest. But Ian might have stopped there, so he pulled in.

The road hadn't carried a dozen vehicles all morning but at least that many nosed the building. A powder-blue sedan that burped steam seemed out of place amid the SUVs. A young Aborigine had squeezed into the shade cast by the car. His smile was animated, as if they were neighbors passing at the grocers, and he flapped a soda can in greeting.

Inside the pub, an ailing window unit and ceiling fans jostled the air. Tables scavenged from cafes teetered around an old blackjack table. In the corner, a group of men wore crusher hats and gumboots and glittering eyes. They reminded Gabe of the dingoes at the wildlife park, predators whose instincts starved on carcass meat.

He turned to the bulletin board. Nearly every pub and hotel had one, and travelers tracked each other along the cork highway. Gabe made room for his flier among ads for cattle stations, last year's camel race, hostels and hotels. A photo of Ian's face, a picture of his truck, and a list of his last known locations condensed all of his and Dob's and Rosie's feelings into shades of black and gray.

He crossed to the phone booth but Dob's line was busy. A conversation with his own mother was brief, just enough to convince her he was fine. When Dob's line was still busy, he thought a beer might help him face the heat. A woman brought a can from the cooler and left the smell of lemons and a spike of ammonia around the lip.

Next to Gabe sat a mechanic whose shirt was stained with oil and a butcher with old blood on his jeans. Whenever they moved, the smell of bread and fermenting potatoes wafted over the bar. Teeth marbled with nicotine leaned from the butcher's mouth as he smirked at Gabe. "Passing through, are ya?" he asked.

"I'm looking for a friend. I'll just use the phone and be off."

"No hurry. We just like to talk, see? We talk to everyone. Where you from?"

"Townsville."

"Didn't know there were tribes in the city," the mechanic said. "Way I hear it, you Abos don't like living in proper houses."

"Watch it," the butcher said. "They don't like being called Abos."

"Right. Abo-riginal, ain't it?"

"Aborigines. They like to be called Aborigines."

Gabe held a sip of beer in his mouth. He could still smell decay.

"Hey, he don't mean nothing," the butcher said. "Go on, show him you don't mean nothing. Tell him a joke."

"Know why they call Abos boongs?" the mechanic asked. "Because that's the sound you hear when they bounce off your fender. Get it? It vibrates when you hit 'em 'cause you hit 'em so hard. It makes that noise, *boong.*"

Gabe walked away. His legs were as stiff as if his tendons were threaded through bamboo. The call could be made from a different roadhouse, one far from this grimy place.

———

"Boong," the butcher hummed. *"Boong!"*

The mechanic guzzled the untouched beer. He noticed the wiry black man who rose from a booth the way a dog notices a fly before snapping its jaws around the pest. The old man left a few bills on the table to pay for his meal then shucked off extra money for his white friend. *Ain't that the way it is,* thought the mechanic. *Always got their hands out when they're sitting on a wad of welfare money.*

The butcher smiled when the newcomer sat next to him. "Say, your best mate just left."

"Not my friend," the elder said. "What did he want?"

"Looking for someone. I thought he was with you, seeing as you're both Abos."

"Yeah, we all know each other." The light shifted along his cheekbones. The skin was taught there and streamed into chalky sachets under each eye. "Did he find what he was looking for?"

"Naw. Must've heard a good tip, though, 'cause he left in a hurry."

The old man's eyes were luminous. The mechanic blinked then blinked again. Each time it seemed the Aborigine flew straight up to hover over his head. His thoughts pleated one against the other until he couldn't decide whether to fight or run.

"You fellows work at Nedermeyer's, is that right?" the elder asked.

"You know old Neddy?" The butcher chattered on, obviously unaware of his friend's predicament.

"Know his name," the elder said, "seen him around. Never met him."

"Oh, you'll want to keep clear of him. Right bastard, he is. Tells a million jokes and ain't one of 'em funny. Like this one. Know why they call Abos boongs?"

He choked as a knife probed his crotch.

"Sorry. I've heard that one."

The butcher hiccupped as sweat gathered under his lashes. His face scrunched up the way a boy's might when he wants desperately to scratch his balls in front of his mother. The mechanic stared but dared not annoy the phantom bird flapping at the edge of his vision.

"You seem like you're not feeling well." The old man massaged the back of the butcher's neck. Their heads were inches apart. "All that hate can't be good for you. I'll let a little of it out. Don't move, now. I might slip."

The butcher yelped as the blade pierced his skin. The tip found a vein and fresh blood fused with the stains.

"Christ." The mechanic gripped the bar.

"Almost done," the elder crooned. Finally he tugged the point free and tapped the wet spot with his knife. "That's what made you say those things. It stuffed up your head, you see?"

The shaman's hand slid down his spine, the touch as mild as a mother's kiss. The mechanic smelled urine but couldn't bear to look down. Instead he looked at the butcher and blushed. His face betrayed the sweet, sweet comfort he felt as his water pooled between his buttocks.

"Don't let me catch you telling those jokes again," the old man said. "Not after the work I've done."

"Christ." The coppery smell stretched the mechanic's brain. He clenched his thighs.

"That's some powerful magic I worked on you. Usually I get paid for a healing."

The mechanic emptied his wallet. The butcher shook so hard sweat rained from his jaw but he didn't move. His friend dipped two fingers into his shirt pocket and added more bills to the stack.

The Aborigine waved for his companion and grabbed the flier on the way out. No one except the men at the bar heard the door bang shut. The butcher grabbed his crotch. The mechanic opened his mouth, shut it, and swiped his cheeks. "Christ on high," he said.

By the time the butcher went to the men's room, the blood would be silt. The mechanic, however, would forever dream of a dark bird tearing out his eyes.

4 Rescue

Barbed wire. Gabe never knew there could be so much barbed wire in the world. Thistles of it bloomed on vines that subdivided the land and segregated the animals. Cattle stretched their necks through to graze on the sweet grass beside the roads while dingoes slipped under its span. Man was the only species truly excluded.

Ravens adored the fences. Bathed in the mercury sun, their beaks were as glossy as the wire and as keen. The birds attended every one of Gabe's stops. A short visit to a pub or hostel found at least one waiting atop the Land Rover when he emerged. They queued up around his campsite to fight for scraps and stalked him while he drove.

At that moment, he was aware of them only peripherally. He'd heard the joke a dozen ways on dozens of days. *Of all the things you'll hit on an outback road, the only one ya speed up for is a boong. Hit 'em so hard, the roo bar breaks. Hit 'em so hard, the fender shakes. It makes that sound.*

Ammonia burned high in his throat. As hot as it was, he wanted nothing more than a nice cup of tea. A canteen filled with rainwater rolled clouds and thunder and the faraway taste of leaves into his belly. He let it cool his anger, condensing and congealing the emotions until they slipped down into his gut. Confrontation had never been his style and he wasn't about to get into trouble now. Not with Ian's life riding on the outcome.

Turning west on the Barkly Highway, he coaxed the truck into a rattling canter. He wedged the canteen between a loaf of bread and the transmission hump, and patted the maps stacked on the passenger's seat. Having everything within reach meant he didn't have to make unnecessary stops. Every minute saved might give Ian another year.

He focused on that idea as he shoved a tape into the deck. Eventually the barbed wire surrendered to distance and the ravens danced in the trees. He pushed his thoughts into a tiny box, and for a time he heard only the music.

～～～

The sun had crossed its midpoint when Gabe turned south on the Stuart Highway. He pushed the visor across the side window and wondered what the skin cancer rates were for middle-aged biracial men with a lifetime of exposure. All those years he'd waded in the ocean, burning the tender skin under his eyes, he'd worried only about jellyfish and sea snakes. What was youth without the careless surety of your own immortality?

Now he was lucky to get through a plate of prawns without worrying how it might affect his prostate. He considered turning back to the nearest town to load up on canned veggies, maybe a few pounds of instant rice. But he hadn't time to spare for mundane chores like shopping or cooking. Every sweep of the sun across the sky, every refueling devoured another slice of the clock.

He shifted in his seat. His hips ached from sitting so long and his neck hurt. Whenever the truck hit a bump he ducked to keep his head from banging the roof. The crumbling road shook alignments out of true, broke shocks two at a time, and burst tires with friction and distance and heat. Even when Gabe drove down the middle, he couldn't avoid cracks made when the freezing desert nights boiled away every morning.

The landscape was tortured by the same forces. Khaki saltbush reminded him of parasitic fish that drained the color from the land for their own dull leaves. Long stretches passed empty of anything except the shells of abandoned cars. To Gabe, the Central region looked like a third-world country that had been bombed by its own government.

Ian lived in this region, in the wild spaces between outposts. Thanks to their friendship, Gabe knew the cockatoo and the corella. He had watched the morning sky flush like the skin of a newborn then turn cyanotic at night. He could taste the depth of a canteen filled from a billabong's sweet, green face. But he knew these things with Ian. Without him, the miracles were witchery.

He jumped as the glove box popped open for the fourth time that day. It was one of the truck's many quirks, and he twisted the knob firmly. As he settled back into his seat, a blaze-red SUV materialized beside him. He slowed only to have the other vehicle match his pace. Squinting against the glare, Gabe sped up as the space between them narrowed.

With a blast of the horn, the driver cut him off. The water jugs hit the back of his seat as the Land Rover went into a skid. Diesel and the burnt-sugar smell of oil filled the cab as the old truck flipped off the highway. He glimpsed a white face and a blur like the wake around a shark's kill. Then there was only the anvil of earth, the ice-glazed sun, and a single ironwood tree that might halt his tumble.

"Hey, mate, you all right?"

Gabe squinted into a world fractured by the windshield. Grit pinched the folds of his right eyelid when he opened both eyes. He didn't need that one, anyway. With the truck on its side, he could see only the window post and the dust that pillowed his head. Gumboots scuffed down to bare leather moved into view.

"Mate?"

When Gabe looked up, he saw his father's wide forehead and heavy cheekbones layered over a young man's face. Then the ghost was gone, a dream that vaporized in the heat.

The soda-pop scent of antifreeze blew into the cab. A beetle explored the earth a few inches from his nose and a jug dripped water onto his arm. He opened his right eye to check the beetle's progress but felt no need to address the other discomforts. "Fine," he whispered. "Just great."

"Right. Let's get you out of there. Seems you've banged your head."

The tick of the engine carried Gabe back through the years into the sighing earth. Voices, laughter and the call of the crested pigeon hung in the darkness. Hands fumbled at the seatbelt, there was a click, and his hips slid toward the door. The day was so bright, he wondered that meteors did not scream overhead.

"Come on then, up you go."

The familiar stranger helped him climb up and out. The young man's hair was mat and wavy, and fell below his shoulders. Swatches the color of tarnished brass braced his face. Gabe's father had worn his hair like that, roughly parted and only half tamed by comb or band. *No, not my father,* he thought. *Some other man from my childhood.*

In the hottest part of the day, he remembered, the men gathered in the shade to share a meal. The round-faced man, his uncle, would throw him up over a branch and call him Little Breeze. "Look, the wind is in the trees," he would grin. Then he would pretend to move on, leaving Gabe stranded and laughing among the leaves.

"You with me?" the young man asked.

"Yes. Just...dazed, I expect."

He leaned on the hood of the sedan, the same sky-blue Ford that had broken down at the pub. The car clearly carried plenty of mileage. But the tires were new, the windscreen didn't have a scratch on it, and it had covered the terrain out to the wreck well enough. Gabe spat blood and broken glass then pulled long draughts from the stranger's canteen.

"I'll run you into the hospital at Tennant Creek." He wiped Gabe's face with a towel then handed him another to hold over the cut. "We'll patch you up, patch up your utility truck, and you'll be off in no time."

"I'm going south. I have to take care of some things."

"Only thing you gotta take care of is that cut. She'll need stitches."

Warm drops fell into Gabe's palm. He thought of Ian's poster, of the truck flaring beside him. His brain woke up enough to set his hands shaking. "A couple of ranch hands ran me off the road. I can catch them if I head south."

"Not in that truck, you won't. How about I take you down to Alice Springs? They've a hospital there, and me friend can fix your truck. Meantime we'll see if we can catch those bastards." He slapped the hood. "We'll be in Alice before you can say 'two jackaroos had too much booze!' Name's Rob, by the way."

Gabe looked at the young man. Rob wasn't as dark as he'd first thought. Instead he was a calliope of harvest hues, plum in the shadows and amethyst in the light. His eyes were the powdery rust of moth wings and rustled without being anxious.

"I'm Gabe." He tried to walk and felt dizzy. "Two jackaroos—"

"And we'll be home before you're through!"

Rob helped him into the car. The interior might have been navy once but decades of sun had parched the vinyl to a thin green. Sisal mats had replaced the carpet, and the firewall was painted a glossy shade of blue. As Gabe sat, the cushion crackled.

"Springs are shot," Rob said, "so I stuffed the cushions with gum leaves. Now I can smell the bush no matter where I go!"

It would, Gabe realized, be a long ride.

***

After settling behind the wheel, Rob had mounted a royal blue baseball cap low on his forehead. The fabric was frayed yet spotless, and the bill was outlandishly long. A patch in the shape of a Vegemite jar was sewn to the front. It was the perfect compliment to the young man's personality. He had a story for every stretch of road and every story involved one of his relatives, each of whom was more outlandish than the last.

Gabe let the words carry him back into the world. He fished a chunk of glass from the corner of his mouth and watched it split the light. There were no thoughts in his mind, only an odd sheen to the world and crisis in his soul.

At every roadhouse, Rob slowed to search for the thugs. By the time they reached Barrow Creek the shakes had receded but there was no sign of the racists.

"Red truck, hey?" Rob's eyes locked on the road. "You might be in luck."

The Falcon surged forward. Far ahead, a smudge grew like a mite filling with blood.

"No." Gabe stared at the bed. "It was newer. A utility truck, I'm sure, not a flatbed or one with a cap."

Rob breezed by. They cruised every pub and gas station, parking bay and pit toilet. Gabe pointed out a gray Subaru that looked similar to the vehicle they sought. Then they flew the highway with the skim of tires the only music.

Billboards assaulted them as they drew closer to Alice Springs. *Take a camel to lunch!* read one but its star had faded to a lurid orange. Another drawing showed a spear-wielding Aborigine balanced on one leg. Gabe read every ad then blinked to excise it from his memory.

Instead he remembered the land. For the first time since starting this trip, he let his thoughts steep in the desert. The Central region was Australia's red heart but many colors rippled in its flesh. There was the sulfuric tinge of boulders shedding their rinds, the purple of sandstone like engorged beef, dead-white saltpans and the sepia fringe around a rock pool. The outback wore many colors, as did the people who bathed in her dust.

Eventually the low outliers of the MacDonnell Ranges appeared. With its year-round tourist trade, the Alice would not be an easy place to track down a single truck. Gabe thought about that face, the gash of its mouth. He thought of his uncle, and of how the bustard's bronze feathers had matched his skin. He looked at Rob and wondered what kind of man would rescue another.

"How you doing, mate?" the young man asked. "Looks like we won't find that truck today."

Gabe twisted the side mirror around to check under the compress. The wound started at his eyebrow and touched the edge of his scalp. His hairline had receded in the last ten years, curving high up on either side but the bold point looked good on his long face. Or it had, anyway.

"I suppose it will scar," he sighed.

"No worries! The sheilas like scars. Makes ya look like a spy or a secret military agent."

Gabe studied his new ally. The young man was and wasn't his memory. His uncle had been the same age and his limbs had also snapped like saplings. But Rob was here, aligning himself with a person he had just met. The man of Gabe's past was lost to dust and time.

5 Message Stick

Among the gentle hills, eucalyptus trees spread a blue-green fever. Their European names were facile—bloodwood for the trees with crimson sap, ironwood for the ones that broke the settler's ax, river peppermint for the scent of another.

Aborigines knew the trees more intimately. They chewed the resin and ate the galls. Wood ash strengthen the nicotine in pituri, and seed capsules became hair beads. Even the grubs found at their roots had different names than the grubs found on the branches.

Names were important. In the *Tjukurpa,* the ancestors created things by calling out their names. In that single act the flower bloomed, the lizard ran, water flowed. Where the creators made camp, a sacred energy called *djang* pooled in the earth. In these places men initiated boys and women bore children. Ceremonies made the tribes strong and brought the prospering rains.

On one patch of sacred ground stood a ghost gum with powdery white bark. The tree's roots drank the *djang* and its limbs twined with the stars. The effort of a whole tribe hadn't enough power to stir the spirits like the rustle of a single leaf. The people sang and danced and carved symbols in the bark. And when the time came, they lay their dead beneath its boughs.

Bush cherry branches and gum leaves were heaped atop embers surrounding the bodies. As fat dripped from their arms and faces and thighs, the dead shrank. At night the women's sorrow mingled with the soot. Each day men cut their arms and thighs to let out their bloody sorrow. The scars would witness their grief the whole of their lives.

After four days the fires were allowed to die. The bodies were hung in the tree and the souls flew up the trunk to join the sky spirits. After Raven had sought out every scrap and Ant had taken its fill, the relatives returned to gather the bones.

Generations offered their dead, carved new symbols and sang the eternal songs. Each Wet, mourners saw the spinifex flowers flush the blanched yellow of early stars. Each Dry season the ground was brittle and ember-hot as they carried corpses to the tree. And as the lights appeared in the sky, the living knew their ancestors were home.

That was all well and good, Dana knew. Now a different kind of work had to be done. He wrapped one leg around the trunk and swung the chainsaw in front of him. The carvings were rimmed in black like the lips of a lamb. Near his foot a series of circles, pools that had gathered a thousand rains, represented the campsites of the creators. A single figure with a halo of wavy lines floated near his toe.

The value of the grouping was incalculable, as were most things of the spirit. Another branch joined the leafy berm on the ground. The shaman sang continuously, both with his voice and deep in his soul. Even when the chainsaw drowned out his words, the spirits knew what lay in his heart.

As he worked, he kept an eye on his shadow. It lay close to the tree, safe from the mule's hooves. Tricky things, those shades. They floated and shifted throughout the day, silent and unnoticed until some whimsy immortalized their afternoon shapes. Yet they were the world atop the world and lived in the space between tangible and phantom.

They also held secrets a sorcerer could read. Some shadows would strangle their masters if only the men would lay atop them for a midday snooze. Kevin had such a shadow. It was thick and jerked with every step, trying to break free. It yearned for independence, days to fly the clouds and nights to ride lightning. Instead it was tied to a man who wouldn't startle if his rutting bed broke through the floor.

Dana remembered the first time he had seen Kevin and his shade. The mule had been outclassed by other men at the pool table but beer and brawn had a way of overriding common sense. He splashed the trickle of his pay across the table and touched the fifty-dollar notes as if they were millions. Urgency flaked off him like mange.

He was motivated by a desire the shaman could feed. As the sorcerer stepped up to the table, the fluorescent light stretched color into the carnal realm. The shades, bent by the artificial light, were sharp and misleading. But Kevin's phantom smelted all the iron of his soul into angles and flat planes. A shadow to beware. Possibly a shadow of some use.

Thus had begun Kevin's lucrative career in international commerce. For the spirit tree, Dana had also enlisted the help of the rancher who ran the property. Like some other pastoralists who were upset that sticks and stones fetched more money than beef and mutton, the man was happy to pocket a little cash to look the other way.

No matter their color, many a man who spent his blood on cattle turned *piranpa* when drought lived for decades and livestock died by the hundreds.

The ranchers did nothing more than answer a phone call, and the artifacts were untraceable. Everyone turned a profit. Especially Dana.

Despite its beautiful name, Alice Springs had been built on broken promises. The Todd River remained dry most of the year. The gold fields didn't contain much gold, the ruby fields yielded only garnet, and the railway took forty years to connect from Adelaide. Only a water hole produced as planned, and by 1929 the population had grown to thirty souls.

Times changed. Tourism and a paved highway turned promise into prosperity. Modern shopping plazas filled the flats, galleries grew alongside import stores, and an airfield whisked visitors from coastal high-rises to the outback hills. In the growing suburbs, Rob parked beside a trim house with whitewashed panels. Kidney-shaped islands gathered blue-green shocks of oat grass near the house while mint bush and sundew bordered the street.

In the shade of a coolibah tree, an elderly man clapped rhythmically. His square beard was immaculate and his hair was combed into a neat puff. A woman a few years younger than Rob danced on the grass. Her hair was teased in all directions, and she wore feathers above her elbows and knees. Gabe could have watched her all day.

"That's Uncle Angus and me sister, Selena." Rob stored his cap above the visor. "Angus might be able to help you but ignore Selena. She's quite mad."

Gabe's shoulder complained when he opened the door. A twinge went through his back and he leaned against the car until his legs loosened. When the clapping stopped, Selena skipped over to pull her brother and his guest into whirlwind hugs. Gabe smelled shampoo and the lilac soap sweat lifted from her skin.

She took Gabe's hand and the trio crossed to where Angus waited. His muscles, though lax, remembered days of labor. Iron-grey hairs steamed from beneath his collar and his eyes were the silver of clouds. The wind, Gabe realized. The wind moved through this man.

"What's your name?" Selena asked.

"Gabe. Gabriel Branch."

"Like the archangel?"

"Not exactly. My mother just fancied the name. Her grandfather's, I think."

"Why do you use Gabe? Gabriel is much more grand."

"Selena talked the leg off an iron pot once." Rob winked and flopped down on the grass. "Uncle, Gabe's from Townsville."

Everything about the elder felt settled and gentle. Even his niece grew quiet as he spoke. "Queensland," he said. "What's your skin? What tribe are you from?"

"I don't know."

"Stolen?"

Gabe winced. How he hated that word, its sibilant start, the exploding "t," the undertone of shame. And he hated that the media had slapped the phrase "Stolen Generation" onto thousands of biracial children the government had forced into mainstream society. Many had languished in missionaries and orphanages, abused by their keepers and beaten clear of their culture. Gabe had been one of the few to be adopted.

"The welfare took me when I was three," he said. "I was held at the Central Brethren's Mission before they shipped me north."

"That was near here," Angus said. "Welcome home!"

A woman bearing a tray of mugs joined them. She was about ten years older than Gabe with a trim figure that predicted how gracefully Selena would age. She had her daughter's large eyes and delicate jaw, the same long fingers and nimble movement. Her hair was captured in a tight roll and a crease had been pressed into her linen shorts.

"I'm Matty," she said. "Did I hear properly? You're from the Alice?"

"I was born near here then spent time in one of the orphanages."

"You're young enough to have been among the last children taken." She offered Gabe a cup of tea, insisted he take a few cookies, and handed Angus a napkin filled with sweets. "There weren't too many group homes left by then. It shouldn't be hard to find your folks."

"Oh, no. I mean, I'm not here to find my family. I'm looking for a friend who disappeared from this region."

She poured cream in a thin, precise stream. "What's my boy got to do with this?"

Gabe recited Ian's last known activities, his days of travel, the accident and the rescue. At some point Matty brought gauze and medical tape from the house to dress his wound.

"A black man alone in those places...." She shook her head. "Things still happen when nobody's looking, you know. You should be more careful."

"Thank you, Matty. For the nursing and your concern. I'll file a report first thing in the morning."

"Police don't much care unless you're a tourist."

"Aw, mum, they aren't all bad," Rob said.

"The ones who picked up your brother were bad. Having a few drinks shouldn't cost a young man his life. He went walking and never saw the sun again." She gathered up the tray, spilling the cream as she returned to the house.

"Me brother died in custody some years back," Rob said. "She was just getting over dad's death when it happened. Officially Mike was already banged up when they took him in. That's what they always say when an Aborigine dies inside. Kicked to death is what we know for true."

A group of magpies settled high in the tree. One began to sing, a tentative whistle different from the bird's normal warble. Gabe spotted the juvenile perched between its parents. It hadn't occurred to him that a bird might have to learn how to sing.

"The white man's been hard on this land," Angus said, "hard on this people. We all carry his mark. Even my eyes, from bad food and not enough of it. But you've other worries. You say your friend worked the Roper Bar region?"

"Yes. Southwest of the river through the grasslands nearly to Alice. He'd stop here and in Darwin to visit friends, most of them transient like him. They'd hook up for an hour, buy supplies, have a decent meal and be off."

"Roo shooters are a breed of their own," Rob mused. "They still draw a lot of attention, and not all of it good. Some of those greenies don't think wild animals should be managed."

"Shooting roos was the only thing Ian ever took to. During the Wet, he stays with his parents or at my place. About three weeks ago he didn't show at the cattle station where he was scheduled to work. The owners figured roo shooters aren't the most reliable lot and didn't report it. Two weeks went by before anyone knew."

"That lifestyle don't attract blokes who live on a clock, hey?" Rob asked.

"I guess not. He tried regular jobs for a while but every time he'd...I don't know, sort of bloat up inside. He said having to do things a particular way all the time made his brain itch."

"He had to be free!" Selena said.

"He had everything he wanted. Most of his pay went to his folks. He kept enough for petrol and food, bullets and the occasional pint. Anything more was fat, he said."

"You been to that station yet, the place he was supposed to work?" Angus asked.

"I was on my way there before the wreck. The police talked to the station manager but no one noticed anything odd. The only thing that seems to hold any promise is an artifact Ian mailed the week he disappeared." He sighed and shifted on the bench. "The police don't think much of it. I haven't a clue what it is, let alone why he sent it."

"Did you bring it?" Selena asked. When Gabe nodded, she ran to the car and pulled his bag from the back seat. He met her on the walkway.

"You'll ruin your feathers," he said.

"No worries! This is my practice gear. The nice stuff stays packed away until dress rehearsal."

"At least let me help." Gabe took one handle as they walked. "Do you dance for tourists?"

"Naw. I'm with the Warlbrooken Company. I'm dancing in town this weekend. After that we'll be on the road for a while. We're touring some pretty remote regions up north, small towns and tribal camps, sort of like a benefit tour."

Gabe fumbled with the zipper and removed a paper bag, the kind a fish-and-chips shop might use to dispense its greasy meals. Suddenly he wished he had wrapped the artifact in something nice or at least had stored it in a box. For all he knew, the chunk of wood was a sacred relic. He shoved the paper behind the bench.

"It's a message stick!" Selena begged to hold it.

"Leave it be," Angus said. "Might be cursed."

"Who would curse a message stick?"

"Might not be a message stick. Come, let me have it." Uncle and niece wore secret smiles, as if they had played this game before.

"Might be cursed, Uncle."

"I know the old ways. I'll be safe."

His fingers brushed the length of the stick before his palms closed around each end. He rubbed the notches and tested the splintered edge with a nail. Finally he sniffed the wood. "It's a message stick," he said.

Selena's sigh would have blown out birthday candles. Angus couldn't suppress a grin. A few of his teeth were missing, reminders of painful initiation rites the younger generations often rejected. Gabe had no idea whether it was polite to notice such a thing and tried not to stare.

"The notches are a code," Angus said. "I can't read them too well because it's from a northern tribe. I do know it's something to do with death."

"Is it a curse?" This time Selena seemed serious, and Gabe felt a peck at his heart. It was ludicrous, he knew, but his fear for Ian was primal.

"These sticks were sent out like letters," Angus said. "It might announce a birth or invite relatives to a ceremony. When there was a death, the message told who died. Curses are different."

"Lucky for us!" She squeezed onto the end of the bench and threw her arm around Gabe's shoulder. When he looked at her, she gave him a wink. He blushed and tried to follow the elder's words.

"I know a woman from the Yirrkala, a tribe in Kakadu. She lives north of here now, out in the desert. It's a hard drive but Rob can take you there."

"We'll have me friend tow your truck first." Rob stood and stretched. "His garage is on the way and ya won't waste so much time waiting for repairs."

"Selena," Angus said, "go see is the guest room picked up. Your brother will get his friend settled."

She flew across the lawn, her arms waving in wide circles, then bowed to Gabe before dodging inside.

"I told ya," Rob said. "Mad as white ants."

6 Family

The shadows were long when Rob carried the tote bag up to the house. Gabe cradled the message stick. He had clung to this link, hoping it would lead to Ian. Now the artifact seemed translucent to everyone but him.

The single-level home sprawled across the center of the property. Under the eaves hung cobalt blue tiles etched with banksia flowers. Delicate mayflies chiseled from slate buzzed over each window and a marble frog crouched on the knocker plate.

"Stonework was me brother's hobby." Rob held the screen door open. "He did construction for a living. Not a lot of call for it here, so he'd spend half the year in Darwin. Saved every quid for his own company. Wasn't enough time in his life for that, though."

The north end of the house was divided by coveys of pine furniture and Berber rugs. The space glowed yellow. The couch was like a split almond, the walls had been painted a delicate butter cream, and brittle light spilled from the kitchen.

Rob led him down the hall. Gabe glanced in one of the rooms to see a bed covered with jewel-bright shoes. Flats and heels, sandals and slides were basted in vinyl with a single pair of black boots the only concession to somber events. He guessed it was Selena's room.

"Do ya think she moves those shoes every night?" Rob asked. "You should see her pack to go on tour. You'd think she was a born diva!"

He threw open the last door. A window over the driveway ran the length of a narrow bed. A table of curly maple and a matching ladder-back chair took up the opposite wall.

"Selena used to be in here. When I moved she took the larger room. More closet space." He set the bag on the bed. "I'll round up some clothes. You'll fit my shirts, no doubt, and Angus will have pants long enough. I'll fetch the stuff I salvaged today and let you settle in. You'll want a proper wash before dinner."

Gabe was surprised not to have noticed his disarray earlier. He was layered in dust, blood streaked his shirt, and his shorts had collected a number of holes. His sneakers had fared well with only a single oil stain. He started to apologize—for his appearance, for the inconvenience—but Rob was already gone.

He sank onto the bed. Just this morning he had felt a connection. Like the suspension of water between waves, he had felt ready to receive something, a message or clue that would focus his quest. Now the truck was ruined and he was hundreds of kilometers off track. If he took another week to reconnect to that flow, any hope of finding Ian alive would disappear.

***

Kevin rolled logs out of the fall zone and sliced away the carvings. Small pieces went directly into the truck. He had to strap larger pieces into a harness then piss around with a real bastard of a pulley. The system was simple but he hated it. Buckling the artifacts into the harness made him think of those videos with fags who wore chaps and leather underwear. He tasted vomit any time he thought of pansies and their shit-sour breath.

The chainsaw kicked back from a knot and bit into his boot. He flipped the machine in time to save his toe and realized the shaman was watching. Bad enough that the old man never let him drink enough to settle his stomach until the work was through. Now his ration would be cut even more. The old fuck didn't care if the guy doing all the work got hurt.

Damage to the artifacts, however, would cost Kevin a week of sly glances. The old man had a temper, sure as flies liked shit. But he'd never do much to a man's face, oh, no. He was always slinking off to plan some underhanded Abo crap. More goddamn chanting and fairy dances to get him hyped up so he could slip the knife in when some poor sod wasn't looking.

Kevin preferred a more manly approach. Put the boot in then and there, knock a few heads, and no sneaky coward tricks allowed. Just like killing that roo shooter. A single bullet and no fucking worries.

His vision blurred. He remembered how the rifle sights had settled on the man's chest, how sweat had chilled his face even as his hot, hot finger moved on the trigger. His mouth was sticky. He wrenched the chainsaw back to life. No amount of beer would quench that thirst.

***

"We're on a good lurk." Rob wrestled a long bundle into the room and shut the door. "I rescued a bit more than your knickers."

"Oh." Gabe looked at the leather case Rob pulled from the blanket. "Dob insisted I take the rifle. He and Rosie gave me the truck, the gear, all the cash they could spare. The bullets are in a box over the wheel well. At least, they were..."

"You all right?" Rob touched his shoulder. "Listen, I'll run you a bath right now. I'll just tuck this under the bed and we can both forget about it, hey?"

He left the door cracked open. Gabe heard low voices and hurried steps then the thunder of water. He willed his lungs to fill and managed to look normal as he walked down the hall. The bath salts were scented with patchouli, and in the great room someone played Puccini's *La Bohem*. After a blissfully long time, Rob tapped on the door.

"I've brought you some clean clothes. All right if I come in?"

"Of course." Gabe splashed his face, careful to avoid the bandage.

"Won't do to have a naked man in the house. Mum might get ideas." The young man pulled a towel from the closet and stacked everything on a chair. "Tea's nearly ready. Maybe twenty minutes and we'll eat."

When Gabe was done, he felt as if he had emerged from a long dive along the reefs. Rob had rounded up white drawstring pants and a T-shirt that swam over his thighs. The canary cloth was trimmed with red, and somehow Gabe knew this was Rob's favorite shirt. Selena met him at the door and added his mangled clothes to the laundry basket.

"Please don't go to any trouble," he said. "I don't think they can be saved."

"No trouble. Now come out here and eat." She whisked him down the hall. "Mum insists we eat as a family once a day. Says it makes children more civilized. We're all grown up now but we humor her."

She ushered Gabe into the dining area. The sun had dropped below the foothills and a whispering light filtered through the bottlebrush trees around the patio. Bowls heaped with peas, mashed potatoes and glazed rolls along with a platter of grilled sausage anchored a quilted runner.

"Your friend white?" Angus asked as he passed the food. "Desert's a big place, too big for men to know every bit of dust. The police will help."

"Actually, the police have finished their inquiry," Gabe said. "They don't have any more leads to follow. Honestly, I'm not sure where to look myself."

"That's hard for any man. Used to be people found their way by following songlines, tracks left by the creators. The really big ones stretch over the whole continent. See, the outback is big enough to own you. You're not big enough to own the outback."

Gabe looked out the front window. The ridges of the foothills were smudged with the first pinks of sunset. The whole of Alice Springs, an oasis of asphalt and imported wood, was the smallest of conquests. The patient seasons would be there when the town fell beneath its own weight.

"Big land out there, big sand and not much law." Angus crossed his arms. "Maybe your friend killed the wrong calf for his dinner. Maybe he took target practice on the wife's favorite ewe."

"He wouldn't kill indiscriminately. He was a conservationist, really. Sounds funny that killing animals could balance the ecosystem. But the artificial ponds let the kangaroo population explode. If the government didn't cull, the mobs would strip the land."

"I've heard that argument before," Rob said. "Never could reckon if it was true. But then, I don't know enough about cattle to say."

Selena cleared the table and put on a kettle for tea. While she was in the kitchen, Matty leaned toward Gabe. "I hope she isn't too much bother."

"Your daughter is delightful."

"A little too delightful for some folks. Alice might be big but it's less than cosmopolitan. I lived in Darwin when I was at university. The city's a long way from here. And not just by road."

"I understand. There aren't many black faces in Townsville. Tourists or transplants, mostly."

"Too damn hot for white fellahs out here," Angus grinned. "The outback was never settled proper. Always had wild land, many clans. That's how the Arrernte survived so well. We were the last to be rounded up, the last to have our beliefs stolen along with the children."

"How do you get along, Gabe?" Matty distributed dessert plates as she spoke. "Even though Alice isn't always peaceful, we do have a community here."

"Oh, I manage. Some of those white fellows aren't half bad." He smiled.

"Your family must be a blessing."

"My mother, especially. She was shipped over from Ireland when the occupation was causing some real trouble, so we both grew up without our parents."

"I meant your biological family. Were you unable to locate them?"

"I never tried."

Some subtle shift circled the table. It was the same hesitant beat he had felt when Matty asked about her son's involvement with a missing man. Angus smiled at him.

"What if you have brothers you've never met," Selena asked, "or a sister who knows all the old dances? Don't you want to see your mother again?"

"Please excuse her," Matty said. "Sometimes my grown-up children forget their manners."

"Oh, I don't mind. How do you get to know someone if you don't ask questions, right?" Gabe avoided looking at Angus. The elder waited, his beatific smile unchanging. "A few years ago I filled out the search forms. It was mum's idea, my adoptive mother. Nothing came of it. My papers had been lost in a fire."

"The minute things turned against the government, all those orphanages suffered fires." Matty pushed away her pie. "Never anything big, mind you. Always just the size of a filing cabinet. Hundreds of lineages gone in minutes. And we still lose the young ones. It's always something convenient, a fire or an unknown assailant...."

"We're here, mum." Selena draped herself over Matty's shoulders then looked at Gabe. "Some day I'll get a place of my own. Right now I'm still learning from my family. Uncle Angus knows heaps of people who teach me dances and songs."

"Are all your routines traditional?" Gabe nudged his plate across the table.

"The ones I choreograph mix modern and traditional styles. Like the brolga stretching its wings, I touch the past and the future."

"And you are perched in the present?"

"Yes. And yes, you may have another slice of Pavlova. It's named for a Russian ballerina, you know. Nothing more than egg whites and sugar. Sweet air, just like her *jete*."

"You two have plans to make." Angus rose and moved into the living room. "Selena, help me make up the couch for your brother. He might not find a soft place to rest for a while."

"I'll file a police report first thing," Gabe said. "Then I'll send a wrecker to salvage the truck."

"We'll pick up me friend," Rob said. "Ramie can fix anything on wheels and he won't charge like a wounded bull."

The young man pushed back from the table and went out to check the car. Matty watched as he disappeared. "He's the only son I have left," she said.

Her face was smooth and unmoving, like a night without stars. Gabe wondered at the depth of her eyes and the bow of her mouth, both of which she had passed to her son. "You'd rather he not go to the police station," he said.

"The keys to my car are on the red strap by the door. Turn left on the highway and follow the signs. I'll find some chores to keep him busy until you come back."

"It must be hard for you. Raising children is tough, even with two to share the load."

"My family sees me through."

"How old was your other son?"

"Eighteen. But he looked twenty, maybe more. Tall and strong like his father, with a mouth like him, too." Her eyes squeezed down. She smiled and touched Gabe's hand. "Family really is the only important thing, don't you think?"

———

Dana's feet gripped the folds of bark where the bough grew from the trunk. Trees could be so much like animals, he thought. They wrinkled with age and bled when wounded. They could even be blighted by their environment, just like human creatures.

He scanned the plains, now saturated with dusk. Kevin would notice the dusty spit of a vehicle but from a distance he couldn't tell a person from a bush. He didn't appreciate how a man could glide through sparse grass and come close enough to touch. Close enough to kill.

For now the vista was still. Dana shouldered the chainsaw and climbed down using only a rope slung around the trunk. His arms were tired but the powdery bark and the sap coating his skin helped control his descent. When he was level with the truck, he pushed off and landed between two large roots.

"Take these three next." He marked the carvings with chalk.

Kevin nodded and belched into his shoulder. The shaman didn't need to smell the beer to know he'd been drinking but the game of sneak-and-guzzle kept the mule preoccupied. When he looked around again, he noticed something new in the west.

It was a dingo, a male whose fur glowed with the coming night. Kulpunya had come. The Dreamtime dog belonged to Dana's clan, the Hare-wallaby people from the Pitjantjatjara tribe.

Long ago, their stories said, the Hare-wallaby men gathered for a ceremony. But the Mulga-seed clan was jealous and tried to create a dingo using bones and the hair of women. Forked sticks became its ears, the tail of a bandicoot was tied behind, and the teeth of a mole lined its mouth. By day songs filled Kulpunya with evil and by night the creature took form.

On the morning of its birth, Kulpunya circled Uluru. It fell upon the Hare-wallaby clan, butchering nearly all the women and children. The bodies became boulders at the foot of the rock, and the hair of the victims grew into fig bushes. The dingo's stalking tracks marked Uluru forever.

At first Dana had been horrified by the bloody tale. As he grew older and began to understand how the world worked, he had adopted the evil dog as his own. He carried a spirit board that channeled Kulpunya's energy. Symbols carved on top of the wood represented the dingo's head, ribs and body scars. Underneath was the windpipe, navel and penis, as well as the crescents left in the dust where the dog sat.

The dingo's presence, Dana thought, was a good omen. The trunk fell and sap the watery red of fish blood welled from the stump. Every whiff of the tree's oils fed Dana more fluently than broth or meat. But the bush was reciprocal. Either the world was sung or there was no world at all. Dana gathered the *djang* and traded it for energy that folded neatly in his pocket.

"There's a prime rib in that one, hey?" Kevin said.

Dana nodded. The trunk was so richly carved Kevin would cut through some symbols to steal others. The Japanese buyer, an entrepreneur who fed the hunger of overseas visitors for young boys, would pay well. The pieces would be smuggled through Port Darwin inside furniture and plaster statues, even framed in shadow boxes as commercial crafts. Kevin wouldn't see a tenth of the money.

Sometimes it was good to team up with a *pi_ranpa.*

The hour was early when Matty suggested they retire. The wreck, the drive and the home-cooked meal had caught Gabe in a sinking spiral. Fortunately the house settled quickly. Only the rattle of the fan kept him anchored in the present.

A bark painting of three large grubs dominated the interior wall. Caterpillar Dreaming, Rob had called it, an important story for the Arrernte tribe. A family friend had given him the painting after his initiation. He had left it at the house where memories of his father were tucked into the baseboards and hung behind the door.

Perhaps that was what made the house so comfortable. Or maybe it was the way the indigo sky had nestled atop the roof, or that Gabe had been on the road too long and missed the familiar rhythm of his own life.

He clenched his fists. It was none of that, he knew, and all of it. Even now, surrounded by Aboriginal faces, he was an outsider. Growing up, he had been the only one without fair hair and pink fingernails. Sometimes his reflection had shocked him. He was bark and river sand, they were wedding cake and opal. Even reaching for a plate could shake him when the sepia crackle of his hand accosted his sister's coral shine.

While still quite young, he took to wearing thin cotton gloves with a rolled hem. He had seen a jeweler at the mall wearing a pair, and for a time he carried a pouch filled with lapis and rose quartz in his pocket. Then one day he put the pouch and the gloves in a drawer, and he noticed how warm the sun felt on his palms.

The child had grown but the adult still ached. He knew the world didn't offer him more or less simply because he was black. But the tourists who delighted in the dives were white. The neighbors who even now watched his row house and watered his garden were white. Until recently, all his lovers had been white. When he went home, he didn't want his family to be white.

And as always, nipping the heels of that wish was guilt. How often had mum stood up for him against school administrators and doctors with their notions of racial inferiority, how many friends had she lost when she'd opened her home to him? She had taught him to march away from the staring eyes at the grocery store, to refuse tourists their requests for photographs.

Yet he could not deny the raw hollow in his belly, the space ground out by a millstone of loss. As fiercely as mum loved him, as much as he feared ever loosing her, some part of him flinched from the blaze of her skin. His betrayal was unconscionable. He rocked, simply rocked, as silence filled his mind.

Finally he wiped his face and crept to the toilet. He felt the airy tide of the house, the combined restful breath of its inhabitants. Returning past Angus' room, he jumped at a voice.

"Gabe."

The elder stood in the doorway with a thin blanket draped over one shoulder. He held out his hand and they clasped each other's wrists. *A rescue grip,* Gabe thought, *for a man overboard.*

They stood, linked in the dark. He felt the heat of his limbs, the warm spot where pain lived in his forehead, the soft kink of his spine. He settled into his body and felt more balanced, more peaceful, than he had in a long time. Their hands slid apart and the men returned to their rooms.

7 Sugarbag

Halfway between Darwin and Katherine, the town of Marbella was a single block packed with every service a traveler could need. A petrol station offered trailer hookups, hot showers and flush toilets without the hotel price. Squeezed onto the end of the block was the post office, a narrow slice of brick sporting a flagpole. Across the street a hardware store and Johnson's Grocer butted up against an aging hotel.

The only roads, one gravel and one dirt, converged west of Main Street. To the east, a double garland of steel trimmed the town. The post master didn't mind the twice-daily rumble of trains, having gone partially deaf from working the mines so long ago. In the hardware store, though, nearly every product was tied down with plastic zip strips. Customers shopped with a pair of scissors and a bit of patience.

While visitors scorned the trains for their noise and the occasional two-car traffic jam, Zack watched for them. From his perch on the corner bench, the teenager could hear the engines nearly a kilometer away. He could identify the freight by watching the reflections of the cars in the shop windows—black bullets for tankers, the white flash of wrappers covering building materials, and the orange sheen of cargo containers.

He even knew their schedules and wondered at how many tasks the rail could serve. The engine that brought the daily milk run crept slowly under the false dawn while freight trains punched through with the fury of time clocks and profits. Passenger trains sliced the kidneys from the desert then were gone. A single track, Zack thought, a single mind. To have such purpose would be grand.

He turned his attention to the road traffic. Tourists were easy to spot. Their hats were always too crisp, their socks too white, and their T-shirts broadcast the name of the last place they had stopped. Their eyes devoured Marbella while superiority nicked the corners of their mouths. They were soft, even Zack could see that, and he prayed for the stupid ones who hauled their families to the Kimberly region without enough food, water or experience to survive an emergency.

The real bushies, ranch hands and miners, were broken in. Their hats were molded to their heads, their haircuts were always a month past due, and their clothes had lapsed into the same dull browns. Every day they squeezed bauxite and diamonds and uranium, cattle and sheep and hay from the earth. Thirty years of that life looked like fifty, and fifty spalled the men down to their cores. They fit the desert in a way the tourists never could.

Zack fit the desert, too. He had been born to it, struggling from the womb during a cyclone. Clouds and power outages had blackened the entire north coast that day. His mother's soprano cries had joined the storm's timpani, the breathy flute of the propane lantern, the oboe wind.

The Aboriginal midwife had laughed at the baby's squall. *He looks like the desert pea,* she said, and pointed to the crimson face blooming around the black disk of his mouth. Then she wiped up blood and mucus, and buried the afterbirth in the damp earth.

———

The boy grew to love the north. It was a land of extremes, with pockets of rainforest crowded around waterfalls. Wetlands welcomed magpie geese, crocodiles and water buffalo. The monsoons brought black-necked storks called jabirus. Great egrets with their long nuptial plumes bred amid colonies of cormorants and ibises.

On the plains stood the tall spear grass. Then came open woodlands dominated by wollybutts, eucalypts with flowers of fire. The stamens smelled so sweet Zack crushed the sticky clusters against the roof of his mouth. The bush responded, sending brush-tailed possums to his window and stingless bees to build sugarbags in his favorite tree.

No one taught Zack of the bush. There were only the men vigilant to every sapling that might shade the precious grass, envious of every kangaroo that faired so much better than the imported cattle. They taught him to drive a tractor, to drag a chain and pull down acres of trees. They taught him to shoot roos and euros and wallabies through the window of the truck. He shot them in the heart and, as he drew better, in the head.

He swung the carcasses onto the flatbed, a half-dozen every morning to feed the station's dogs. Blood pooled on the metal like pudding. Their feet were tufted with fur of russet and gold. The colors of the dry, the colors of the men's despair. All for the Brahma with their pointed hooves and meaty mass, their sluggish blundering over the hills.

There came a day when his rifle lay untouched. That morning his father parked beneath a stand of stringybark on the crest of a hill. As usual, roos had gathered at the cattle pond. Most days Zack could hit two or three before they fled. On this morning the barrel stayed between his feet.

"Ya missed!" his father laughed as the animals disappeared.

Under the rising sun, the trees were cosmic blue. Zack would be thirteen soon, man enough to make his own decisions.

"I ain't shootin' no more roos."

The engine rumbled steadily. His father eased the stick back to neutral. "Hey?"

"Dogs can eat dog food. I ain't shootin' no more roos."

"They eat the grass, Zack. They mate faster 'n rabbits."

The locusts began their deafening burr. The cattle, half wild and always hungry, circled the feed trough. Tugging at his hat, his father drove on.

As if in conspiracy, roos swarmed the property that morning. They outpaced the truck with a flip of their tails as Zack felt the blood in his cheeks. His father remained grim even when a female gray sailed over the hood. Zack thought of their eyes, white-rimmed in death, and the way their guts shone purple and yellow on the sand.

***

That night Zack's parents had a big row. It was the same argument as always. The price of beef was rock bottom, the rains rarely came far enough inland for long enough, they couldn't pay enough to get or keep good help. Their words spilled off the table and streamed under the wallpaper, and the house was sodden with ire.

His mother knew of things other than finances and livestock. Rita had lived the rosary of empty days when beads of work couldn't save her from the bush closing in, closing off the roads, closing down the phones with black river mud and monsoons. She knew the tuck and ruffle of rain on the roof, the pull of its weight in her clothes, the warm run of it like blood on her skin. If her own burden had become too heavy then it was unconscionable for her son.

"He has too little company, Tom." She watched from the window as Zack escaped to the shed. "It was all right when he was small. He's grown up independent, knows how to care for himself. But he's changing."

"I know, Rita. I see it in him every day. He's taller than me already." He picked at the upholstery. "But what am I to do, love? I've sunk everything into this place. We can't just up and go. What'll be left for him?"

"That's just it. Twenty years we've run cattle here and every year prices drop. It was different when we started." She pushed her hair behind her ears. "The lease is up for renewal soon. We should just go."

"This is all there is, Rita. A few buildings, some cattle, and a bunch of bleeding roos with their bellies full of grass."

The lame bull in the paddock lowed. Rita kept her eyes on the creature as it hobbled to the feed trough. "We could get a place closer to town. Find other jobs. It would be less work than this with better pay. I've saved a little here and there. Never knew for what but Zack needs this."

"You tell me what that boy needs." Tom stomped into the kitchen but his anger wouldn't cool. "He's gotten the best the both of us could offer. You just tell me what he needs."

"Friends, for one. People his own age for a change. Not those stockmen who come through, the lot of them drifters and bagmen."

"Now, Rita, they're as hardworking as you or I."

"And they drink their wages come Friday. Zack needs to see that life's not all picking through the dust for a little money. Hell, Tom, we can't even keep the child in books." She banged the kettle onto the stove, then gripped the counter. "He needs more than we can give him here."

He stopped pacing. "Twenty years, Rita. That's a lifetime."

"Our lifetime." She turned toward him and softened. "Now it's Zack's turn."

<hr>

And so began the tallying of trucks and tractors, the price the homestead would fetch at auction, the money Rita had stashed in a tin. The cattle were bought by a corporate station closer to the coast and the few pigs were slaughtered for meat. A neighbor took his pick of the horses in exchange for helping with the muster, and the rest went to a tourist ranch near Darwin. Last to go were Tom's prized breeders, three blue tick bitches and a cur he had hoped would grow into a champion sire.

The business of closure brought more people to the ranch. Neighbors came from as far as Oenpelli in the east and Victoria River to the south. They brought tikes too small to reach the stirrups and adult children with kids of their own. The teens Zack chatted with on the short-wave came, and the ones from farthest away met each other for the first time.

Every evening the porch was overrun, and Rita's sister lived in the kitchen making endless meals. Rita herself only budged from the drift of invoices and receipts when a new arrival or departure occurred, and that was often enough to chaff her thin. Tom was constantly outside haggling, hauling equipment, and raising every last dollar from the musty pockets of the bidders.

Zack helped where he could. Occasionally he slipped away from the homestead, carrying his sandwich or a thermos of soup into the nearest pasture to eat by the creek. Each bite seemed more savory sprinkled with the gurgle of water or spiced with dappled light. He knew the meals would be some of his last memories of his birthplace.

The balance in the ledger grew not by leaps and bounds, as the sheer bulk of the equipment might suggest, but with the patter of rain. A new balance pooled at the bottom of each sheet until there was nothing left to sell. The visitors trekked away with promises to write and the flush of their purchases bright on their cheeks.

Tom looked for opportunities where he and Rita could work together. Darwin offered little that was affordable but satellite towns around the Stuart Highway had the perfect mix of neighbors, community and affordability. They bought the Marbella Hotel, and the building became both shop and home.

Three years passed in a world populated by a hundred and fifty souls. Tourists and newspapers taught Zack about far-off places, about the angry way people lived when they had too much stuff to keep and not enough to give. Mostly he learned about people, townsfolk and bushies and vacationers who passed through like the trains, a little less hurried, a little more worried. For three years he had watched, even as he watched now.

A flame-red Toyota parked in front of the hotel and a pair of men got out. Even from a block away Zack could see that the white fellow was trouble. He looked like the typical drifter, men barely above vagrants who wouldn't even shear sheep for a living. Pirates of the bush, his dad called them, scavengers who'd offer you tea then siphon your petrol dry.

The Aborigine was different. He slid through the gloom like a king snake through spinifex. Zack had the feeling that if he looked away for an instant, the man would simply disappear. The Aborigine turned toward him with eyes like quicksilver moons. He nodded at the teenager and led his partner into the hotel.

Zack waited while a few more cars pulled in. Tom didn't like him hanging out in the pub but if enough people were there, he let Zack stay. When the bar had filled a little more, the teenager cut across the street. A fog of eucalyptus oil, heady with the strength of sunlight, engulfed the Toyota. Zack gave the rear gate a tug, never expecting the door would actually swing open.

He whistled as he touched the carvings. Symbols like this had been chiseled into rock and wood on their homestead. He didn't know what they meant but he did know they were sacred. And the Aborigine, the one who moved like a king snake, had stolen them.

8 Police

The morning sun pierced the coolibah and filtered through the bay window in the guest room. When Rob was dispatched to locate a particular tool in the shed, Gabe slipped out with the keys to Matty's car.

The old Holden, a restored classic, had a flat-edged sixties style that made him smile. As he rubbed the corduroy upholstery, he remembered family trips in a similar vehicle—long afternoons at the ocean, his sister's first rodeo, brushing marmalade from his collar as his father swerved around college students protesting the Vietnam war.

And later came Kayla, his first love. She had been a spider mum with spindled limbs and a bold, round face. Her whisper-fine hair had been his obsession until she wrapped it in black bandanas to honor the Stolen Generation, dead to their culture. As she spent more of her time volunteering for any number of efforts, Gabe frequented the movie theater.

After the relationship ended, they sometimes passed each other on the street. She was always with her protester friends, so happy to be so sad about war and poverty and injustice. Gabe spent more time at the water's edge collecting the spiral cone shells and bits of coral that rolled in the foam.

Kayla had been as far out of his control as the government's attempt at genocide. Love and war, he knew, were like the tides. They rose in gyres then subsided. Friendship, on the other hand, was a tree that rooted more deeply with each year. Its demise left a hole that would grow over but never quite be filled.

He parked across from the police station and wandered down the echoing corridors. In the main room, a single counter separated the waiting area from the bullpen. The receiving officer wore a uniform of rigid cloth.

"I'd like to file a report," Gabe said. "I was run off the road yesterday."

"Fill out this accident report and we'll notify the insurance company."

"This was more than an accident. I was forced off the road."

Her name tag, its letters as crisp as bullets, flashed in the fluorescent light. Officer Burney folded her hands and her cuticles frowned at him. "Perhaps you should tell me what you think happened," she said.

"It was south of Three Ways. These men I met forced me off the road."

"So you just got into town?" She eyed his clothes. "Why didn't you report this at Three Ways?"

"I wanted to find the men."

"They live in Alice Springs?"

"No...well, I don't know. When I stopped at a roadhouse, we had a confrontation of sorts."

"Is that how you got that cut?" Officer Burney's face was flat and the arcs of her cheeks were tinted green. Gabe took a deep breath.

"No. That's from the accident."

"So what happened at the roadhouse? Were you in the pub?" Her eyelids closed the width of a hair.

"I had one beer. A few sips, actually. They started harassing me the moment I sat down. They told me a racial joke." Gabe glanced behind him as an elderly man in Bermuda shorts and a light duster limped through the door.

"Hey, Steve." Officer Burney smiled. "Charles will be back in about ten minutes."

The man nodded and shoved the chairs into a circle. His feet went up on the seat of one and he leaned out of the second onto the back of the third. After a pause, he retrieved the newspaper then made even more racket readjusting everything.

Officer Burney watched the whole episode. Gabe waited for her attention to return to him as the resin of a thousand such encounters bubbled in his legs.

"A joke," she finally said.

"A racial joke. I didn't want any trouble, so I left."

"What was the joke?"

"You want me to repeat it?"

"I need to establish the level of harassment, sir."

Gabe stared at her, the model of proper law. Very respectable, she was. And painfully respectful of him. Her nails were so pale he could see the outlines of her fingertips through them.

"He said, 'Why do they call Aborigines boongs?'"

"All right, sir, I know that one. No need to finish it. Did these men say or do anything else, make any threatening gestures?"

"Like I said, I didn't wait around."

Steve had become surprisingly still. Gabe turned, and the man ruffled the paper and mumbled about Parliament.

"You said 'he,'" the officer continued. "The driver was male?"

"Yes. I only saw the passenger but they weren't with anyone else at the pub."

"So you didn't see the driver at all?"

"No. I had just shut the glove box when they showed up."

"What makes you sure it was the two from the pub?"

"Who else could it be?"

The tar had risen past his hips, wrapped around his torso and crept into his fingers. He felt needles behind his eyes. He didn't move as Steve cleared his throat.

"Is it at all possible, sir," Officer Burney asked, "that you simply lost control? You were distracted, driving an unfamiliar vehicle on a rough highway."

"I was run off the road." His voice was loud, clogged with ire, but he didn't care. "Will we be filing a report today?"

Her head tipped the tiniest bit as she pinched a form from under the counter. Gabe ran through the story again, this time without her questions. The commissioner arrived and glanced at the report.

"Gabriel Branch? From Townsville?" His voice was strong, like the push of oil around pistons, but the warmth was cultivated. "I'm Commissioner Dawson. Did we talk the other day about a missing person?"

"Mr. Branch has filed a different complaint," Burney said.

"Had a bit of trouble up north, I see. Why didn't you report this in Three Ways?" The Commissioner leaned against the counter. The move was calculated to set him at ease but Gabe knew his every word and gesture was being scrutinized.

"I was in shock. Anyway, I thought I might be of some assistance in finding Ian."

Dawson tugged a business card from his shirt pocket. "I'll be honest with you," he said. "If this were a sheila or a young bloke, some student or foreigner who might get into trouble easy, we'd assume kidnapping. For someone a bit older who knew his way around, we don't jump to conclusions. If I remember the case correctly, your friend looks lost."

"Yes, but where?"

Dawson waved away the receiving officer. His face was sincere but he wouldn't jump at the chance to enlist a civilian in the search. He pitched his voice low enough for their words to be private.

"I know this is a tough situation for you. But I don't think you can be much help. Just go home. He'll turn up sometime."

"You mean when a tourist finds his body." Gabe pushed back from the counter. "I'm not willing to wait that long."

Steve rumpled the newspaper furiously to make up for all the rustling he had forgotten to do. A few more platitudes and a practiced crinkle of the commissioner's eyes propelled Gabe into the hallway.

The door clicked shut. His anger curled upon itself like rawhide left in the sun. The police had their rules to follow, the same rules that kept Gabe from banging back into the station and demand they do something, anything, to bring Ian home. But hysterics would only net him another crepe grin from Steve and the hard glint of Burney's gaze.

If that's all rules are good for, Gabe thought, *then to hell with them.*

<hr>

At the grocery store, Gabe wandered the aisles looking for something more elegant than apples. He wanted to thank Matty for her help and he wanted to calm down before going back. A collection of imported spices finally caught his eye. The cashier, a spiky redhead with facial piercings and a tattoo firing her throat, caressed his palm when he took the change. He returned to the house with her smile still in his mind.

"Made your report, then?" Rob shut the Ford's trunk.

"It's done. We can go any time."

Selena bounded off the porch and grabbed his shoulders. Tipping her head down, she studied his face from under her dark brows. Finally she stepped back.

"I can see your totem animal in your face," she said. "It's definitely a bird, probably a pigeon. I thought as much over dinner last night but I wanted to see your face in natural light to be sure."

"What's a totem?" he asked.

"It's like an energy you're born into. It could be a plant or animal, a rock or waterhole, even a type of storm. If you know your totem, you can call on its energy." She waved at her brother. "Rob's a possum 'cause he's always getting into things."

"I'm not sure how useful a pigeon can be," Gabe said, "but it's nice to know."

She rolled her eyes. "Everything has power, Gabriel. You just have to respect each totem's special traits."

"You'd best come around," Matty called from the back yard. "Angus wants to say a proper goodbye."

The elder was painting the picture of a dingo on a piece of bark. The tips of his fingers found the ridges of dry paint and used them to guide his new efforts. Rob had said that, along with caterpillars, the wild dog was an important Dreaming ancestor for the Arrernte. When Angus handed Gabe the artwork, a peculiar vibration raised the hair on his arms.

"Possum will take you to the songwoman, a keeper of Law. She'll be able to tell you about the message stick. Until then, take this." He offered Gabe a twist of red cloth. Inside was a tooth nearly an inch long. "Dingo. For protection."

"You really think I'll need protection?"

"Maybe. Maybe not. Keep it with you just in case."

The highway wound north through foothills that measured the pulse of the earth. Soon the land lay flat under a blanket of saltbush and Mitchell grass. Nothing moved except lizards and snakes and the occasional semi, each hauling three trailers, blasting south.

"There's cold meats and fresh bread in the back." Rob was wearing his Vegemite cap again.

"Did you bake the bread?"

"Baking's not me best. Give me a casserole dish and the end of your grocery run, and I'll make your belly bigger."

"What's your best meal?" Gabe wedged a blanket under his rear. It didn't help much but at least his pelvis was cushioned from direct contact with the support bar.

"Roast bustard with wild orange sauce. Bustards kill snakes, even poisonous ones. Anything that can do that is pretty strong. Makes for a nice meal, to take that energy inside you."

"So you hunt the bustard? Gather the fruit?"

"Yeah. It's me job, really. I run tourists into the desert to find tucker. No hunting, mind. We pick fruit, dig roots, and find the occasional grub." He patted his stomach. "I will admit, me first attempt at bustard was a disaster. Used the wrong kind of fruit. All three wild orange species are good but one has an aftertaste like kerosene."

"I expect you wouldn't get many repeat customers that way."

"I tried the recipe on me family first. Angus never said much but he walked around with this funny smile for a few days. Selena, though!" He screwed the cap sideways on his head. "Cor, she didn't let me forget that for a long time!"

The conversation turned to Selena's early obsession with shoes and Mike's artistic talent. Rob discovered that he had seen Gabe's sister compete in a rodeo years before, and talked about his cousins. Gabe noticed that the young man's self-depreciating humor had the softest edge, as if he forgave his own flaws as readily as he recognized them.

Sooner than either expected, they neared the crash site. A pair of ravens worrying the metal strip around the windscreen left only when Rob waved his arms. They recovered dented cans of food and a single shoe from under a shrub. The maps and notes, still wrapped in a binder, were wedged between the seats. With a little creative packing, everything fit in the Ford.

"Not one to travel light, hey?" Rob palmed sweat from his face.

"Didn't know how long I'd be out or where I'd be going. Besides, the more Dob gave me, the less worried he seemed."

"He must like ya. It's nice to have someone in this world care about ya, hey?"

Gabe looked at the shattered glass, the bits of paper blown from a notepad, the gum wrapper overlooked by the ravens. If he found Ian's truck, would his friend be a bloodied mess? Or dare he think, as he sometimes did, that even now Ian lolled beside a rock pool roasting wallaby and waiting for a search plane?

It's nice, he thought, *so long as no one gets hurt.*

〰〰〰

Gabe and Rob pulled into Tennant Creek, a gold-boom town that survived the bust by changing its tastes to copper. The dinner rush was on and the petrol station crawled with customers. The garage was a Sydney hut, a portable building of corrugated steel once popular with pioneers. On one side, *Ramie's Wreckers* was stenciled in forest green.

Ramie himself stood beside the pumps, ready to service and squeegee the next car. He was lanky the way a box of straws was lanky, as if his bones never quite connected while they clattered around inside his skin. Added to this internal unrest was the tendency of his eyes to drift without ever hooking the object of interest. Combined with a few tics—a toss of his right hand while walking, a tug of his shoulders when still—he seemed perpetually off balance.

By the time the men hauled the truck back to the garage, the light was a wispy blue. The mosquitoes were out, and bats sliced through the edge of Gabe's vision like fish in the bubbles of a respirator. They retired to an adobe house with sun-baked walls nearly three feet thick and a roof thatched from wire grass.

[49]

The entire structure was a single room smaller than the garage. All around the ceiling, miniature halogen bulbs had been recessed into earthen ridges, and the kitchen was a slim alcove defined by a granite counter. Everything about the structure had been planned, right down to the coin collection molded into the walls.

The money Ramie saved on construction had gone into electronics. A band of recording equipment, everything from eight-track and reel-to-reel to DAT and CD burners, was built into the far wall. A satellite brought in reception for the television, cell phone and internet, and a ham radio was evidentially as valuable as any other piece. For one man, at least, remote didn't necessarily mean secluded.

"How long will the repairs take?" Rob asked as he dropped the last ingredients into a soup pot.

"A week?" Ramie's statements ended with an inflection that made them sound like questions.

"I can't wait that long," Gabe said. "I'll rent a car tomorrow. Can you give me directions to the songwoman's place?"

"You're off to see the witch?" Ramie plucked a cigar from a recessed glass box. "Like her, love her? Says I'm too young for her, she's too old in the soul for me. Old soul. I'd go with you. Except for the repairs?"

"Except she scares you," Rob laughed. "You should see him when we visit. All moony-eyed and ready to pass out every time she blinks."

"No help for it? She's a witch and a beauty." He stared through the door where the burgundy air fed the stars. Without looking back, he wiggled his fingers and stepped outside.

"Don't mind him," Rob said. "He takes a lot of walks when he wants to think. I know he seems to have a few roos loose in the top paddock but he's a good mate."

"It's fine. I expect most people find Ian a little odd. With luck, you'll be able to judge that for yourself."

Rob flashed a half-smile so unlike his usual snappy expression that Gabe winced. The odds against finding Ian were staggering, and the idea that they might all come together on this journey sounded desperate.

But Gabe could be stubborn about those he loved. It was why he'd stuck with Chance even when he'd known she would one day tire of his cultural ignorance. It was why he'd returned to the police in hopes that the case might be reinvestigated. If the officers actually spoke to one of the friends or family, he'd thought they might try again.

But Charles Dawson hadn't budged from the rule book. Commissioner Charles had never seen the pale of Rosie's skin or the way Dob's eyes had recessed into haunted pits. Dawson didn't know how the loss of a son bankrupted a family.

Gabe did. He would wear the tires down to the rims and the rims down to the axles. He'd barge onto every cattle station and Aboriginal reserve, and he'd keep looking even after Rob went back to his own life. Gabe might never know the truth about his own mother and brother but he would learn the truth about Ian. If he didn't, the pain of not knowing would overrun his life like a secret organ crowding his heart.

9 Whirligig Woman

In the 1930s, mining companies tried to persuade Aborigines to leave the Tennant Creek area by dynamiting oil drums. When the tribes failed to see that the black drums represented black people, the government stepped in. Some two hundred Warumungu were corralled at the Phillip Creek settlement. But the creek ran only in the Wet and the meager food rations were siphoned off by greedy wards.

The Dreaming Law was timeless and the government's strength waned. When the original people returned, they celebrated the songlines of Snake and Crow and Lightning in a mural. The painting was triumphant, and Gabe turned away before his tears could attest to its beauty.

After a short stint on the highway, Rob turned onto a gravel road. The stones gave way to dirt then even the track faded. A series of turns pointed them south again, and the Ford crawled over a snarl of ruts into the northeastern tip of the Tanami Desert.

Amidst the sand and rock, the slightest rainfall transformed the land. Rob described acacia blossoms glittering in seasonal swamps and wildflowers that roared across the ground in waves of blue and pink. Over thousands of years, Aborigines had farmed the land with fire, setting controlled burns to encourage the growth of edible plants. Communities of hare-wallabies and bilbies, supported by the management of plants, had flourished. Now, though, the system had collapsed.

For the first time, Gabe understood the extent of the changes caused by settlement. He stared out the window as if he could conjure the past. He saw only the imported rabbits that stole the grass, the feral cats that decimated native species. The air was stale with the lack of cooking fires and the drought imposed by industry. He stared as if he could will it away, as if thousands of songmen and songwomen had not already tried.

Deep in his chest, he felt something like sorrow. He did not yet know it was the absence of song.

Dana led the mule into a shallow gully. Striking a site so soon after raiding one in the same area broke his cardinal rule. But the buyer had requested rock art related to men's ceremonies and the deadline was short. The station manager's morning rounds were finished, so the thieves would be safe until evening.

Deep in the shadows, Dana rolled sheets of newsprint into tubes and sealed the ends with tape. He added fuses, fertilizer and detonating caps to create homemade dynamite. After the charges were set, the men hiked out for a last look around. The flash of glass or metal would alert Dana to vehicles but he also watched for animals. A burst of cockatoos or the scatter of roos would reveal movement on horse or by foot.

Everything appeared normal, and the explosion sent a dingo bolting from the scrub. Dana had learned how to free sections of rock during a stint as an opal miner. He rarely damaged the art but pieces sometimes split when they hit the ground. Salvageable carvings disappeared into rucksacks or were dragged out.

As Kevin loaded the truck, Dana leaned against a boulder. The mule's veins throbbed beneath his skin. A cigarette was clamped between his lips, and he puffed angrily as he hauled the larger pieces. He paused between each for beer, the trough that kept him sedate and pliant. Dana watched an aimless cloud and barely heard his grunts.

<hr>

Shortly after noon the Ford reached Rachel's house, a cabin dropped onto a clay pan nestled between sand hills and the horizon. A gallery of whirligigs, given life by the heat rising off the ground, lent a surreal touch. Spring-loaded ducks promenaded around the soffit, rocket ships launched from the propane tank, and a circus lined the walkway. They glutted the yard with their wooden chatter.

A woman appeared on the nearby hill. Her feet were bare and her hair was a flossy bouffant held with a twist of cloth. She wasn't strong so much as monumental. Her piedmont thighs thrust up her torso, while the ridge of her shoulders were solid and calm. At the summit was her face, with eyes that indeed belonged to an old soul.

"Where you from?" Her "f" sounds came out like the letter p, and Gabe remembered that many tribal languages lacked the sharp letter.

"Townsville. The Alice, really. Or a settlement close by." He shook his head. "I don't exactly know."

"I met Angus long time ago at an outstation. No telly there, you know, no phone. No toilet to gobble up water. Just land an' quiet."

She waved the men inside where a wooden chest topped with a straw mat doubled as a sleeping platform. The dirt was swept and rafters of peeled timber held canned vegetables. Herbs bristled from the eaves and jerked meat was strung from a rope spanning the center. Gabe saw flashes of light everywhere. Insects, he thought, or dust motes catching the light.

The men sat at the table in the center of the room. Rachel had killed a snake for her meal, a python with the colors of an Eastern brown. When they had talked for a time, Gabe offered her a jar of yellow-box honey and set the message stick on the table. "Angus thought you might know something about this," he said.

"Him not so special." She tapped the artifact. "Him tell my great-granny's death, just before I were put in a girl's home. Weren't much of a girl after that. Grow up quick in them homes."

Gabe stiffened. "Why did they take you?"

"Same reason as all the others. Neglect, they say, but they mean poor. Some baby were stole without tasting mama's milk. Mama wake up at hospital, no baby no more. Baby were inside, mama sleep an' wake up empty." She shook her head. "At least you know what happen when the welfare come to camp. But sometimes mama got shot because she not let go of the baby. White power always were the power of death."

The wind picked up but Gabe had no concept of the change. Instead he felt a heat that wasn't from the sun. Rachel's voice sounded distorted and compressed, like light through the wrong end of a telescope. He wanted her to stop talking, to stop catching him with the thread of her gaze, to *stop.* It was all he could do not to jump from his chair as she continued.

"My baby were stole young. I keep him some time, nurse him two nights. Girl's home train me to sweep, wash, cook an' mop. Clean a house I weren't to go in otherwise. Sleep in a shed by the water tank, same as a dog. One night station man come late. Never say no word, then or later. Like nothing happen 'cept my belly got big." She rolled her nipple between her fingers. "Two nights."

The cabin was dark and the western sky had turned rheumy. The urge to walk frayed Gabe's muscles. Rachel began to sing, a long call followed by a repetitive rise and fall. The melody was the coils of a river deep and cool, and the words were hidden flowers in a woman's perfume. Fires burned in that sound as ghosts shook free from the air.

Gabe was desperate to dam the cascade of his memory. He wanted to incise the words on his heart like a lullaby. He pushed away from the table. The message stick pointed west, far across the clay pan, and he followed the invisible track out onto the plain. His feet slapped the earth as lightly as if he were three, as quickly as if the welfare would snatch him again. A spinifex pigeon, its harlequin face red at the eyes, flew from his approach.

He fell hard in front of a mulga. The wind rose to a scream and the galls on the branches popped like tumors. When he looked up, he saw a cloud as livid as crows. The wind was grief, it brought him wailing mothers with full breasts and empty arms. The dust storm swallowed the sky and Gabe was alone at the beginning of the universe.

They had been on their way to aunty's, he and his brother Andy. Gabe was young, too young even to know his age, and his brother was in charge. Andy was everything to him, with skin that glowed apricot and teeth that flashed white, white, white. With a whoop, he grabbed a dead snake from the side of the track. It was a lovely prize and their cousin ran over to claim his share.

"Grandfather showed me how to kill it." The cousin pinched its tail between his toes and jerked it through the air. "You throw it like that so it don't get ya. Then you bite its neck, kill it quick. Then you eat."

The boys giggled and lashed each other with the corpse. Gabe hung back until a truck rounded the curve.

"Run here!" Andy cried. "*Iparrpe,* quickly!" Their cousin was already gone, hidden by scrub or running low through a dry creek bed.

"Wait!" The driver held candy out the window. His hands were puffy and unformed, like those of a sick person who did no work. "Come on, then, have them all."

"*Alaye!*" Andy yelled. "*Apetyaye!*"

Gabe stood suspended between his fear and the sweets. This man was not the police, he knew, but he was *mperlkere,* white like the police. The children were supposed to run into the bush where the *mperlkere* couldn't see, where the *mperlkere* wouldn't go. Then he noticed the snake, its mouth open and drained of threat. The older boys played with dead snakes. He would take candy from the white man.

He marched to the truck and snatched up the treasures. One of the sweets was the color of the pictures he had seen of the ocean. The rock holes near his house were black and as still as a sheet hung to dry. But the sea bucked and rolled, his mother said, and the candy shimmered just as he imagined the endless water would.

"*Apetyaye.*" Andy darted forward. "Come here, little one."

"Your mum's sick," the driver said. "Get in and I'll take you to her."

Andy froze. Never before had he acted anything less than certain about what the brothers should do and his cheeks turned ashy. Gabe thought he might be sick, perhaps with the same illness that had struck his mother. Sweat mingled in their palms. Finally Andy helped Gabe into the back. "Other way," he called as the truck lurched forward. "We live other way."

"She's in hospital, mate." In the mirror, the man's eyes were filmy and subdued. "You understand? She's bad off. That's where we're going, to see your mum."

When Andy settled down, Gabe juggled the candy. They were the same golden yellow as the hairs on kurrajong seeds, the lilac of the flowers tucked into headbands during dances. And their taste! They were as sweet as conkleberries.

When they passed the footpath to their aunt's house, he wondered who would tell her where they had gone. Would their neighbors know the *mperlkere* had picked them up or would they worry when the boys were not back by dark? Perhaps the white man would drive his neighbors to the hospital as well.

Soon the land turned strange. The wind smelled the same but the hills were none he knew. The ocean-blue candy, the one he had saved to show his mother, had turned sticky. As they turned onto the highway, he stuffed it behind the seat. The road screamed beneath the tires.

Softly, so softly Gabe wasn't sure at first that it was a voice, Andy began to sing. It was a child's song, one to ward off the cannibal who snatched up youngsters when they wandered too far from the fire. If Andy had been older he might have known a man's song, something with more power. But this was his only psalm.

———

Gabe hummed as dust shook down his spine. The pulls and stops of the Arrernte language were lost to him. Only the melody remained, as precious and comforting as his brother's voice had been that day. In his mouth, the dust was a bitter candy.

When a hand touched his shoulder, something moist percolated through the fingers, some damp core of memory like the heat of a brother's palm. Gabe opened his eyes to air the misty pink of Kimberly diamonds. He followed Rob back to the cabin, and the men left two sets of tracks where once there had been one. Their footprints were already crumbling back into the desert.

"They lured us away." Gabe fell into the chair. "The welfare told my brother and me that our mother was ill."

Rachel palmed the sweat from his brow and smeared each tear as it fell. When the sorrow retreated, there was only a refreshing dampness on his cheeks.

"Where you from?" she asked.

"I don't know. I was three, maybe four years old."

"Where him take you?"

"To an orphanage. Everything was dirty and crowded. It was so dark at night, darker than outside, it seemed. I just cried and cried." He blinked back fresh tears. "They made us sleep in separate dormers but I could hear Andy through the wall. Every night he sang, always the song of the cannibal woman."

"What your mama do? Sure she come for you, yeah?"

"No. My brother said it was too far, that we hadn't a car. A man came to the fence every day, though. Andy said he was our uncle."

The dampness had evaporated, leaving his skin a tight mask. When Rob made fresh tea, Gabe let the cup burn his hands. He wanted no milk this time, only the tannins on his tongue.

"We weren't allowed to talk to anyone through the fence. I was afraid to go over there, anyway. So many people came every day. All those faces lined up just to look at us kids. My family tried to get us back but the court said it was neglect."

"No hope." Rachel thumped the table. "The only way were to hide the baby or rub 'em with ash to make 'em real black. Or run, like ya mama said. Run an' don't never stop."

The sky shook off its veil and the last whirlwinds danced over the hill. The mugs were empty before anyone spoke again.

"At least you and your brother were together," Rob said.

"After a few days they shipped us to Darwin. We were separated and given out to different families." In the jar of honey, Gabe saw the apricot color of Andy's face. His limbs felt baggy, his knee throbbed from the fall, and he wasn't sure he'd ever feel strong enough to stand again.

He remembered, though. After moving to Townsville, he no longer sang the cannibal song.

10 Wanampi

The Rainbow Serpent, a creator spirit known to nearly every tribe in Australia, often crawled atop Uluru to sun itself. When a hunter attacked the snake, their struggle was so violent that blood misted the sky. Any bird that flew by was painted with the different colors of the Serpent's blood.

Gabe had heard that story from his mum. He didn't know if it really had been set at Uluru but he supposed it didn't matter. It was one of the scraps she had been able to offer about his past, a jumble of tales gleaned from the edges of another culture. They had little to do with each other and offered nothing to an orphan without a tribe.

He held up his hand. His skin was cocoa, a color that wasn't in any rainbow. Nor was it the black of the night sky that swallowed the sunbows. His was the color of the ground that supported the rainbow's ends, the earth that nurtured all life. Surely that was good enough.

"Eat now," Rachel said. "Eat an' rest."

As Rob prepared to serve dinner, the songwoman handed Gabe a box. Inside lay perhaps a dozen cloth balls. "Pick," she said.

The bundles were paisley and hide, nylon and fur. Inside a ball of gray flannel lay an opal with flecks of red and apple green. He heard Selena's laugh and snapped his head around but of course only Rachel smiled back at him.

"That one magic," she said. "A man with special Dreaming owned that." She seemed pleased with his selection, and with the care he took wrapping the opal in its muffle.

Using a sheet of tin as a tray, Rob bustled in with the python. The snake had been roasted on coals then split down the spine. Canned tomatoes stewed with walnuts brought out the meat's sweetness and damper, bread cooked in the earth, sopped up the juice. Dusk was still a few hours away when they finished.

"Your friend played hard games," Rachel said. "The man you're chasing got different Law, him got the old spirit. White law is young an' weak. Rob, are you a man?"

"I've been initiated, yes." He settled down completely—not just his usual holding pattern contained by a tapping foot or restless fingers but a total resolution of his attention. "The *djang* stretched out all around me. All of a sudden I understood what Angus says. It's everywhere and in everything."

"Yeah, and that Dreaming power is dangerous. Remember, Gabe, a sorcerer got clever ways. You got a question. The answer will be hard, and hard to get."

He nodded as ravens fluttered around a tomato that had escaped the pot. The birds seemed unsure whether the morsel was treasure or trick. It was inevitable that they would fight, and Gabe turned away.

"Go to Halfway Downs," Rachel said. "Annie will show you the *bora* ground, the place where ceremonies were held."

"Are you two kin?"

"I worked for her a long time, and a long time ago. I say Annie my flour baby 'cause she so white. She got a soft face, too, soft spirit." She found a possum pelt for the message stick and after a little rummaging produced a piece of twine. "You ought to make hairstring for this but you got no hair. Take a long time to make string from your head!"

They stepped outside. The world was gentle with dust and late sunlight. Gabe realized again how subtle the colors of the desert were, how they mirrored the colors of his own organs.

"Your friend," Rachel said. "Him show you the bush?"

"Yes. We camped in the desert a lot."

"Red is sacred. The color of blood an' land." She rubbed his arm. "Dust is in you, Gabe, sand is in your marrow. Find the country in your heart. Then you'll find your friend."

She handed him the rest of the python and a tin of beef. Rob slipped him a few folded bills, which he passed to the songwoman. As they pulled away, dust streamed from the Falcon like the ashes of ancestors.

Everything about the Marbella Hotel let travelers and townsfolk know it was family owned and operated. The parking lot was always clean, the curtains were hand-embroidered, and the pub was well-lit. In the corner of the tidy establishment sat Dana, alone and unnoticed.

Invisibility was an art. Of the different veils a man could use, tricking the eye was easy. Invisibility of intent could also be simple, except with children. No matter their race, children were closer to spirit simply because they were so pure. They could detect a violent motive even if they didn't understand the source of their fear.

Tonight Dana had no such concerns. The customers were all older, all Europeans, and all gullible. They were, in fact, the antithesis of invisibility. They seemed bred to bluster like a typhoon and stampede like water buffalo. Perhaps the journey from an overcrowded island to the expansive plains had caused them to decompress too quickly. They had burst and now dragged their gut heaps behind them wherever they went.

So easy to read, those *piranpa*. Loose and messy, with eyes that spilled the sum of their souls. They huddled about the oases of pool tables and clanking coolers. They laughed loudly to convince themselves that their presence would not be annulled when they stepped into the desert. They were conspicuous by choice, feeding a drive to exist in ever larger numbers.

That boy, though. Zack had an innate talent for invisibility, the same as an adder is born knowing how to kill. His manner was humble enough to be unthreatening, confident enough to make people ignore him. Good magicians understood that the audience wanted to be fooled, wanted to see a harmless teenager or a black man so old he couldn't cause trouble. Every twitch and step should convey only what the viewer wanted to read.

In the days when the Law still held sway, such a boy would have sought out a shaman's knowledge. His trials would have been held in places no ordinary human dared enter, places like burial grounds or caves. If he endured the spirits might send a vision, and in it the gift of healing, the art of herbs, the speech of animals.

Dana's own training had been unconventional. By the time of his birth, most tribes had been locked down on reservations. It was the Killing Time, a twenty-year period when retribution parties rode out like the monstrous Dreamtime cannibals. Whole tribes were slaughtered for the crimes, real or perceived, of a few Aborigines.

The worst part about those pale riders was how quickly rival clans helped them. Centuries of dickering over hunting grounds and curses ended with the roar of black powder. Trackers worked rock and river where no European could find life, let alone the signs it left behind. The skill of the men was so refined they could identify individuals by their footprints.

Sometimes trackers were brought up from Adelaide or New South Wales. They were the worst of the race traitors, for they tracked for money alone. Often they were given uniforms and membership in the black police force. No matter how shiny their buttons or how numerous their medallions, the splendor was as shrill as a mourner's grief.

Some would say Dana was the modern equivalent of the tribal police. But there would always be fools who saw only a site's symbolic value. Nostalgia offered nothing to the owners or the country if the *djang* was not regularly sung. The old were dying off too quickly to preserve the sites, and the young were too busy to care. Why shouldn't Dana salvage the energy?

It hadn't always been that way. Tjamu, the elder who started Dana on his mystic path, told of different days. Once the seeds of quandong and solanum were scattered after the fruits had been eaten, and pituri was used to bring rain. Songs and ceremonies danced the world out and back in again.

Then the Dreaming turned. The witchetty went lean and the mulga sap bittered. The white man eliminated the raven that ate his crops, the dingo that chased his sheep. The Law demanded a bloodletting, the sorry cut, in exchange. But the white men, for all their command of guns and steel, didn't know how to dodge a spear. The resulting wounds were deadly. No spear, not even the broad-pointed weapons used for war, could match the bullets that flew in return.

"One day," Tjamu had said, "*Wanampi* will return. The Rainbow Serpent's beard will be poison from its chin to the tip of each hair."

"Will it kill the white men?" Dana asked.

"Quickly. Without pause, without malice, it will punish the *piranpa*." He leaned forward, his face glowing over the embers. "Our people will die, too. Those who have forgotten, who turn away from the *Tjukurpa*. Many have not been taught. Others throw their Dreaming on the trash heap. They, too, will be swallowed. That is why I teach you."

The government-issue blankets were thin, and the pair huddled close to the fire. Dana lay awake, watching the stars and thinking about the creator sleeping in its earthen lair.

When *Wanampi* woke, Dana would be ready.

———————

Halfway Downs lay only two hundred kilometers southeast. The roads leading there, however, were too rough for the Falcon. They would backtrack to the Stuart Highway, run south nearly to Alice, then turn onto the Sandover Highway. The route took them over plains where blue mallee and desert bloodwood bent into fantastical creatures. Temperatures were so extreme that minerals varnished the surface of the stones. *Exceptional beauty,* Gabe thought, *created by exceptional stress.*

Rob offered tidbits about the land and its history as they drove. None seemed to obligate a conversation, and Gabe wasn't inclined to start one himself. He sat with his head tucked under, afraid of the dull rage bloating his muscles.

He had been angry before, yes, but out of fear for Ian. What he felt now had a sticky, primordial quality, as if it had been pumped from deep beneath an echoing cave. He longed for the Coral Sea, for the saline precision that would wash him clean. If he never saw the outback again, it would be fine with him.

Eventually they turned onto the Sandover Highway then pulled behind an outcropping some distance from the track. Rob assigned Gabe a few easy tasks and plenty of time to do them. By the time he completed the chores, the young man had spread out their bedrolls, put the billy on to boil, and was halfway to dinner.

Gabe watched the sun drop through the earth. Camping makes you wait, he realized. Wait for water to boil, for food to cook and embers to form. It slowed him to the speed of life, the place where the layers of the world peeled back. The unveiling was much like the peace he felt waiting for clients to come up from a dive.

He sat now in stillness woven from ants and rock and Dreaming. The barest breeze touched his hair and the fire's pageant shocked him. It was a raw, vulnerable core he was seeing, the fragile nuances lost to the everyday crush. He saw, and somewhere deep inside, he bled.

***

"Honestly, Dana, you always find the poshest places to land."

A woman plopped onto the stool at the end of the bar. Her nervous energy had not quite been subdued by her years behind a desk. Although she might have entered middle-age a handsome woman, too many nights perched on a bar stool had scorched her looks. Her face layered debt, divorce and frustration over a bedrock of disappointment.

"Next time, you reckon we could meet in Darwin?" She lit a cigarette and winked. "You can even stay at my place."

"Too risky, Bev. Too many tourists nosing around. Besides, you might be recognized."

"A clerk for the artifacts registry is hardly famous."

"No, but if you're seen during a transfer, it won't be long before someone asks the wrong question."

"I suppose." Her hand found his thigh. "I just know that if we spent more time together, you'd see we have a lot in common."

Dana had come to expect her clumsy advances as often as Kevin's thirsts. It was, in fact, one of the things that ensured her loyalty. Even if Bev were caught, she would martyr herself before she would divulge his name. He wedged an elbow between them.

"Well, what'd you get this time?" she sighed.

"We found more than was listed in the society's description. The top of one boulder was used to mix ochre and a depression had been worn into the stone. It's perfect for that fellow who's interested in coming-of-age rites."

"If you ask me, it's the boys who undergo the rites he's interested in." She beat her cigarette against the ashtray. "Last time he called, he asked could I get a foreskin."

"Bodies, bones, hair...what's another piece? Men like that will line our pockets."

"He's a pervy old bastard who want to wank off with little boys. It's disgusting."

"Man-boy love, black-white love, it's all part of the same world. Some of it's farther from Law." He watched Zack carry a cola to a nearby table.

"Is that why you won't look at me twice? 'Cause I'm white?"

She inhaled furiously. She had confronted him before and knew he would not respond. Clutching her twin pacifiers, she spun off the stool.

"Six o'clock?" he called as she stormed away.

"Half past."

She wriggled into a clutch of men around the pool table. It was always the same with her—charge, skirmish, then retreat to a night of random encounters. She was fairly trim, with a belly that remembered her babies and hair dulled by the decades. But her skin was sweet with decay, and Dana's work demanded purity.

Besides, her desire was for power, not sex. Dana's flesh, though deceptively vital, would hardly appeal to a woman generations younger. Her lust was for his wizard eyes and the slow cycling of his energy. She didn't understand her attraction and knew no other way to bind him to her except through intercourse. It was another illness caused by the white man's ignorance.

On top of that, Dana never touched a woman outside of his race. Not sexually. Although Aboriginal women had always crossed racial boundaries with Pacific Islanders and Spaniards and even the colonialists, Dana found it so repulsive he would rather lie with an animal. At least then there would be no children like that mutt at the Carrara pub with his corrupted blood. Dana would never bring that kind of filth into the world. It was all he could do not to go looking for him now and finish the job.

He shook off his thoughts and leaned back. There was work to be done and more important people with whom to contend. One of them was in the pub right now, inching his way around the room. Dana settled in to watch the boy and the crowd.

By midnight Zack had memorized the order of songs on the jukebox. A37 was his favorite but he had to be careful. The 7 was sticky and if he didn't push it just right, the machine registered the 8 button. A38 was a rock song that had moldered on the juke since the late sixties. Tom liked it, though. He must have been pleased that his son played A38 as often as he did.

When Zack ran out of coins, he cozied up to the dart board and scanned the room every time he walked up to the line. Never the best of players, he put an abnormal number of holes in the wood paneling but he figured it was for a greater good. Things went well until he almost nailed a patron. Zack decided to take a lower profile and sat by the door.

He had found the Toyota parked on the street, its paint deeper than the mist of night. The vehicle shed an acrid odor he couldn't quite place and the bed hung low over the tires. This time the gate was locked. Despite the setback, Zack was sure the lumpy bundles in the back were sacred.

He nursed a soda that had gone stale hours before. The pub was rowdy this close to the weekend, and he didn't want Tom to send him to the kitchen or their private quarters. He watched as the white thug sank into his grog. The men had registered with their initials and had given a post box in Darwin as their address. Zack overheard someone call the thug Kevin, so he knew part of the white fellow's name.

The woman denied her age with too much mascara and lipstick a shade too bright. Her walk, a loose-hipped stagger, was meant to cover how drunk she was. She had approached the black man with a sexual urgency Zack had seen between strangers before. At first he thought she was a prostitute but the way the Aborigine greeted her, fixing her in his vision without soaking in details, proved they had met before.

The way they argued hinted at the length of their acquaintance. Their voices never rose and the fellow never let off his clockwork scan of the crowd, yet the conversation had ended abruptly. After a few hours at the pool table, during which the woman checked a dozen times to see if the Aborigine was watching, she picked up a truckie with a face like butchered lamb. The elder didn't look over, and the woman seemed annoyed to be with the truckie if he wasn't going to notice.

Kevin had fallen in with a group of backpackers. Besides belting out beery laughter that overpowered the music, they didn't do much. Then the elder motioned for Zack to come over. The teen's fingernails tingled and he had the overwhelming urge to scratch his throat but he walked over and managed a greeting that was Sunday casual.

"I must be up early tomorrow," the man said. "Can you wake me? I'll pay you for your trouble."

"Yes, sir. What time?"

"Six sharp." He laid a five-dollar note on the bar. Tom eyed the exchange from the sink but left them to their business.

"Six o'clock, sir. You can pay me then."

"Put your money away. You look strong for your age, Zack. It is Zack?" His brows rose, yet his eyes remained hooded. He was patient and poised like the king snake in his spine. "We could use some help tomorrow. It won't take long but it's heavy work."

"Sounds fine, sir. Six o'clock?"

"Half past, out back. By the red Toyota." He lay some coins on a napkin for his tea. "But you knew that already, didn't you?"

He slipped behind the boy and was up the stairs before Zack could catch his breath.

"I see you've got a gig lined up," Tom said as he cleared the bar. "Do a good job, son. You'll never go wrong giving an honest day's work."

Zack nodded. His heart would eventually return to its normal pace. Even then, he hardly expected to sleep any time that night.

11 Legacy

Zack circled the parking lot, walking off nervous energy until his watch read 5:59 a.m. Gulping his breath, he mounted the stairs to the upper floor. The Aborigine opened on the first knock, as if he had been waiting for the exact moment the teen's knuckles touched wood. Zack swallowed so hard his eyes pressed back into their sockets.

He thought the man might say something about his eavesdropping last night. Dana only asked if he still planned to help unload the truck. When Zack said yes, the man followed him downstairs. It was unnerving to have someone walk behind him without making a sound.

At this hour, the pub was filled only with breakfast guests. Zack bussed tables while Kevin buddied up with Sinclair, a hard-drinking regular who spent his days spelunking for bat guano. Organic farmers liked it but it smelled like a pit toilet with a kangaroo stuffed down the shaft. And as much as old Sinny claimed the work paid, he rarely parted with the extra few dollars for a shower.

"Bat piss and bug juice," he said. "No job for a beauty queen but it pays me tab."

"We sell shit, too," Kevin said. "Only we spell it a-r-t."

"Oh, that boong shit. Yeah, that ain't worth the ass off a chicken." He looked up as Dana appeared beside his chair.

"Oh, I don't mean you. It's them black fellahs on the reservations what get me. 'Gimme some land. Gimme some food. Gimme some money for me dog 'cause me grandpappy's grandpappy lived with the dingoes.'" He wiped his wet, wet lips. "You, though, you're not one of them."

"Yes, I am. I'm boong through and through, *piranpa*."

"Hey, now, I don't mean nothing. You look decent, is all. You're clean and you're clothes ain't tore up. No cause for calling names."

"I called you a white man. You are a white man? Skin the color of urine, eyes like the scum on bird dung..."

Tom popped out of the kitchen. Tending bar had given him a radar for trouble, and Zack knew this group threw sharp little rockets across his screen.

"Fellahs," he called, "if you'll take a seat over here, I'll bring your food out. Everything's set up for you, cream and hot tea, everything you'll want."

The Aborigine didn't move. Sinclair's knee twitched, a muscle in his cheek fluttered. Finally he looked away.

"Just trying to make conversation," he mumbled into his beard.

Zack slipped out as the three settled in for breakfast. He passed through the kitchen and around the back stairway, checking the clock as he went. He had almost fifteen minutes before he had to be out back. *Time enough,* he thought. Just barely.

Creep, creep, little mouse. Zack eased up the back staircase. He knew every dip and loose nail, every splinter and crack that would pop or groan. His mother didn't like him to be out after dark. Too many transients, she said, too many rough-and-tumble jackaroos blew off steam in Marbella. But when the moon called to him, he snuck down the back staircase to wander the bush.

All those nights avoiding Rita's sharp ears served him now. He didn't know exactly why he was being so sneaky, though. He was *supposed* to be there. He checked the guest bath and toilets every day, cleaned up any mess, set out fresh towels and soap and shavers for the next round. His presence was perfectly normal, perfectly expected, and perfectly hair-raising.

The oddball travelers made him twitchy. Kevin was no more than a thug. Harder than most, maybe, but incapable of disguising even simple lies. The other fellow was rotten, him and his cargo both. If he had left his door unlocked like many other travelers did, Zack might find something. He wasn't sure what to look for. A bill of lading, perhaps, or orders from a museum. Anything could be forged but at least he'd have a clue.

With those thoughts spinning behind his eyes, the teen miscounted. The next riser groaned horribly. Not so small a mouse to have made such a racket. Shaking the ice from his legs, he stepped rapidly up the rest of the stairs. He would do better not acting like a thief in his own home. Rapping smartly on the toilet door, Zack stepped into the cubby.

Dana stood in the shadows near the main staircase. He had noticed the boy's look as they began eating, had felt him slip from the pub in a casual way. Zack was good. Fear radiated from him like the firestorms that swept the bush but he controlled it better than most men. The boy's history had yielded to Dana's discrete inquiries, and the shaman knew he must have connected with the bush at an early age.

The *piranpa* who heard the earth whisper beneath their heels were rare. In fact, that roo shooter had shown some of the same skills. Enough to remain hidden while Dana looted the cache of artifacts and to track the Toyota despite their meandering path. A man like that could be dangerous.

As a teenager, Zack was more amusing than threatening. He lacked the training that might mold his ability into a useful form. Still Dana admired the teen...and even the roo shooter. He could teach the smartest man every song and ceremony, show him how to find quartz and make magic with animal bones. But memorization and repetition would yield nothing without the music of the country in a man's soul.

White men, with their metal and machines and their mania for conquest, never understood the Aborigines or their land. One of their first efforts to wipe out the native population had been the Black Line, two thousand soldiers and civilians who tried to drive Tasmania's tribes onto a peninsula. After months of effort, two Aborigines were captured.

If Zack had been there, he could have said why the effort failed. He would have appreciated how a woman familiar with every inch of her country could slip between the trees and beyond the soldiers' grasp. He might have spotted the mark made by a child as he squeezed into a crevice where the *piranpa* thought only a possum could hide. But without the proper ceremonies, Zack would remain a boy. Dana watched, wrapped in stillness, as the teen padded toward room five.

⸻

The door was ajar. A wedge of cheddar light fell into the corridor. No matter what kind of bulbs his father put into the fixtures, the upper floor was always filled with an orange glow. Zack peered into the room and noticed that the closet door was slightly off true. If anyone showed up, he could claim maintenance duties. He glanced down the hall and pushed the door open the rest of the way.

"Hello?"

Silly nit, he thought as his voice echoed against the ceiling. Did he expect someone to step out of the closet or roll from under the bed? Even if someone was hiding, he wasn't likely to step out with a wink and a smile. Blocking his shoulders with official intent, Zack stepped inside.

The room was a showcase of military neatness and financial efficiency. The cotton coverlet wore a row of geometric flowers his mother had cut from cloth scraps. Across it lay the brown leather jacket Dana had kept in his lap the evening before. The shelves held a layer of dust deposited by yesterday's windstorm, a set of keys on a braided strap, an apple, and nothing more. Zack pulled the door shut and glanced over his shoulder as he hustled back to the rear staircase.

Sweat pricked his cheeks as something clicked in his head. Some fine texture to the shadows at the end of the hall was different. He knew without looking again that the Aborigine was there, that he had watched Zack's every slinking step. The teen forced his feet to move as the trio of leaded glass windows cast spirits on the risers. Not knowing whether the silent man followed, he descended into the smoky heart of his father's pub.

***

"How ya holding up, mate?" Rob asked.

"I wouldn't mind a shower," Gabe said. "And a decent cot would do better than this bedroll."

"You sure you're not from England?" Rob grinned. "Because the only other person I've heard gripe so much is a Pommie."

"Nope. I might have an Irish bent from mum but that's not the same." He peeled oranges while Rob fried the tinned beef. "I was lucky she adopted me. She was able to help me through some tough times when I was a teenager."

"I bet your brothers and sister were a help, hey?"

"In their way. My sister thought I was an oversized doll, so she was delighted to play with me. My brothers were too old to bother. Being the only black face at school or on the mall...that was the hard part. Summers were better because some of the tourists were black. It kind of helped without really helping, if that makes sense."

"Ya felt like ya blended in more?"

"Yeah. But there wasn't any depth to it, no meaning I could hold onto after they were gone."

Gabe suddenly realized why he had looked forward to trips with Ian so much. Oh, he had griped about the flies and mosquitoes, worried about snakes and spiders, and had put up with more than his share of teasing because he always took a flashlight into the bush when he relieved himself.

For all the hardships, real and imagined, Gabe enjoyed the excursions. Ian knew a great deal about the bush and with his healthy appreciation of Aboriginal culture, he seemed to know a story for every star. Ian had taught him a lot and had fed some hunger Gabe had hardly noticed was there. Or perhaps he had noticed the need and only now understood its source.

Which meant, of course, that Chance had been right. How could she have seen something in him that he had missed? He stared at the embers creaking under the ash. Slowly, very slowly, he pushed dirt over their liquid glow.

At precisely six-thirty, Dana pulled the truck behind the hotel. The sun promised to flare into an angry blue but the morning was bearable yet.

"Beverly, this is Zack. He's going to help us today."

"Hello, lovely." She squeezed his arm then his shoulder. "How old are you? I bet all the girls are after you."

"Watch out," Kevin grinned. "She'll eat you with hot sauce."

Zack unraveled from her grasp then helped carry the first stone to an industrial-grade flatbed. Dana jammed a straw into a can of spray paint and marked the artifact with a number. As the rock was packed away, Bev transcribed his comments.

"Number one. Three depressions where ochre was ground." Dana marked the second rock. "Two. Painting of snake, red ochre and charcoal. Note blood sacrifice."

The process continued until the larger segments were evenly distributed across the bottoms of the crates. Kevin brought loaded knapsacks to the truck while Zack sat on the flatbed and packed away the smaller artifacts.

Dana watched closely. The teen was fascinated, possibly even astonished. The *djang* in these rocks was male Dreaming. It was, in fact, the power that made boys into men. Upon touching the first stones, his fear had visibly melted away. From then on he appeared to see nothing except the carvings, the drawings and the blood.

Oddly, Dana felt gratified. Nearly his whole life, the sorcerer had kept his distance from his own people. He respected the Pitjantjatjara, to be sure, but his years at the mission had corrupted some delicate part of his spirit. He rarely entered the region where he had been born, and even then he avoided contact with his clan.

His self-imposed exile had been meant as a temporary solution. The bitterness that had etched his soul at the mission was too caustic. To return with all that poison inside would destroy what he so desperately loved. He stayed away for years, then decades, but the toxins sank deep into his bones. Soon a lifetime had been upon him. He had been in his sixties when he'd realized there was no cure.

Among the countless things he had lost was the opportunity to pass along his knowledge. Of course, the *Tjukurpa* would continue regardless; even a skilled clever man couldn't save or vanish that *djang* on his own. But the Law was as real as the water that filtered through the substrate and the wind that moved the stars. Training a novice created a legacy. In Zack, the sorcerer caught a glimpse of what might have been.

"Slow down," Bev said, "my hand's tired. How much of this is true, anyway?"

"How much is it worth if it's wrong?" Dana smiled.

Bev laughed and ancient cigarette smoke rose from the bottom of her lungs. The smell was that of damp iron, and Dana turned away.

"She's with the Preservation Society of Adelaide," he said to Zack. "We're moving these to a safe place where many people can enjoy their beauty."

The teen wouldn't buy that story but at least he'd have an easy answer for his father. Most people, Dana knew, were happy with solutions that were as basic as primary colors. But they lived in a rainbow world, the nuances of which were appreciated only by a few. There would be no one to catch Dana's errors in the reconstruction of objects or their meaning. And, of course, he would be paid the same even if he were wrong.

But the shaman was never wrong. Not about *djang*.

They broke camp as the last of the night burned away. Gabe thought of it as the changing time, when colors and sounds retracted like coral hiding in their bony cells. Bird song stopped, the golden tone faded and the day turned functional. It happened as smoothly as a curtain drawn and allowed the world to commence with its fiction. It was the closest he ever came to the divine.

When they stopped for petrol, Gabe found his favorite brand of caramel cookies behind a bin of sugar wafers. He didn't dare check the expiration date. He would eat them even if they were gummy.

At the counter, the cashier talked around a wad of chewing tobacco. "That yer mate at the Bowser?" he asked.

"My friend's getting the petrol. I'll pay when he's done."

"What I said. Bowser's the pump. Yer a Yank, ain't yer? One a' yer Americans invented that pump. It's named after him, Bowser."

"I'm Australian." He shot Rob a look as the younger man came in and snagged a frozen custard from the cooler.

"Don't sound it," the cashier said. "Yer pick yer words all fussy like a Brit. But yer ain't rude, so yer can't be a Yank. Yer Canadian?"

"My mother was Irish."

"Hah! One a' them black Irish, was she? That explains yer color *and* yer accent."

Rob hit the door running. Gabe followed the trail of custard out to the car.

"So." The young man gripped the wheel so tightly his arms quivered.

"So."

"Your mum. Black Irish."

"Apparently."

Rob spilled the rest of the custard as laughter burst out in waves. Gabe stared at the lot. The insistent clarity of the sun hurt his eyes. The ancient Bowser, the hand pump for water, even the scale of eucalyptus leaves seemed surreal. Slowly, like the cracking of earth, he began to laugh.

"Black Irish!" Rob roared. "Your mum! Black Irish!"

The sedan rolled back onto the highway as the ravens fled from their laughter.

<hr>

Another hour passed as they packed the artifacts. The whole time, Kevin did nothing more than lean against the truck and drink, although Zack assumed he would run interference with curious tourists. The teen touched the shapes made by one stone chipping out the face of another. He fell into the rhythm of Dana's voice until he could almost hear the songs crying out from the Dreamtime. Finally he nailed the crates shut.

"Do you like the carvings?" Dana asked.

The elder's hair was so thick he looked decades younger than his age. There was, however, a powdery quality to his skin, like rubber left in the sun, that made Zack think he was older than anyone he'd ever known.

"You think the rock art should be left in its original place." Dana peeled a number of bills from a roll. He leaned forward, his eyes curiously aglow.

"Things in this world," he said, "are not always as they seem."

Zack stood staring as they drove away. When the trucks disappeared along the track, he was surprised to find the money in his hand.

12 Halfway Downs

Four dusters hung in the mud room, all muggy to the touch. Shrimp-colored water, a mixture of a sudden downpour and the endless dust, pooled on the floor. Annie sighed. *So much work around the station,* she thought, *and so much of it running just to keep up.*

Annie was a lean woman whose sturdy bones ransacked her flesh for room. She was strong enough to lift fifty-kilo sacks of feed, yet she never failed to look delicate. Women who didn't know her often thought she was pregnant, and men of all ages immediately felt comfortable in her presence. She was the kind of person strangers made every effort to help but who wound up helping the strangers.

Not that she met new people very often. The closest town was fifty kilometers overland or twice that by roads nearly as rough. The ranch was populated year-round by two hired hands, her family, and a trickle of visitors who wandered up the drive on the off chance she might let them camp in her yard. Additional jackaroos were brought in twice a year to muster cattle for shots or tick baths or the long trip to market.

The work was never easy. Cows had to be monitored during calving, weaners had to be separated from their mothers during dry spells, yearlings had to be castrated and branded, lame bulls had to be culled. The windmills that pumped water from underground and the berms that held the water had to be maintained. Trucks and tractors needed attention, fences wanted mending, and the cattle were always hungry. Always.

Then there was the freezer shed with its six-month store of food; the ductwork that funneled rainwater from the roof for drinking; motorized pumps that pushed artesian water to the toilets and showers; and a host of other maintenance demands. Successful agriculture, she knew, was the management of problems that cycled with the seasons. Cleaning was slotted between calls to the accountant, tracking beef prices, and juggling money. Dirt was always in season.

This far into the dry, the grass was nothing but hay so poor the cattle starved with their bellies full. Euros drowned in the wells and dingoes scavenged the livestock that dropped from exhaustion. With dust feathering her tongue, the meals tasted of tin and fatigue.

As usual, her husband had been right about how soon the rain would stop. Bret and the hired hands had returned to work without their dusters, leaving Annie to wrangle with the creditors. She took a moment to watch the shadows glide off the pools on the road. Tomorrow the ground would be tinted with lime, and in two days the pasture would be flush. By week's end it would be gone, eaten or trampled or seared by the sun.

It seemed like such a little thing, this greening of the land. Stations lived on little things and often were broken by them. Annie didn't like how hard Bret worked. He never complained, even when bushfires burned off the last bits of grass or the cattle caught fever. She worried that his silent dedication would drive him until his heart burst.

Now the pressure in the new well was dropping. Their son Collin needed money for books and food at university, the main generator had yet to be replaced after the spring blowout, and the backup wouldn't run much longer. Even without the drought, Annie couldn't see how they would make it.

She sighed and put the kettle on. The kitchen window framed the barn lot, the space between the house and the other buildings. Directly across from the verandah stood a stone barbecue and a picnic table for their many cookouts. Further on lay the corral for the weaners.

A sound like the rubbing of onion skins announced a flock of birds. As Annie crossed the porch, a shoal of galahs encrusted the buildings. Ropes of them wound atop the corral; they huddled by pairs on the fence posts and blanketed the shed. The trucks were a mass of red and gray lit by a shining rain of eyes.

And the noise...my God, the noise! Claws gnawed the rooftops. Wings cracked the air inches from her face. Even the mutter of their feet could be heard as they waddled through the lot. The sheer weight of their unearthly numbers sent the gutter crashing to the ground.

They screamed, Lord God how they screamed, and the ones on the clothesline dangled upside down. It was the sound of coins, of metal sheering from fatigue, of a locust plague. From above and below, from gum trees in front of her and the house behind came their cries, as holy and dreadful as a monsoon.

Finally a group rose and banked around the house. The smell of feathers, like earth motored with fish oil, like air stored underground, bricked up

Annie's mouth and nose. Their calls drifted back from the horizon, and she wondered at her waking dream.

<hr>

"Cor! I've never seen this before!"

Rob steered around galahs and in the confusion, wound up parking on the lawn. A woman stared from walkway. At first Gabe thought she was angry that the car was crushing the only patch of lawn for hundreds of kilometers. But he realized she had also been shocked by the size of the flock and now wondered that the sky-colored car had dropped into her world with such fanfare. They got out and introduced themselves.

"We're looking for Ian McCabe," Gabe said.

"Of course!" Annie's face brightened. "A real charmer, that one. All the ladies from here to Golwing come runnin' when he's around."

"I'm afraid he's gone missing. Rachel sent us here to look for clues."

"Sorry, I don't follow. How does Rachel know Ian?"

"She doesn't. Ian sent me an artifact. Rachel said it had been hidden on your station." He showed her the message stick. Annie stood for long seconds, her hand holding loose strands of hair against her head.

"No one knows about that except the tribal owners and my family. Perhaps you'd better come in." She waved at the gifts the birds had left. "And watch your step."

A verandah wrapped around three sides of the spacious rambler. In the middle of the porch a trio of wing-back chairs mingled with humble stools and a wooden rocker. Annie invited them to sit while she prepared tea.

Her hospitality apparently won only a partial victory over her curiosity because she didn't let the water come to a boil. Gabe drank the weak tea without comment, feeling rather than tasting the roll of cream and the spur of lemon. More of Annie's hair escaped its chignon, and as she talked she brushed it repeatedly over the top of her head.

"This is a horrid, horrid thing," she said. "It means someone's been snooping around the property. No telling what else they've gotten into."

"Did you know the storage area had been broken into?" Gabe asked.

"It wasn't really secured, I'm afraid. A collection of ceremonial objects was hidden in a cavern in the north pasture."

"I thought things like that would be secret."

"Rachel showed me the sites so we could preserve them. She told me little things, if it was all right for me to hear. Apparently her brother-in-law came from this country. Did Ian say how he found the message stick?"

"No, and I'm not sure why he sent it to me, of all people."

"Perhaps he thought my hired hands weren't trustworthy. I know Ian was not the type to steal."

Gabe nodded, relieved that he wouldn't have to justify his friend's actions to her, at least. "Rachel said we're to see the *bora* grounds."

"Yes, that's the place where the things were hidden," she said. "It's best we get started right away."

Rob wrapped the remaining cookies in a napkin and followed Annie across the barn lot. The truck was a recent model with plenty of miles already stacked on it. A horn-shaped dent, ending with a neat hole, marred the fender.

"Will there be any cattle at the *bora* ground?" Gabe wriggled into the middle. "Any bulls, maybe?"

"A few. They shouldn't bother us much. If they do, just hop in the truck."

She offered him a stick of eucalyptus-flavored gum, the same brand he had chewed by the yard when he'd run track in high school. Running had been his specialty, the one area where he could excel without an audience to validate his performance. He remembered the sound of the starting gun, the powdery staleness of new sneakers, the wobble of his cheeks with every step. Even when the gum became rubbery, he could detect none of the brine that had fletched his formative years.

"We just passed a birthing cave," Annie said. "It's really a space between the rocks. The ground is scooped away underneath, whether from erosion or to help the mother, I don't know."

"A little of both," Rob called with his head half out the window. "And you shouldn't be looking over there, Gabe. That's women's business, strictly off limits to us blokes. Now, my sister says nobody has to tell her where the sacred sites are because she can feel the *djang*. I reckon she's joking."

"I thought you said she was mad," Gabe said.

"That, too."

Annie stopped before a mound of branches circling a stump. When she cut the engine the silence, so denuded of bird call or breeze, was stifling.

"This was a spirit tree, where the dead climb up to the sky world." She covered her mouth. "Who would do such a thing? Have things changed so little?"

Rob circled the tree, spiraling outward a meter at a time. He touched the cut ends of the branches, dug his thumbnail into the bark and sniffed. He turned over a cigarette butt with the tip of his penknife and excavated piles of sawdust by brushing away thin layers. Finally he followed some invisible trail back to the road.

"How would they know to come here?" Gabe asked.

"Bush telegraph," he said. "When tribes got moved around, everything went to hell. Anthropologists published our sacred lore to dress up their diplomas. Added to the killings and the fevers, that's a heap of lost Dreaming. What's left is dear but not everyone reckons the importance of a secret."

"What're you looking for?"

"Everything. Nothing. Tracking is as much what's not there as what is." He pointed to the road. "See those tread marks? They're shallow, sort of smoothed over by the wind, but they're still visible."

He pulled Gabe into a squat with the tracks between him and the sun. The angle of the light raised the dust into high relief. Gabe leaned over until his face was inches from the ripples and scars. Suddenly he saw it: the crosshatch left by the tires, the mountain kicked up by a sudden start, the dunes blown into the tracks. He followed the trail back to the site where scuff marks whispered of boots and shifting treasures.

"Thought you were a city kid, Rob."

"Me family took us kids out bush on weekends and holidays. Cousins, uncles, aunties, even me grannies came. They wanted us to talk to our land, and to listen. Uncle Angus taught me everything I know, and he's the best."

"Except now, I expect."

"Wrong, mate. He works by touch. Makes him harder to shake 'cause he can track at night."

Rob smiled but Gabe had the feeling he was only half joking.

13 Magic Tea

The truck struggled up the rise. Runoff ruined the track every Wet, and Bret hadn't had time to do more than a cursory job grading the road this year. The whole hill was a sacred spot, a tediously large sacred spot, among the many Annie insisted they preserve. Tomorrow he'd bring the dozer out, cut a pass and be done with it. Annie'd be out of her head but something had to give. Besides, a hundred years of family history on the land surely gave a man some rights.

The Ford parked on the lawn kept him from fussing too long over the calves in the corral, and soon he was crossing the barn lot. He would have been justified in driving the distance but he enjoyed the walk. It was the one time of day he could relax. Otherwise there was always an engine running, or a discussion to be had, or his focus was on whatever was broken. The stroll let him smell the green scent of mangoes and hear the buzz of bees.

Lately the habit felt like stolen time, with his minutes of leisure heaped atop the stack of undone chores. He shook off the urge to tighten the handle on the screen door and went inside. From the mud room, he could see that the table was set for five. That meant two visitors, probably backpackers looking to spend a few days on a working ranch. Annie took in anyone who stopped by, just as her neighbors would. The loneliness could be crushing, especially for women.

Instead of the foreign visitors he expected, two Aborigines were in his home. The older one, perhaps ten years Bret's senior, looked up from the overstuffed chair. Collin was talking with the younger man, clearly happy to have someone closer to his own age around. But eagerness could override caution, and Bret studied the stranger closely.

Not even teenagers looking to try the jackaroo lifestyle smiled so generously. Perhaps because the two were seated together, Bret suddenly realized his son was an odd-looking lad. His mother's complexion, so pale as to make any other man sallow, had mixed with Bret's iron-gray cast. The result lay somewhere between honey and cream, like the fur of a spinifex mouse.

Collin majored in social anthropology, yet there he sat talking about animal husbandry and agriculture, wildlife and urban development. He was much like his grandfather in that way, concerned equally with the affairs of people, land and animals. Bret's sole focus was in that room. If he were concerned about the livestock or the environment, it was only for the impact it might have on his family.

At that moment, his lately pensive son was more engaged with a stranger than he'd been with his father in months. Bret stepped into the bathroom to scrub his face and arms, changed into jeans and a clean t-shirt, and returned to the living room. He wanted to know why these men had come.

———

After some shuffling, everyone found a seat at the dining room table. Bret took the end nearest the living room. His wide shoulders and angled jaw were guarded, and Annie shot him a look anyone would recognize as a warning.

"Dad, this fellah says his uncle can track by feel. That's not right, is it? No one can track if they're blind."

"You've heard of Braille, yeah?" Rob asked. "Same principle."

"My Pappy always said if you're lost out bush," Bret said, "you'd better hope the fellah looking for you is black. That way you're sure to be found. 'Course, I've heard plenty about what Aborigines can do. Doesn't make it true."

Annie peered at him then passed a basket of rolls.

"Me uncle takes a mate. Once the helper finds a track, Angus reads it with his fingers. He can tell you where the animal was looking, how fast it was moving, and where it was headed."

"I've heard about them witch doctors, too," Collin said. "I've heard they can run faster than any man and disappear when there's nowhere to hide. My friend says they carry magic sticks and such."

"Like a message stick?" Gabe asked.

"Naw," Rob said. "He means like a pointing stick or a bone. It helps 'em cast spells, maybe put a curse on ya."

"Is that what you fellahs are doing out here?" Bret asked. "Playing fancy tricks?"

Annie thumped the teapot onto the table. "They are looking for Ian McCabe."

"He's finally gone walkabout." Bret's teeth formed a glittery, slippery sort of smile. "That's no surprise. He always struck me as wild."

"How so?" Gabe sipped the broth, woody with barley. Somehow he didn't think he'd be able to stomach solid food at this meal.

"You'd think he was in a shooting match out there, killing anything that moved."

"That's what he was paid to do."

"He was paid to shoot roos. He shot anything that would turn a quid."

Annie and Collin stopped eating. Rob shoveled on but his eyes flickered.

"McCabe may have talked that save-the-koala crap with you," Bret sneered, "but around here he was the devil with a gun. Word was that his roo-shooting gig was a cover to get him around the country easy. Word was he poached crocodiles off the Roper Bar River, right on top of an Aboriginal camp. Maybe you should talk to them about your friend."

Annie studied her husband, quite analytically, until he felt her gaze.

"You never went out of an evening," he shrugged. "You never saw him on his rounds."

"I didn't need to. That man has a good heart."

"Maybe with people he does. 'A real charmer.' You said so yourself."

Rob dropped his spoon into his bowl. "Right lovely stew, missus. Not even me mum could do better. We'll be heading off now."

"Oh, but you'll not get far before dark. We've quarters for the men who come during muster. Nothing fancy but you'll be comfortable."

She moved squarely between the guests and her husband. Collin smiled as she led the men outside.

<hr>

As Gabe stepped off the porch, he still felt Bret's animosity like the rasp of water during a dive. His neck was terribly stiff and he wondered if the accident was catching up with him. It was hard to believe he had left Townsville less than a week before. His skin felt as brittle as if he'd been in the desert for months. The breeze promised a cool night, though, and he watched cockatoos haggle for space in a stand of eucalypts.

"Please, you mustn't let my husband make you feel you're not welcome," Annie said. "I won't apologize as there's no excusing rude behavior. But he's been under so much pressure lately. We're all feeling the push."

"Is there anything we can do?" Gabe asked.

"Oh, it's the cattleman's cry, is all. Not enough rain, poor grass when there is."

She mounted a walkway in front of a trailer and opened the first door. To the right sat a cot with a patchwork quilt folded at the end. A dresser and a folding chair took up the opposite wall.

"Sheets are in the bottom drawer. Kerosene lanterns are in every room. I'm afraid there's no electricity. These rooms are only used a few weeks out of the year."

"Are you sure we won't be intruding?"

"I'll be upset if you leave now. Take your pick of the rooms. Shower's in the shed around back and there's a pit toilet to the right."

"Really, much nicer than camping ever could be. You're very kind." Gabe stepped aside as she moved down the stairs.

"Don't mind Jocko." She waved at a shaggy pony. "We keep him on the lawn so he can graze. I suppose you think it wasteful, to water a lawn just so I can have something green to look at. But the pony gets something fresh to eat, too. Come to the kitchen in the morning. Breakfast is at seven sharp."

She disappeared into the house, shutting the door a little too forcefully. Bret's voice returned her anger, and the men stood quietly until Collin's stereo drown out the argument. They waited a few minutes more but no one came out to tell them to leave. Finally Rob shrugged and investigated the remaining rooms.

Gabe pulled a change of clothes, his towel and the overnight bag from the car. Besides the usual toiletries, the bag held a book he had yet to open, a miniature flashlight, and earplugs for nights at noisy pubs. Everything smelled of the cedar soap Chance had made for him. The scent was soothing, and he was glad of its comfort.

He opened a small double picture frame. On the left was a photo of the McCabes at a picnic. Ian was wearing the asbestos apron Dob had received after scorching his shirt at the company barbie. The other picture was Gabe's family a year before his father's death. The patriarch stood, as he always had when presenting himself to the world, touching mum's chair.

To his right were Danny and Bob, and Bob's wife and toddlers. To his left stood Gabe and Nancy with her then-beau Sam. Or was it Steve? Her passions, intense and brief, had always left him dizzy and a little anxious. He wished he had brought a larger picture of mum. She was small in the group shot and while her smile was a beacon, he couldn't see the rest of her face clearly.

The day he'd left Townsville, she had made him eat a big breakfast. She had been in her slippers, and dawn had made petals of her wrinkles. When he peered past the hydrangea bush, he saw that the lawn wanted cutting and the rubbish bin was about to lose its wheel again.

"Tell Danny he'll have to take care of things while I'm gone," Gabe said.

"Oh, he's so far away. I won't bother him."

"Halifax is not so far a drive. You'd never know you raised four children for all the help you get."

"You always have done right by others, Gabe. You who've been so wronged." She patted his hand and eased herself into the chair. "Must you go?"

"Ian's my best friend, mum."

"Yes, I suppose. Only fellow you ever took after. Rosy will thank you. The poor thing, her only son gone and no body to mourn." She retrieved the cream from the counter and rubbed her neck. "Remember when you'd come in from those nighttime swims? I'd have tea and you'd have cocoa. You never let me fix it proper, you never wanted milk."

"It was too light otherwise." He smiled. "It had to be the same color as my skin."

"Do you regret having had a white mother? I did my best by you, same as for all my kids. We never would've taken you if we'd known the truth. We didn't know any better back then."

"I know, mum." He lost track of the sugar and added one lump too many.

"You've always been so fair about it, never said much nor acted out. For the longest time after I was sent here, I was so angry with my father that I wouldn't write to him, I only wrote my mum and my brothers. All these years, I've never seen you angry."

"There was no point. I couldn't change the past with screaming."

"So you've never screamed at all."

They stared across the teapot. How could she ever imagine the anger that bubbled inside him, the rage that had curled up like the tiniest seashells and plunked deep into an empty place, weighting it but never, ever filling it up? She couldn't know. No one could, and talking about it wouldn't soften the kernels one bit.

"I'll be going now." Gabe drank off the tea and stood. "I've arranged for the grocer's to deliver."

"Oh, I can still walk up the block. You do make a fuss over me."

"At least we know where it comes from." He leaned down to hug her. She pressed his hand between hers, and the fire in her joints was fierce.

"Come back to me, Gabe. Do what you can for Ian and his family but don't you get lost out there."

Even now, it was her hands Gabe remembered. He wondered how she was. She had sounded so tired during his last call. Worried, of course, but that was normal. Ian's disappearance had changed things between them. A subtle change, to be sure, so subtle that until this moment he hadn't recognized the shift. But a wistful quality had crept into her words, like the sigh of tides under the waves. They still drifted on the same ocean except now they were in separate boats.

He folded the clothes across the chair. They would leave right after breakfast, so there was only this night to survive. He thought about how little he really needed to live. His lifestyle must have seemed extravagant to a man who lived out of the back of a truck. But if that were true, what might drive Ian to poaching? Rob's knock kept him from following his doubt further.

"Looks like the end units have extra windows," he said. "Might be best to stay close tonight, so I'll be right next door."

"I don't doubt it. Bret acted like we were criminals the second he walked in."

"We're black, mate. For some blokes we don't have to be or do anything more."

"Did he think we might attack his wife? He looked at you as if you were about to kidnap his son."

"He was probably afraid we'd steal his land. He can get another family." He flopped onto the cot. "You know how touchy all this land claim business is. Two black fellahs come on your station these days, more's your worries. First we look at a few sites then we come around with our friends for a corroboree. Then the whole tribe camps out until the government gives back the land."

"It's a reasonable fear, isn't it? You hear about it on the news every week." Gabe leaned against the doorjamb. "I know a lot of those things look how the reporters want them to look. It's accurate enough, though."

"Is it now? Have ya heard about the backlash? Sacred sites are being vandalized. They spray paint the rock art, shoot up the carvings, and steal anything that's not nailed down."

"I heard some bones turned up in Cairns."

Rob sat up and shook his head. "The worst part is that it costs too much to figure out where the old ones belong. Those bodies will end up in the storage bin of some museum. First our land, then our songs, now our dead."

"At least it's the dead they're taking."

The sweat on his back went cold as the breeze finally reached the building. Night was coming. Somewhere in the bush, creeping, creeping, was the old cannibal woman. Gabe felt her sliding between the bushes, each step hushed by the soft dust. He smelled her hunger, like mildew riding her breath, as she waited for him to wander too far from the fire. When Rob resumed talking, a part of Gabe feared the grip of her icy hand.

"Without songs, the land can't live. But without ancestors there's no link, the cycle is broken. We can remember the songs or learn them again from the trees and earth. We can hang on in a strange place until we return to our country. But if the dead are gone, there's no place to go back to." He looked at Gabe. "As for stealing the children...."

He walked to the balcony and leaned against the rail. The house was quiet now and the lights in the barn lot went out. Gabe continued staring into the room, his eyes filled with the rainbow quilt aglow in the lantern's light.

"You'd have to talk to someone like Angus," Rob said, "an elder who's got wisdom. What the government did...it just doesn't seem human."

14 Spider Lightning

Gabe heard the clack of crabs breaking coral. Birds of every kind scrambled through his dreams—screaming gulls and whistling swifts, cockatoos and corellas and lorikeets. He wondered where the pigeon was, the bird Selena had said was his totem. The grass in his dreams was impenetrable and the crab kept tapping, *rickety-tickety-clap,* until Gabe stumbled to his feet.

Opening the door didn't clear his head much. The light was too sudden, as if morning had struck with the speed of a snake. He squinted at the lawn, at the potbellied Shetland eating, endlessly eating, and Rob's beaming face.

"Jocko's a hungry horse," Gabe grumbled as they moved down the path. "He kept me up half the night trying to eat the screen. When he finally figured out it wasn't made of hay, he stood under the window chewing his cud."

"Do horses chew a cud?"

"Whatever he was doing, he was bleeding loud." He jumped as the pony rubbed against his thigh. "Quit! Damn thing's lucky I didn't run it off."

"Cor, that's all we need. The man of the house goes for a snack and sees a half-naked boong chasing his pony. He'd take the rifle after you, true!"

"I was wearing shorts."

"What kind of barbie do you get off a Shetland, anyway? Short ribs?"

Gabe wiped green spit from his pants and tried not to laugh. Rob found a trio of galah feathers, shards of fog, and tied them with a thread from the hem of his shirt. They were almost to the porch when Gabe touched his arm.

"Why do you use that word?" he asked. "Why did you say boong?"

"If I don't, someone else will."

Collin waved from a table on the west side of the porch. "Tell me about the magic men," he said while the group settled in. "Is it true they can do all those things? Like be in two places at once or fly through the trees?"

"They'd like you to think that," Rob said. "Magic is mostly a game you play with reality, yeah? Some slight of hand, a little skill. And an audience, of course."

"So it's all kiddy tricks," Bret said as he stepped onto the porch.

The temperature rose so quickly Gabe thought a brazier had been shoved under his chair. Normally he dealt with people like Bret by walking away. This morning, though, with the birds still screaming in the basement of his brain, Gabe thought of a few choice words he'd like to share with Bret. For Annie's sake, he stayed quiet.

"I wouldn't go so far as that," Rob continued, as calm as a koala. "It's illusion and reality mixed up together. Let's say a shaman leaves for another camp two hours away. There's no horses or pushbikes or camels but he gets there faster than if a regular bloke ran. The shaman moves so fast, you think he must be in two places at once."

"How could he do that?" Collin asked.

"He ran."

"You said no one can run that fast."

"OK, so he walked." Rob shrugged. "Shamans move in a special way that eats up the distance. Like you're doing with that sausage."

"You're fooling. Tell me true, please?"

"That's as true as a gift, mate. Clever men learn different ways of doing things. Can't tell it better than what me uncle told me."

"Yogis can do something like that," Gabe said. "It's a form of meditation, I think. They walk all day and never get tired."

"Annie. Forgot the cream." Bret's voice was as hard as ironwood. After she disappeared, he turned to the men. "About time to move on, fellahs."

"Right you are," Rob said.

Gabe swallowed what was in his mouth, folded his napkin, and stood just as Annie returned. She took in Collin's slouch, Bret's Gorgon pose and the hovering guests. She set the cruet carefully on the table. "You'll have tea before you leave."

She folded her hands and sat only after the men had taken their chairs. The cicadas geared up with the shrill of a sawmill. Otherwise there was only the dunk of spoons and the plunk of sugar cubes diving to safety.

"What's the weather been lately?" Rob finally asked.

"Gentlemen," Annie said. "Surely there are more interesting topics than the weather."

"Knowing the weather will help me sort out what I saw at the spirit tree."

"You're a tracker?" Bret asked. "Who taught you?"

"Angus Kamare."

"How good are you?"

"Fair enough. You lose someone?"

The cicadas broke their song. The morning hardened and the weaners bawled piteously.

"Come on, Collin. Calves are waiting." He lifted his hat from the bench beside the door. "Annie, track the weather from the log so these fellahs can be on their way."

Collin paused on the steps. "You'll stop in next time you're out this way? I'm going back to university soon but you can always write me here."

"Count on it, mate," Rob grinned.

The teen followed his father across the barn lot. For the first time since waking, Gabe relaxed. He and Rob would be far down the track before Bret returned.

When Annie brought the station's daybook from the office, Gabe learned that the past week had been fine and bright with stronger winds than normal. A calf named Duffer wasn't weaning, a whippet had lost an ear to a possum, and the fish pond they had struggled with all year had officially been abandoned. Nothing much out of the ordinary, and certainly nothing to explain the theft.

Rob asked for a visitor's log. After Annie went inside, he flipped to the previous summer. Gabe peered over his shoulder. Annie had recorded the loan officer's birthday, their trips to town, and the pregnancy of a jackaroo's wife. Finally he caught a familiar name.

Ian McCabe came, none too soon. Many boomers about. Ellie will be over soon. Maybe she'll catch his eye this year.

Bret's notes from the same summer were squeezed into rows of baby teeth that gnawed at the page.

Shooter busy last night. Quarantined heifer 6511. Lump jaw? Two sows dead, boar sick.

And the next day, in the same print:

Boar dead. Fixed pump well 15. McCabe made quota, left this a.m.

"Sorry it took me so long." Annie bustled back and Rob shut the record. "The visitor's log is never where I think it should be. Seems we had a family of Swiss here about that time." She flipped through the pages.

"Yes, here it is. Such careful print foreigners always have. There was a teenage girl, two boys and the father. The girl writes, 'The animals are all so pretty. Must you shoot them? Can you not trap them for a petting park?'" She handed the log to Gabe. "I think she had a crush on your friend. Broke her heart to find out what he did for a living."

"It's a touchy subject." Gabe reviewed the weeks before and after Ian's visit. "For such a remote station, you seem to enjoy a lot of company."

"Everyone comes when you're too busy to visit, and when you've time there's never a soul." She pressed Gabe's arm. "A shame we've met for such a sad reason. Do come back after this is over. Bret is usually the model host, I promise."

She offered the men a jar of marmalade and walked them out. As Rob turned the car around, he gave Gabe a sly grin. "Sheila's sure like to feed you up."

"Oh? I hadn't noticed."

"Something special, you are, all wide-eyed and proper. 'No, thank you kindly' this and 'yes, please' that. They eat that up and you with it. Don't tell me it's not an act."

"OK, I won't." He held the jar up to the sun. "Why didn't you want her to see you checking last year's entry?"

"Bret made it sound like your friend had come out just the once but she talked like it had been at least two years running. And didn't you call them from Townsville?"

"Yes. I talked to a man, probably Bret, although it could have been an employee."

"He gave you stuff-all for leads and there was no note of the call in the log. Someone asks about a fellah gone missing from your property, you'd make a note, hey?" He hung the galah feathers from the mirror. "At any rate, with a husband like that, I thought it best she didn't get any ideas from me."

"You think Bret has something to do with this?"

"Let's say I don't trust the man. If I'm right then the less his family knows, the better."

◆━━━◆━━━◆

Dana pulled into Katherine as smoke filtered between the buildings. To the northwest a bushfire skimmed over hundreds of acres and its glow was visible from the outskirts of town. The air was peppery and bold, and reminded residents of the outback's sudden moods.

Bushfires were never much of a threat to lives but the structures and possessions the *piranpa* held more dear were of concern. Dana wondered if the Vanishing would be like that, with everything the Europeans valued consumed while they watched. They would be as helpless as the tribes had been when white plagues shattered the world.

Normally he would take a cup of tea at a sidewalk cafe and watch as the town monitored the flames. Now, however, he was tired from a day spent on the docks of Darwin and a night spent over a noisy pub. Whenever he visited

[88]

Katherine, he played the role of a senior weak enough to need help getting off the toilet. Right now the feeble act wasn't much of a stretch.

A few days of down time had always been enough to help him manage the next round of thefts. Lately, though, the breaks had become longer, the energy expended higher, and the finances less of a boost. His age, of course, had been creeping through his bones for some time, and he had sprained his ankle on his last trip into sandstone country. His control of the *djang* remained steady, however.

No, some other ache threaded the core of his muscles, some support cable in his being had frayed. Seeing Zack again had brought it into focus. The knowledge he would take to his grave was a burden. Only other song keepers who died without passing on their skills would understand.

He blinked deliberately and pulled behind the Fox and Hounds. The proprietor knew Dana by now, of course, but he never tried to play tour guide or nose into a guest's business like the owner of a smaller place might. Over the next week, the shaman would have the tailgate fixed, restock supplies, settle accounts and plan their next job.

Then Dana would slip into the bush. He would net birds for their feathers—the yellow-tinted wings of cockatoos, handfuls of breast feathers, and whole hides from the occasional emu. Depending on the country and the season, he might gather plant silk from the fist-sized nuts of the kapok tree or from *tjulpun-tjulpunpa*, wildflowers like daisy and billy button.

The ceremonial objects would be prepared before he dared approach the next site. Like many people these days, Dana bought string from the store and rolled strands of his hair into the twine to saturate it with his energy. Fat was another resource. The emu provided lard in quantity, with the grease of lizards and snakes the most prized. And, of course, he always painted the spirit board, his touchstone.

The work was exhausting, truly, and screening new buyers interested him less and less. But the next site would feel as sweet beneath his feet and its treasures would yield to his expert hands. A week's rest would find him back on the road with new vigor.

***

Gabe pulled into a roadhouse that clung to life in a creaky, groaning sort of way. The gas pump leaked, the showers were screened by a mosaic of hoods from different cars, and a goat looked down from the roof. Tiny bells on its collar offered the only festive touch. Rob filled the drinking water and returned the jugs to the car.

"She's as full as a possum carrying twins," he said.

"Where do you get these sayings?"

"Uncle Gummy."

"Your uncle's named for the gum tree?"

"Named for he hasn't any teeth. When he eats, he chews with his mouth open. Mashes stuff up, really. He just eats soft things. Anyway, all ya can see are his gums. And whatever he's eating, of course. That's Uncle Gummy."

"That's...logical." Gabe smiled until the goat appeared and nibbled at the fliers. "Go on, you smelly thing."

"Seems you're popular with *all* the sheilas. And this one's all dolled up for ya. That collar's covered with beads and hand-sewn, I'll wager!"

Gabe caught the shivers as he imagined more spit adding to the equine contribution on his pants. He slipped inside, leaving his four-legged fan club doe-eyed at the door.

A bulletin board hung near the cash register. Tacked to the cork were the now-familiar faces of other missing souls. Most recent was a flier for Tammy Castor with her sulky mouth and wide forehead. Next to her was John Bastinini, the yellowing paper still faithful to his Roman chin and forest of whiskers. Then the color print of Jeremiah Blakely at his *bar mitzvah,* the glint of the flash like twin suns in his eyes.

Gabe pinned a flier next to these paper neighbors. Ian's wheat-gray hair and carrot highlights had gone white on the copies. The striking way his cheekbones formed chevrons had flattened until he looked Asian. Gabe turned from the board, unwilling to imagine the flier as brittle and old as John's. He wondered if every copy he hung sealed Ian's fate. *Lost,* the paper said, *never to be found.*

At the register, the cashier's swollen knees held the drawer at bay. His eyes soared around the room like a glider without a pilot while a second man worked a miniature fry vat stuffed into the corner. The very end of the counter held a single catsup container oozing a substance too much like grasshopper spittle to be appetizing.

"No rooms," the cashier said. "C'n sleep out the back. Nice camper hookups."

"You have any tinned meat?" Gabe asked. "We could use a quick lunch."

"No specials. C'n eat out the back. Nice barbies, sell ya some wood."

"Your cook served a man while I picked out this mutton," Rob said. "Don't tell me there aren't any specials."

"Gotta have proper clothes to get proper service." He pointed to a handwritten sign that read *no shirt no shoes no service no holes no dirt no drunks no smells no spitting no sleeping GOATS OK.*

"You'd serve a goat but not a black fellah, is that it?"

The cashier's eyes settled on the register. "Barbie's 'round the back."

Rob slid the meat off the counter and turned away. The clerk was painstakingly slow with the change but Gabe waited. The choice words he had been so ready to throw at Bret had buried themselves far from his tongue. At least Bret had made his feelings clear. But this cashier—this feeble, addled, creepy cashier—acted as casually as if he saw Gabe every day.

"Stay the night," the clerk offered with the coins. "'Round the back."

Gabe stepped into the heat and immediately felt deflated. Except for the *tick-tap* of hooves, the day was utterly quiet.

"What took you so bloody long?" Rob wrenched the Ford onto the road. "And what the hell was that, standing there with your mouth open like a girl waiting on a lolly? 'No specials,' he says. 'Serve ya 'round the back,' he says. Christ, mate, is that the way they treat Aborigines in Townsville?"

"What was I supposed to do?" He squeezed his fingers until his knuckles cracked. "We're in the middle of the desert. We need petrol and food."

"Is that all you're worried about? Filling your belly and having it easy?" He glanced over and his face softened. "We've extra petrol in the trunk and we can always get food or hold out a bit. You don't have to take that from anyone, let alone some skinny cunt with the lazy eye."

Gabe bent his fingers backwards. He felt he should say something, maybe make a joke at the cashier's expense. But his throat was so thick his breath blistered his lungs.

"Damn it. God damn it!" He punched the dashboard repeatedly. His curses burned with all the heat in his chest and he stopped only when a chunk of foam flew into his lap.

"Damn *him.*" He wiped the sweat from his face. His hand was numb but the first ache woke in his bones. Rob seemed unfazed. Perhaps because he was so angry and embarrassed, or because he was so tired and the day was so hot, Gabe didn't think about what he said next.

"You didn't do much about it." The blood doubled in his face as Rob, his expression as mild as milk, simply drove.

A monitor lizard watched them from a boulder. *Land of reptiles,* Gabe thought, and every one of them with serpentine heads. He looked at the dents in the dashboard and wondered what could have brought him to such extremes.

Rob held up his hand. The lavish collar, smelling faintly of goat, dangled from his fingers. It was silly, the feeling of vengeance that cooled Gabe's ribs as quickly as a seaside breeze. But for the longest time he laughed whenever they hit a bump and the bells sang their crystal song.

15 Soot

In his second-floor room, Dana had little time to relax. Bev said the station owner who had given them the Tree of Life was calling every hour. Dana wasn't worried. Occasionally a pastoralist got to thinking about the money he'd been paid and how much more he might have made. Once they discovered the law would prosecute them as surely as the thieves, they usually backed off. He dialed the number Bev had given him.

"It's the treasure hunter," he said.

He recognized the way Bret blew air into the receiver as the phone was carried somewhere private.

"Two Aborigines were out here poking around that tree. They were looking for a roo shooter who went missing, maybe from here. What the hell is going on?"

"Why do you think the events are related?"

"Those blokes sure thought there was a connection. They had an artifact, a stick of some sort. I've never seen it before but my wife swears it came off my property." His voice rasped into a whisper. "You said all that crap would leave the country. How the hell did it end up back here?"

"How is Annie, by the way? Still putting in those lonely hours at the house while you're out running the wire?"

"Goddamn you! I don't care if you cut down all the trees from here to Perth. But I won't have my family dragged into this."

Dana waited while the man pushed two heavy breaths into the receiver. Then, very clearly and not too quickly, he said, "How is your son? Collin, right? He has a long drive back to university. Alone."

"Stay away from my family. If I see you on my land, I'll shoot you dead."

"Don't worry," Dana said. "If I come on your land, you won't see me."

He cut the connection. The man wouldn't talk to anyone else but his wife might. And Bret had told Bev that two men, the mulatto from the roadhouse and some young fool, were heading up to the Roper Bar to check into reports of crocodile poaching. Poaching Bret had laid at Gabe's feet to deflect attention from his family. Poaching Dana had done just that year.

Damn those *piranpa!* Damn their meddling, sticky beaks and their childish, undisciplined ways. And this Gabriel, the biracial mutt who had their thoughts in his head, their intentions in his heart and no Dreaming in his soul...damn him, too. Next time Dana tracked him down, he'd do more than run him off the road.

The rest of Gabe and Rob's stops were utilitarian, gas and go, and at each roadhouse they switched driving duty. Their lunch was bread and tinned meat bought at another roadhouse and they stored extra cans in the trunk.

Further north bands of black cockatoos appeared. Unlike their clownish cousins, these birds were subdued. The males shared the glossy feathers of crows while the females were speckled with gold. They were throwbacks to the shadowy jungles that once covered Australia and remembered a long-ago time when being black was not a burden.

All around, heat squeezed the world flat. It was one of those brittle days when the sky was chalk and the earth a mirror. Even a bushfire didn't elicit a comment from either man. The world was in cinders and words would not quench the inferno.

Every dip in the road lulled Gabe further into his brooding. He remembered the year Ian had taken him north to watch the seasons change. When lightning had spidered over the clouds, the bolts had chilled him more than the centipedes that shared his sleeping bag.

That was the year his father had died. Gabe's brothers hadn't stuck around long enough to help mum in any meaningful way. Their jobs were demanding, they said, and with a slap on his back they loaded their cars. Mum didn't say anything but Gabe knew she'd been hurt. The electric arachnids reminded him of his brothers' faces, of the venomous light beneath their skin.

When the wind rose, the grass feathered like the hair on a dog's belly. Then the rain was upon them. For perhaps half an hour the men sat transfixed. Gabe had no memory of his thoughts during those storms, no concept of the sorrow that brought tears to his cheeks. He felt now like he had then, as if some creeping sadness was erupting in his limbs. He clenched his teeth against the sores.

"Me mum seems to think I'm leading you into trouble," Rob said.

"Oh, no. You're actually quite useful. You're always turning out to be someone's granny's sister's ex-husband's great-aunt's cousin. Out here, people respect that."

Rob laughed so hard his cap tipped back over his ears. "All right, mate," he said. "You'll do all right."

"You have many friends in Three Ways? A girlfriend, maybe?"

"A few."

"Liar."

"Me Aunt Paddy's a liar. She'll tell ya the ridges on a clam shell are caused by erosion and make you believe it. She'll tell ya she rode to school in a kangaroo's pouch and you'll beg her to tell you more. But me and the sheilas are no lie." Rob turned toward the window where his words were nearly lost to the wind. "A bit of an exaggeration, maybe."

"Just one girl in every town, then?"

"An act of discipline, you know. For them, not me."

"So you're not seeing anyone right now."

"Naw. Haven't found the right woman. And you?"

Gabe gripped the wheel. He hadn't had time to figure out how he felt about the breakup, let alone call Chance. He turned onto a gravel road and hoped the silence would bury Rob's question.

"She means that much to ya, hey?" the young man asked.

"She did. We broke up right before I left Queensland."

"Ya lost your best mate and your sheila? That's hard, very hard. Was she pretty?"

"Stunning. Like a chocolate sea."

"Oh, you're a poet now!" He propped his foot on the dash. "What happened?"

"It wasn't happening. In the long-term, I mean. We were together two years but...."

"Two years isn't so long. There'll be others."

"It's the longest I've ever been with the same person."

"Crikey. Ya sure go through 'em fast. No wonder you're still single."

"There were always...problems. Things outside my control." He flexed his legs. "It's different for you. A lot more Aborigines live in Alice, and you have a network of friends. You haven't had to deal with the same things."

"Like what?" His tone was curious, concerned, hardly confrontational. Nevertheless, Gabe's heart squeezed shut.

"Like taking your date to the theater and some git tells her she shouldn't have half-caste children because they'll be disadvantaged. Or going to parties where her white friends look at you as if she's slumming. The first time I got up the nerve to ask a girl out, her father told me I could pay for dinner, take her dancing and give her flowers but I could forget about marrying her. I was fourteen years old."

"Some people are bloody fools. Surely that didn't happen with all your girlfriends."

"Not to my face. But I always wondered what the friends and family said when I wasn't around."

"What, even when you dated Aboriginal women?"

"I never dated Aboriginal women."

"I thought you said this last one was 'a chocolate ocean.'"

"Chance was Jamaican. All the women before were white."

"Some people would say a Jamaican woman's not the same as an Aborigine."

"I know what some people say." Gabe's voice was nearly muffled by road noise. "I know damned well what some people say."

"Why the sudden change?"

"It wasn't a sudden change." His voice was too loud now but he couldn't control it. "We fell in love. I didn't suddenly decide to date black women, or date other women because they were white. There just aren't a lot of Aborigines in Townsville."

"So you said."

"What the hell does that mean?" He steered around a channel cut by erosion. The sun sat at the precise angle where the glare blinded him.

"It seems like an excuse, is all. You can meet Aborigines if you try, even in the city. We don't all live in the bush, ya know." He forced a smile.

"For God's sake, now you sound like Chance! She was always after me to study my heritage and find my family."

"Sounds like a smart woman."

"Listen, friend." The word sounded like a curse and Rob winced. "I didn't grow up with a father and a truckload of uncles to show me the proper way to do things. But I'll be damned...I'll just be *damned* if some kid half my age—"

"Hey, mate, back off a little."

"—*half my age* is going to tell me how to live. No, I've not been initiated, and no, I don't know any songs, and no, I'm not the keeper of some twelve-hundred-year-old stump in the middle of the goddamned desert. But I've made a good life for myself with the hand I was dealt."

"I never said you didn't. Did I ever say you didn't?"

"You have no idea what I went through." The road blurred and there was no glare on which to blame his tears. "You had all the fucking advantages."

"What the hell are you talking about?"

Gabe pulled off the track, crunching the fender against a rock. He bailed out and slammed the door so hard he spun halfway around. He didn't know why he was so upset but if he didn't get away from Rob he would punch him right in the face.

The smell of ash was all around. Behind him the engine cut out then the other door slammed. "Hey," Rob called. "Hey! Where ya going? What the hell's eating you?"

"I didn't have what you had!"

"So? You can't sit around feeling sorry for yourself."

He stepped back. Gabe knew that the clouds moving across his face were torrential.

"You've had it so easy, you take everything for granted. Everywhere you go there's Auntie So-and-so or Granny Joe. You have this whole network of relatives. *I didn't have that!*" The soot tasted like medicine, a bitter, bitter medicine, and he coughed.

"It wasn't easier," Rob said. "Just different."

He turned and walked away. Gabe stared, still heaving, as the young man squatted in the shadow of the car. He looked in the opposite direction, far off to the horizon, and Gabe could only guess at his thoughts.

"Fuck," he said, and spat dust. "Fuck all."

<hr>

Despite the hotel's upscale atmosphere, the pub was the dim, smoky enclave Australians craved. Certainly the tables matched the chairs and the selection included beer on tap but the womb and its amber milk suspended the *piranpa* in perpetual childhood. The shaman knew he would be ignored in the buildup to the noon rush and selected a table behind a row of booths.

The mule shambled off to call Rowdy, a former prison guard with contacts low and lower. Rowdy dealt parcels of heroine and the occasional snippet of information. Dana was known to him only as the *karadji,* the executioner. Inside the prisons, Rowdy had seen men sung to death and others tormented in ways that made death seem sweet. The *karadji's* requests always received immediate attention.

So few people accepted the real system of power, Dana mused, even when they saw it firsthand. He nodded as the waitress waved away his money. She saw only the scale of years on his face, the way his skin was nearly translucent in the light from the bar. She saw him and she didn't see him, so willing was she to play the game of kindness to an aged black man.

Yet Dana couldn't fault her for that. He had, after all, spent a lifetime playing the game he learned at the mission. After being "rescued" from a settlement near Pukatja, Dana began his lessons. First was that, to the *piranpa*, his value was less than that of a draft animal. The priest and nuns, the building and the property rested on the backs of the wards. Nearly the entire operation was financed by hiring out children as ranch hands and domestics.

Dana learned how to dig post holes and mend fences. He knew a little English already, and what he didn't know the nuns and priests were quick to beat into him. He talked to the other children using the tribal dialects he spoke fluently then tried scraps from other languages. The boys avoided him, muttering, "no, no."

When he persisted, the overseer tied him to a post in the yard. Dana felt his damp breath and the insistence of the man's erection against his buttocks. The overseer's hands lingered on the boy's hips, rubbing a bit too much against his nipples as he tucked the shirt up into the collar.

The matron, meanwhile, lined up the other children to watch. Then a leather strap branded Dana's kidneys, wrapped under his armpits and punched his ribs like a baton. When they cut him down, half conscious and bloated with welts, his hands signaled defiantly. He cursed them with finger talk, the silent language of the hunt.

For weeks he spoke only the braying English aloud. But he signed repeatedly, flashing messages to the boys who said nothing in return. The overseer crushed his fingers inside a coil of barbed wire. The nuns forbad anyone to help him and sat him at the table in front of food he could not eat.

That night, he chipped three molars trying to open the hitch at his wrists. A Yankunytjatjara boy crept over to help. "There are graves over the hills," he whispered. "Follow the rules if you want to live!"

He was expected to work the next day as usual. It was cleaning day, and Dana washed his own blood from the floors as he scrubbed. The Yankunytjatjara was flogged for helping him and his screams mixed with the gurgle of the slop water.

Dana knew then to keep a secret heart. He wiped up his blood before it stained the boards and emptied the bucket as soon as the water turned pink. He would speak the English better than the whites. He would mutate into their notion of the redeemed savage. Their own expectations would camouflage his burning soul.

An older boy, a Pintupi, had told the overseer about the Yankunytjatjara in exchange for a bit of cake. When Dana found out, he sang. The Pintupi withered so quickly even the overseer became alarmed. The teenager was sent to a hospital where no doctors could help him, and the dorm was steamed with formaldehyde for fear of an epidemic.

Now Dana had another boy to sing to his grave, a half-caste mutt who needed to learn when he was outplayed.

16 Golliwog

The breeze died as the day grew. Every inch of shrinking shadows clicked away more precious time but Gabe couldn't go back to the Falcon. He walked circles instead, heading away from the sun before curving back to the track.

The bush flies were unbearable. They clung to him by the dozens, by the hundreds. The sleeve of his shirt swung under their weight and when he stopped to rest, they sipped from the corners of his eyes.

He had fucked up. It wasn't a slip of the tongue or a stress fracture in his temper; he had plain fucked up. The fact that Rob hadn't driven away without him was astonishing.

It was just like that business with the Golliwog, he realized. It had been his curse that his favorite brand of marmalade had a coal-faced, kinky haired mascot known as the Golliwog. Its smile was clown white and its eyes wide enough to swallow coins. And wherever the Golliwog lurked, it seemed, there was also some wisecracking white kid to say, *Look, Gabe, you're famous! Your face is on the marmalade jar!*

At those times, his heart had clutched in its need for other friends, ones who knew that *none* of them looked *anything* like the Golliwog. Yet he had avoided other Aborigines. At least Gabe knew where he stood in white society. Chance had been a big step for him but the whole two years had felt like a bandage stretched over a massive wound.

So there he was again, digging open the incision and blaming someone else for the pain. He shuffled back to the car. His face was so hot his brow felt molten. "I'm sorry," he said. "I had no right to say those things."

Rob peered out of the shade with narrow eyes. For a moment Gabe's heart beat double as he read disapproval. Then he realized the sun was behind him. Without a word, the young man picked up a crowbar and set off into the bush.

Gabe sighed. He'd probably have to make some ritual gesture of apology. They hiked into a stand of witchetty bushes where Rob circled a different shrub with wide, flat leaves.

"Dig here, here and here," he said. "Straight down about half a meter you'll find bush potatoes. I'll get the meat."

The young man headed deeper into the desert. Gabe hoped he brought back a nice wallaby or some bush fowl. He had a feeling it would be something repellent, something meant as a penance. Even if it was week-old roadkill, he vowed to eat it without complaint.

The ground might as well have been concrete, and the vibrations that ran up the crowbar stung his fingers. When his hand slipped, the new grip gave him more force for less effort. Eventually he learned to throw the iron rather than hammer away, and he found a rhythm in the work.

Nearly two feet down, the dirt was cool like cocoa powder. It was darker, too, and smelled of something stored in a freezer. Eventually he had to sit beside the hole, and he didn't mind when the earth he scooped away formed hillocks on his thighs. Eventually he uncovered a lump shaped like a yam and moved on to the next spot.

"Cor, those are big," Rob said as he returned. "We'll have a good feed tonight."

"Exactly what did you catch?" Gabe eyed the paper sack tucked under his arm.

"Lamb chops. Tender as pudding, I'll wager."

"Who wrapped them? The ewe or the ram?"

"The sheila at the pub. She knew I had a hike and she didn't want them to spoil. Quite a looker, that one."

"I'm out here shoveling dirt while you're chatting up some girl in an air conditioned pub?"

"I had to give you time to dig. Ground's hard as a bleeding brick out here. Come on." He headed back to the track. "Don't forget the potatoes!"

Gabe gathered the tubers and caught up with Rob.

"Is that milk on your lip?" he asked. "You were having a milkshake while I sweated my life away for potatoes when you could have bought chips?"

"You've got to be self-sufficient out here, mate. I'm helping you learn."

"That kind of help I can do without." He handed Rob the crowbar. "At least you could carry this. My arms are killing me."

Rob shouldered the iron. Whenever Gabe looked at him, he saw that same press of lips that wanted to be a smile. He stared off into the bush, not wanting to be the first to laugh. Finally he did, and Rob offered to carry the potatoes as well.

"Oh, no," Gabe said. "You got the meat. The least I can do is carry these."

Rod clapped his shoulder. They walked a while like that and even when the young man's hand slid away, Gabe felt the friendship between them.

"The young cunt's a bush guide working out of Three Ways." Kevin returned, already stinking of beer.

"Bush guide," Dana snorted. "I doubt he can fix a flat, let alone say much about the desert."

"Probably makes it up as he goes."

"Tourists don't know any better. They see a black face, they think you're the spirit of the outback. That or the shit on their shoes."

The mule crumpled an empty while he pulled a fresh beer from the pack. It was the most coordinated move he ever performed and was a tribute to the power of habit. Foam sputtered over the web of his fingers as he worked the tab loose.

Dana scanned the crowd. Standard fare, except the ratio of tourists to regulars was higher. Any black faces would belong to loose-limbed West Indians, uptight Brits or hawkish Americans. They were hardly black at all. They lived the same lifestyle, bought the same products, and wore the same clothes at the *piranpa*. Australia's indigenous people spent less, demanded more, and didn't go away at the end of the season.

If Aborigines were second-class citizens underrepresented by the patrons, women were barely a step up the rung. The few present worked in the back room, lugging out meals and hauling trash. Occasionally a female trucker, her jaw set in concrete, took a meal. At the next table a middle-aged woman with the piercing eye of a station manager talked beef production and hauling fees with two male employees.

The *piranpa* had no concept of the power women carried. The blood let during men's initiations mimicked the birth fluids, and the subincision of the penis copied the shape of the vulva. The Europeans feared that creative power. When they subjugated their women, they blocked yet another path to *djang*. A pity their self-destructive tendencies weren't stronger.

A couple entered the pub. The woman, as blond as money could buy, simpered at what she surely thought was an old boong too senile to know he was supposed to buy his alcohol off-sale and eat his meals on the sidewalk. A crooked incisor chiseled a triangle from her sneer.

The shaman's eyes remained heavy and without emotion, yet she recoiled. The songs rose in him, thrumming from belly to breath to tongue like the drone of a didgeridoo. They carried him through the enemy's camp, past cairns of curses and death straight to their sacred hearts. All so some tourist could sneer at him in a pub.

She looked at Dana while her date ordered, looked again when their drinks arrived. Each time her gaze flattened more quickly. He held quiet. This game was simple, the standoff between hunter and hunted. He was the dingo waiting for the prey to break.

Fumbled with a pouch of tobacco, she rolled a lumpy cigarette. She hated him for his power. For moving beyond his place. Most of all, she hated him for waking her fear.

"Time for another killing?" Kevin's speech was heavy. One more drink and he'd be loose enough to start a fight and forget what he'd done by morning.

"Not yet. A man comes all this way to find a friend, he should get a good chase."

"I don't care about the old fuck. It's that kid I want. The bush guide." He crushed another can. "He sounds like this prissy little boong I went to school with. He was always saying things to make the other kids laugh at me. I bashed him good one day. Just say the word and I'll shut this fella up fast."

"Fair enough. But at the right time and in the right way. Otherwise their bleeding pool club will come out looking for them."

Dana smiled at the blond. Kulpunya's teeth were his. She recoiled and her cigarette singed her date's arm. The usual yammer ensued—the protest of the wounded, the frantic apology, the conciliatory touch. It took but a moment. When she looked again, Dana had slipped through the shadows. The panic in her eyes brought a true smile to his face and he closed the door before she could see him.

Patience, he thought as he walked to the elevator. *Patience.*

<hr>

When they pulled over for the night, Rob parked behind an apron of bushes. Gabe attacked his chores as a way to keep himself under control. By the time he found a decent pile of wood, Rob had collected twice that and was laying the fire.

"Did Angus teach you that?"

"Naw. Dad was the fire maker. You could give him two bits of straw and he'd cook a kangaroo. At least, that's the way it seemed when we were kids."

"I thought your dad died before your brother. If you were too young to have known Mike, how can you remember your father so well?"

"Oh, I wasn't so young. We say that to help mum. Selena really was too small to understand much but she missed him. I was just old enough to grow up hating the police." He put water on to boil. "I'm over that hate thing now. Still don't trust 'em, though."

"How did your mom fare?"

"She said the men of our family always had warrior's blood. But today's world doesn't have any challenge, there's nothing for the blood to leech out its metal on. Mike was bound to it, she said, bound to push the reeds until they bent. Except the reed he pushed snapped right off."

Rob grabbed the crowbar and the pair hiked down a gentle slope to a soak. The young man chopped a trench along a patch of plants with whip-thin leaves. When he turned the earth, papery bulbs rose to the top. He called them *yalke,* onion grass, and Gabe tried the word on his tongue. The men easily filled a bucket then smoothed the seeds into the ground.

Back at camp, Rob pulled a box of dried fruit from the trunk. He reconstituted screws of garlic, apple rings and a resinous clump of bean paste to rub on the meat then buried the *yalke* in the embers. The meal was wild and strong with the flavors of grass and scorched earth.

"Heavenly," Gabe sighed.

"Sure, ya pour it on thick. I bet the sheilas swoon for old Gabriel Branch, named for an angel and twice as divine."

"I'm hardly an angel. They're always as white as their wings with gowns of snow."

"Yeah. To go by the telly, you'd think there aren't any black people on earth. Except on the educational programs."

Gabe looked at the bloated horizon. It would be night soon, with only the wind stepping through the grass. Dingoes would circle and howl before leaving the men to their patch of domesticity. And as he watched the stars pivot on some distant celestial axis, the stillness would rush into his ears and memories would raze his dreams.

"I remember those programs." He thought he smelled blood but decided it was the onion grass. "It was the only time I saw faces like mine. My skin is lighter and my face isn't as broad but those people looked like me. My face, my head, my hands. And all they ever did was winnow mulga seed or eat ants or carve toys."

"That didn't seem like you either, hey?"

Rob leaned back and let dusk bring the silence. Overhead, sheathtail bats dodged the stars.

17 Twin Stars

The map rated the final leg of their trip for four wheel drive vehicles but Ramie had assured them the route was passable. At times Rob walked the track to map out the best route and they made fifteen kilometers in an hour.

When they crossed a dry watercourse, Rob cut branches from a red gum. Gabe copied the young man as he lifted the white lerp scales from the leaves, and the flakes dissolved in their mouths like crusty frosting. Gabe's enthusiasm waned when he realized he was also consuming the tiny nymphs that excreted the scale.

"Ian may have served up some strange creatures but at least he never fed me bugs," he said.

Rob polished off the scale, nymphs and all, then tossed the leaves out the window. "It's OK, you can look now. Any lerps in my teeth? Don't you hate it when you're talking to some bloke and he won't tell you there's a big green bug caught in your choppers?"

"Piss off, already." Gabe checked the mirror and tried not to smile when Rob slapped his arm.

Was there something about the desert, he wondered, that made clowns of the men who loved her? The bush severed him from what he had spent a lifetime learning. Townsville was a cup of ocean breezes, the chatter of palm fronds and gulls brimming above mountain peaks. The desert was painfully bright, razor dry, and pocked with silent water holes.

The northern part of the country was different. Here tropical rainforest grew on red soil. Tablelands rolled up from the Katherine region until the land fragmented into bays and coves. At first glance, the estuaries were like reefs that created curving atolls. But coral islands were fragile countries on foundations of bones. Mangrove swamps churned earth and sea and air together to create new land.

It was similar, in a way, to what Chance had always said about Gabe's family. She hadn't meant that his adopted mum was less valuable than his biological mother, just different. The traditions he grew up with—the Catholic religion, the holiday haze, those school breaks spent in Canberra or Sydney—

were as valuable as the sea life that swarmed the reefs. But there was another, neglected part, one with roots as ancient and a spirituality as strong.

He watched the sun roll across the sky. If he wanted to share those outback trips again, he'd better find Ian soon. A pang that lately had become a gnawing made his arms hang weakly from his shoulders. What if it was too late? What if he had waited too long, frittered away too many nights in fear and indecision as the sea ran its endless waves up the beach?

He dug his fingers into his arms, pulling the muscles up and away from the bones until he thought they might tear. What if setting out even a day earlier would have made a difference? Gabe suspected that even then he would have been too late.

Thin Creek Crocs stood near a river. One bank was a limestone escarpment that exposed the earth's secret colors. There was the tan and gold of reptiles, cream and ivory and chalk for feathers and teeth, and a thousand shades of red: rust and amber for fur, ruby and garnet for petals, claret for sap and blood and fruit.

Against this backdrop was a clearing filled with huts of canvas and wood. A cinderblock building with blazing white paint sported a cap of solar panels, and a half-dozen SUVs mingled in the parking area. As the men dropped into the valley, dogs and children tumbled from the woods. All arms and legs and cheerful slips of clothing, the group ran beside the Ford while the tallest boys slapped the fenders.

"Guess they don't see many visitors," Gabe said.

Faces bobbed at the windows as Rob parked. The older children arrived last, having walked the final meters so as not to seem too eager. A girl pushed through the crowd. Her brother, identical except that his hair sprung up in thick curls while her hair was wavy, gave the men an ecstatic smile.

"I'm Mary," she said. "He's Zephyr. We're twins. Who're you?"

"I'm Rob and this is Gabe."

"He your brother?"

"Nope."

"Didn't think so. You don't look nothing alike. He your uncle?"

"Naw," Rob said as he opened the door.

"He your dad?"

"Hardly," Rob grinned.

A woman with a small cooler in each hand emerged from the trees. She was of average height, around middle-age, with the calves of a runner. "Who's that, Mary?"

"Don't know."

"What do they want?"

"Won't say."

"Well, don't leave 'em there like a mouse with no paws."

Mary marched them across the clearing to a bamboo lean-to. Zephyr trailed behind and slipped his hand into Gabe's.

"To your chores," the woman called, and all but the twins scattered. "My name's Fancy. Mary, find some mugs for our guests, please. And mind they're clean!"

Gabe noticed the woman's extraordinary skin, which was the color of fresh ginger. She offered tea and cookies warmed over a propane stove. "What brings you to our camp?" she asked.

"We're looking for a crocodile," Gabe said.

"You've come to the right place. We're one of the original cooperatives supplying eggs and hatchlings for the leather and meat trade."

"Actually, we're here about the poaching."

"How do you know about that?"

"My friend's gone missing. A station owner accused him of poaching on his ranch and along the Roper Bar River. He thinks that might have made someone angry enough to do something."

"You police?"

"No, ma'am."

"Government?"

Gabe shook his head. Fancy's outline was chiseled smoothly from the shade and she was perfectly still as she sized up the men. "Mary," she finally said, "find Corrine and Herman."

The girl sighed mightily and half ran, half stomped into the woods. Fancy chatted lightly about things that had nothing to do with crocodiles or disappearing friends until the girl returned, breathless from running.

"They're coming." She frowned at her cookie. "It's cold."

"A habit of mine," Fancy said. "I warmed the cookies once and now it seems I've spoiled them."

"What else are kids for, if ya can't spoil 'em?" Rob pulled Mary onto his lap. Zephyr patted Gabe's hand and left traces of cream filling on his fingers.

"Tell me," Gabe asked, "how did you get such an unusual name?"

"He whisper to me what he wants," Mary said. "One night a wind come fast, flash! Off the cliffs. He wants to be fast like that wind. I asked Fancy what it were called. He said that's what he wants his name to be."

"How old are you, Mary?"

"Eight. He's eight, too. We're twins."

"So you said." To burn so bright so young. Surely at twelve they would eclipse the sun.

"All right, off with you," Fancy said. "Here's Corrine and Herman."

The pair fled, their thongs clapping like wings. Walking the opposite direction was a woman whose spine had locked in a permanent bow. Hair the color of distant rain was tucked behind a band, her only article of clothing besides a pair of shorts. Her breasts had been emptied by mouths now as old as Gabe. The rest of her flesh hung neatly, as if she combed it every morning into long folds.

Gabe could hardly stop staring. There was a light around her like sunshine through fog. She was the most beautiful person he had ever seen. Behind her plodded a broad-faced man with a tangle of wet curls, the length of which seemed calculated to offset the enormity of his frame. He was around Gabe's age, perhaps a few years younger, and nodded as he eased a pack to the ground.

"Corrine, these men want to know about Kumoken," Fancy said.

"Who?" The word was both question and command.

"Gabriel Branch, ma'am. I'm looking—"

"Who?" she demanded, this time of Rob.

"Possum Rob Kamare from the Alice. Wagner was me granny. I'm the nephew of Angus Kamare."

"Not met 'im. Hear 'im name. Renegade." She waited but Gabe looked blank. "You ask on Kumoken, crocodile. Renegade shot 'im. Near died, near killed Thin Creek with 'im."

"The critter's still alive?" Rob asked.

"Aye." She sat on a log and her back straightened somewhat. "Kumoken big snapper, got big power. 'Im made man. This area part of 'im Dreaming. When renegade shot Kumoken, everything got sick. Trees wilted. Moths gone, birds stay away. The crocs no mate. Roar all night, horny as Herman—"

"Mother!"

"Roar like Herman before 'im fed but no mate. No mate, no eggs. No eggs, no sales."

"Crocs don't breed well in captivity," Herman said, "and wild harvest nicks the skins. We manage a resource at its point of origin. The cash lets us buy what the land here doesn't give."

"Balance," Gabe said.

"The kids benefit the most. They grow up on the land, get an education on the two-way, and can choose what they want when they're older. They'll be some of the first to have that choice in a long time."

The sun spun behind the escarpment as groups emerged from the forest. A teenager struggled with an enormous jackfruit until a young man traded his basket for her burden. Their movements were shy and breathless and as they walked, they smiled at each other's feet. The crowd contained people from every nation.

"Renegade," Gabe whispered.

"Yeah," Corrine said. "Kumoken holed up in the banks. Renegade took another croc near as big."

"Did anyone see them?"

"Naw. Found 'im killing ground, 'im blood and such."

"Why bother?" Rob asked. "You can buy all the bits you want. Teeth, claws, hides, even stuffed crocs. They must've wanted a big one, hey?"

"Aye, or 'im heart or kidneys. Strong magic in the kidneys." She sucked her teeth. "Some just like to kill. Why you ask?"

"A friend of mine's gone missing. A station manager accused him of poaching."

"Your friend white? Hair like river sand?" Corrine heaved herself up and threw her fingers at Gabe. Zephyr broke from the crowd, a single syllable of protest constricting his throat. Mary tackled him before he reached the lean-to.

"No," she cried, "don't go near him now!"

Corrine waved the children back and disappeared inside a cottage. The whole community, it seemed, had witnessed the scene. They returned to their work but monitored the visitors with sidelong glances.

"What was that?" Gabe asked.

Rob gave him a pitying smile. "I think you've been cursed."

<hr>

Gabe stared and stared but nothing seemed to fit. Shadows had tinted everything a soft blue, and the windows on the central building lined up like Cheshire teeth.

"That's silly," he finally said. "Isn't it?"

"Sorry." Herman gathered up the pack. "She's been a little wobbly since the croc was shot. She says your friend did it. Of course, we can't know either way."

"What kind of curse was it?"

"Oh, just a little one. Quite a shock, this poaching thing."

"It's no bloody picnic being cursed!"

"Our healer will be by later. He'll smoke you then we'll all have dinner." He pointed out the path to the pit toilet. "Unless you really must, please stay here. I'll ask Rob to fix your tea. Until you've been smoked, anything you touch will be cursed."

Gabe wrapped his arms around his knees as Herman walked to the camp kitchen.

"Oh, come on," Rob said. "It's only a curse."

"Because someone thinks a friend of mine was poaching. What if she thought *I* shot that croc? She might have come after me with a knife."

"I reckon she would use her trowel. Besides, the *karadji* does all the killing. And he uses a spear, not a knife."

Rob was joking, yet Gabe felt something stir beneath his words. Rachel had said the men they would meet knew a different law. He was glad he had left the opal wrapped up with the message stick in the car.

Damn it, he thought. Was he actually giving in to all this talk about *djang* and charms and hexes? He hadn't fallen for it as a child when mum had taken him week after week to mass. The rosaries and candles and ritualized workouts never impressed him, so why should a magic stone or a curse?

He was tired. So bleeding hot and so bloody tired. He hoped the healer would come soon, if only so his world would seem normal again. "Do we just wait until some voodoo priest takes care of things?" he spat.

"Why don't I make you some tea?"

"I can make my own bloody tea."

Rob lowered his voice. "Listen, mate, I don't believe everything I hear about the old lore, either. I know you got caught in that bleaching process but you've got to respect what others think. I will make the tea."

"Sorry. And don't say that! About the bleaching. It sounds as if I was thrown in the wash and came up white. I'm as black as any."

"That you are, mate."

Rob dropped a cookie into his hand. The wafer was dyed a chemical black that absorbed all light. He dared not eat such a thing and set it aside.

An older man wearing jeans and a shirt reading *Surf the Gold Coast* appeared. Without speaking, the healer built a fire. From a possum-skin pouch came dried pituri and scented bark. As the fire grew stronger, Zephyr came as close as he dared. His sister didn't look worried. Perhaps this wouldn't take long. Herman had said it was a *small* curse.

The healer began to sing, a low intonation punctuated by a falsetto call at the beginning of each refrain. Or was it the same chant, Gabe wondered, and the call marked its repetition? The smoke thickened until the men could see only each other's faces. Gabe felt saturated and drifted like a turtle in a river. The shaman dusted his scalp and face with a feather then cleansed the log, the mug, even the ground around their feet.

There was a pause as the healer stored the feather with his other tools. Then he bent Gabe over the fire. The smoke was honey and tobacco, eucalypt and bitter cherries. He inhaled, a gulp at a time, as the heat crusted his skin. Something sour in his belly unraveled. He leaned forward, half swooning, and the snares spun through his body dissolved.

Then it was over. The healer pulled him up, the fire was kicked over and Rob appeared with a mug of clear, cool water. Gabe drank, greedy at first then grateful for every sip. Hands rubbed his back and chest and arms and thighs. His muscles were warm and his joints loose, as if he had run a far pace.

"Done." The healer swept up his bag. "Now we eat."

<hr>

Herman pulled the limbs from a pit-roasted wallaby then shoveled wild onions and quandongs from the bed of green leaves. On the serving table, a delicate broth of herbs sat next to river crabs and foot-long crayfish called yabbies. Pies of geese and duck emerged from stone kilns. Dessert was damper heavy with fruit, figs stewed in condensed milk, and slips of coconut still wearing their woody skins.

"You've come at a good time." Herman handed Gabe a banana leaf to use as a plate. "We're celebrating the purchase of a new incubator. It'll double our production of live young."

Gabe was famished, yet he ate carefully. He learned the name of the snake-necked turtle and how it was prized for its fat. The life cycle of the bream forged the background of its flavor and the wallaby tasted of fragrant grasses. Corrine wandered into their circle and offered him a yabby.

"Is it cursed?" he asked.

She laughed, repeating his question over and over as he sucked meat from the tail. The yabby was sweet and earthy, unlike the briny crab of the coast.

"Your friend, how long you know 'im?" Corrine asked.

"Fifteen years."

"Long time for a white man. Europeans, 'im come, 'im go. We stay. Many people visit this year. 'Im one of many."

"You remember him, though. How long did he stay?"

"Two...nah, three nights. Always out on river. 'Im ask questions, always questions 'bout Kumoken. What is 'im Dreaming? Do 'im live here? 'Ow big?" She studied Gabe's chin. Her gaze was nearly a challenge. "'Im truck stank like blood, it not cleaned too good. No good man can smell death all'a time."

Gabe knew with certainty that she hadn't seen Ian. He might have killed for money and lived in a truck most of the year but he was finicky about his things. While other shooters hung the roos on their trucks to bleed out, Ian never loaded a carcass until it had been gutted and the abdominal cavity salted. His clothes were always clean, if somewhat ragged, and his favorite hat was reblocked every year.

Whatever sandy-haired man had visited Thin Creek had been no relation. Yet Bret had clearly felt there was some connection between Ian and Thin Creek. As dusk fell, Gabe listened to everything people told him about visitors and crocs, stories and histories, wondering which bit of information might lead to the truth.

"Rob teach you?" Corrine asked. When Gabe nodded, she howled. "You 'im daddy," she said to the young man, who smiled broadly.

"Under traditional systems," he said, "a person who helps you learn is related to you in specific ways. I'm teaching you bush ways, so that makes me your dad."

"Great. A twenty-something father with no fashion sense," Gabe muttered. "Just don't expect anything special come Christmas."

As the night wore on, a dog flickered at the edge of the firelight. Gabe caught only the yellow blaze of its eyes and a flash of teeth before it disappeared. Then Zephyr pointed at the sky. A meteorite appeared, as white hot as magnesium. It lasted the longest time, half a breath at least, and the boy and the man held hands.

"'Im got clever tricks." Corrine touched Zephyr's head. "That why 'im not talk. 'Im got another kind of thinking."

She waved goodnight as the clearing emptied. Soon the kerosene lamps were doused. Gabe looked at his fingers, twined so securely with the boy's. They could, he thought, stand there all night. Even forever.

18 Killing Ground

Tjamu had taught Dana about anger. Of all the hungers that devoured men, rage consumed completely. If a man harmed another, the victim had the right to revenge. A sorry cut, a little wound to let out blood, evened out the suffering. If rage took over, the cut was made too deeply. Things escalated.

Dana didn't drink or take drugs and he refrained from intercourse during times of magic. But other passions—the anger, love, grief and hatred, hope, jealousy and pride that were rabid in every man—also had to be tamed. Anger was the shaman's one excess. In him it was otherworldly, like the charge that creased the air around lightning.

"Let it go," Tjamu had said. "Yer magic is there at yer middle. If yer angry, yer got no belly."

Anger was the one thing Europeans could read from a black face. The days when men slaughtered white families in the night were over but the *piranpa* were still edgy around their workers. After leaving the mission, Dana had worked the southern sheep sheds, cleaning the shearer's blades and gathering the wool in enormous bags. He stayed quiet, worked hard and kept to the shadows.

Yet his rage glowed like moonlight in a dog's eyes. The manager saw the teen's potential and counted the shears every evening. Until that angry glow could be dampened, Dana knew he would not be invisible.

He found strength by remaining true to the Law. Whenever chores took him to another station or out to the pasture, he dug bush tucker. If he could break a goanna against the ground or kill a snake, all the better. The meat kept well enough in a hollow log or weighted in the cool depths of a bore hole. At night he bribed the ranch dogs with his rations then snuck out to feast. Through these foods his body remembered its ancient connection to the desert and his face grew smooth and blank.

Now he was wealthier than the men who ran the largest ranches. Yet his audience consisted of a drunken mule, an oversexed bureaucrat, and a Yugoslavian with so much money he paid someone to sluice his nostrils whenever he took the sniffles. Except, of course, the roo shooter with the fussied-up hair and that long goddamn nose he had stuck in Dana's pie.

Now this amateur detective tag team was poking around. The mutt dropped so much spoor, fliers and questions and phone calls, Dana could have found him in a dust storm. The young one wasn't much more than a chauffeur. Possum's relatives and friends were useful but would the young blood be so helpful if the stakes were raised?

He would soon know. Dana lay high on the escarpment beneath lacy ferns. He had watched Gabriel welcomed at Thin Creek as one of their own. But the half-caste had no Dreaming. He clung to the boy like a ship to an anchor. Surely his soul was as porous and chalky as limestone. With a little pressure, he would crumble.

～～～

Gabe unrolled his swag on the porch of Fancy's cottage. The sunscreen kept out the mosquitoes, so for one evening he wouldn't have to worry about scorpions under his bedroll.

"The kid's taken with you," Rob said.

"We stood on the hill for a while to watch the lightning. Do you think the Wet might come early this year?"

"Hard to tell. The signs are there but you never know." He yawned expansively. "We'll have your truck soon. Even if it does rain, we'll be jake."

"I appreciate everything you've done for me. Otherwise I'd still be driving around hoping for a break." He touched the message stick through the canvas tote. "I wouldn't even know what to call this artifact."

"Cheer up, mate. We'll find him."

"I know you have your own life. After the truck's fixed, you don't have to help me anymore. I'll either find him or I won't. But I won't ask you to take on this burden."

"Oh, don't worry. It's sort of an adventure, really. I reckon as long as you pay for the gas, we can go from here to Black Stump and beyond."

"But you didn't know Ian and you hardly know me. Why are you out here at all?"

"Dunno. I'd like to say it's because you need the help. Maybe it's because you remind me of me dad."

They lay back in silence. Perhaps the young man knew as much about this trip and the reasons for it as he did. They both had lost their brothers, and now Gabe was determined to find the man who had become more like a family to him than anyone else. It seemed logical that Rob would want to help him.

"Ya know," Rob said thoughtfully, "when me dad came back from the mine every month, he'd spend time with each of us kids, just me and him or just him and Selena. He'd tell me stories about things he'd done. A lot of those stories were about Aborigines and a lot were about white people. But they were all about mates."

"So he wanted you to be friends with everyone?"

"I think he was telling me to treat people like I'd want to be treated. Golden Rule and all. 'Sides, he always reckoned that all we've got in this world is other people." He rolled onto his side. "I guess that's why I fell in with you."

"Well, you certainly got sucked in deeper than either of us expected. Thank you."

"Don't thank me until it's all done." His eyes lit up and he slapped the floor. "I'll make you a deal. I help find your mate then you tell your customers what a great bush guide I am. There's only so many times you can show tourists how to harvest bush tomatoes. I'd enjoy doing guided trips like this. Only for pleasure, you see."

Gabe watched strange insects gather on the screen. Rob was young, not yet thirty, and young men often started things they never finished. Still, he was relieved Rob would stick with him, at least for a time. "You're not getting much of a bargain," Gabe said, "but you've got a deal."

He blew out the lantern. A moth battered the screen, devastated by a twist of the wick. Without hope, there isn't much point in having wings. He forgot that the heat could incinerate such a tiny life. His dreams remembered, though, and he quivered in midnight's chill.

***

At dawn, a sound like an ailing lawnmower bounced off the cliff. Gabe wondered if the crocodiles were fighting and shrugged into his jacket.

"Ever think a croc could make so much noise?" Fancy brought a tea tray onto the porch. "They gape at each other, showing off their teeth or some silly thing, and growl. Herman will have the tinny ready after breakfast so you can visit the killing ground."

"We're going out in a fishing boat?" Gabe asked. "Those little two-man things?"

"They hold four and a bit of equipment if you pack them right. Don't worry, Howard hardly ever tips the boat." She patted his knee. "Even if he does, crocs don't eat much. A hand, a foot, usually something you've got a spare for."

"Morning, morning, could you pass me a cup, please?" Rob stretched and tucked the blanket under his chin. "What is it about eating that makes ya want to eat more? I stuffed myself at dinner and now I'm famished."

"Maybe you're a croc," Gabe said.

"Or a man," Fancy laughed. "Be in the clearing in twenty minutes or you'll have to fill up with porridge."

"Mmm, porridge." Rob smacked his lips. "Like a hot milkshake with butter."

After breakfast, Herman led the group to a dock built across the wandering trunks of pandanus palms. Overhead, crimson finches flustered in the trees like strange fruits. Rob wriggled his eyebrows as they settled into the boat.

"We won't be here long, so just quit," Gabe said.

"Wazzamatter? You can't dance?"

"No. I mean, it doesn't matter." He stuttered as Fancy looked over her shoulder. "Just be quiet, all right?"

"Rightio. Just pointin' out the obvious."

They motored around sandbars while crocodiles watched from beaches carved into the banks. When the creatures flopped into the water, Fancy armed herself with a sawed-off broomstick.

"The wounded croc holed up here for a time." She pointed to a cubbyhole in the cliff. "He was tucked so far back we didn't see him for a week after the shooting."

Perhaps a mile downstream, Herman turned the boat into shore. The flood lines of various Wet seasons had jumbled driftwood and leaves and stones together.

"They gutted it under those trees," Herman said. "They staked a wallaby as bait, so I'm guessing the shooter hung out in the canopy. You've got to put the bullet in a croc's brain if you want a trophy, and their brains are pretty small."

"I reckon the poacher shot from that gap along the cliff," Rob said. "Limbs have been cut there and there to make a peephole. Then they dragged the carcass through this break in the flood line into the woods."

He moved into the jungle. The ground had been soft when the killing had happened, and deep ruts were still visible.

"These tracks are wider than the ones at Halfway Downs but they could have deflated the tires for extra traction." He plucked a piece of metal from the ground. "I found three of these at Halfway Downs. Not every bloke pulls the tabs off his beer cans."

"Could be from a soda can," Gabe said.

"The ones at the station smelled of beer. I'd say our poacher likes his grog. Let's see what else we can find."

When they returned to the clearing, damper and cold yams waited beneath a woven basket.

"Do you know what happened to the carcass after it was hauled out of here?" Gabe asked as he passed the marmalade.

"Nothing's definite," Herman shrugged. "A teenager in Katherine saw the croc in the back of a truck. She didn't stick around long. Some of those tourists don't take kindly to the locals unless they're cooking their meals or serving their beer."

"Can we get up on the escarpment?" Rob asked.

"Yeah. Our men have a ceremonial site near there, so Fancy will have to stay here."

"I've calls to make anyway." She smiled at Gabe's look. "Satellite phone. Solar powered and a clear hookup every time. Unless there's an eclipse, or a solar flare, or a storm. Fortunately our buyers are an understanding lot."

The men piled into an SUV. The drive didn't take long, and they hiked up a terrace of broken rock and boulders softened by rain. At the base of a palm lay dozens of cigarette butts, all smoked down to the filter and pressed flat. Rob wrapped several in a twist of dry grass and pocketed the mass.

"They must've used a scope to get that shot from here," Herman said. "Probably an old Army issue rifle. They're cheap and powerful enough to do the job."

"That's not a regular rifle like a roo shooter might use, hey?" Rob asked.

"Oh, no. These fellows really knew their job."

Gabe shook his head. "If killing can be called a job."

Lunch wasn't quite ready when they returned, so Herman slipped away to catch up on his chores. Even though they would save time by eating there, Gabe paced around the clearing. Nearly four days had passed since the men had left Alice Springs, and his legs pistoned round and round.

As the heat grew, Rob dozed and Gabe padded over to the pump. When the warm water in the top of the pipe yielded to an icy stream, the twins told him to get under. He gasped as the water squeezed his neck, and the children's laughter dissolved his grunts.

"Looks like a croc drug you under," Rob called.

Gabe eyed Mary as she danced in place. Hadn't he pulled the same tricks on his own parents and felt the same joy when they'd gone along? With a roar, he snatched up the twins and spun them until their thongs flew off their feet.

Giggling and barely mobile, they staggered off to help with the meal. Gabe watched them, both so confident. They had no doubt that everyone, even strangers, would love them. If Gabe had one wish he could use in the whole of his life, it would be that they never lost that confidence.

"I wonder," he said so softly he didn't know if Rob would hear, "I wonder whatever happened to Andy."

"It must be hard, to think about him all these years," Rob said.

"I didn't remember anything about my biological family until two days ago."

There had been dreams, scraps of another life that tumbled from his grasp and pulled him sobbing from sleep. But there had been nothing as concrete as the sweets he tossed away, nothing as warm as the hands of the mother he had traded for those watercolor candies.

Thin Creek Crocs was his fantasy world come to life. His biological family had been in the desert, of course, surrounded by mulga and saltbush instead of nutmeg and ferns. But the feeling was the same. The warmth of the community embraced every meal, and the chores of children and adults strengthened the whole.

Gabe strained toward Ian, yet he already ached to know he would leave here. He would miss out on this seemingly perfect world. Hell, he would miss out on this imperfect world. Perhaps that was the way it should be. Sometime, he knew, it was best not to look back.

The meal was ready. Zephyr loaded his leaf with the same food Gabe selected. The boy ate in the same order, drank tea at the same time, and wiped his mouth with the same precision. By the end of the meal, Gabe was smiling again.

The travelers offered the last jar of honey to their hosts. Corrine gave them smoked crocodile meat wrapped in leaves, and Zephyr waited until they got in the car to give them each a cookie.

Gabe glanced in the side mirror a final time at the twins holding hands then forced himself to look away. The fliers stacked on the floor shifted between his feet. He would hang the posters in every roadhouse and pub in Australia. He would dredge his friend's likeness from the soil, if it came to that. As he studied the photo, he knew the posters should really show Ian's hands.

***

Dana watched the Ford trundle up the hill. That young blood was a nuisance. He had found the sniper's nest almost immediately. Cigarette butts were hardly evidence of poaching but the fact that he knew where to look could mean trouble at other sites.

When the village had converged for lunch, the shaman had watched as the mongrel was given everything: food to eat, tea to drink, a place to rest. And words. They spoiled him with words, stuffed him with information, fed him with their thoughts and opinions and ideas. Even the young ones flocked to his side. In just a day the brittle layers Gabriel wore, the glaze of European ways that had hardened in grim fires, had softened.

The men wouldn't get far before nightfall. Dana eased down the escarpment and set off on foot. As he drew his awareness into the center of his mind, his spine became fluid and his pelvis floated over his thigh bones. He never paused, not for shade or water or rest. Nor did he let off singing, and the spirits gathered around him like charms.

19 Butcherbird

The men drove until the sun threatened the horizon. Gabe parked beside a stand of paperbark trees where the air tasted like chicory tea. While Rob collected bush tucker, Gabe soaked dried carrots and tomatoes with the smoked crocodile. Bush onions added flavor to the stew, rice created bulk, and Rob returned with quandong fruit for a sweet kick.

"I've never had these before this trip," Gabe said. "Most bush foods Ian fed me were meats."

"Ah, you've missed a world of flavor, then. I live on seeds and fruit when I'm out and about. That and the occasional lamb chop. Or three"

"If I've learned nothing else on this trip, it's that I shouldn't have you to dinner without enough to feed a herd of jackaroos."

"Glad to know I'll be invited." He stored the under-ripe fruit in the car and cleaned the rest. "What do you think of Bret now that we've checked out his lead?"

"I'm not sure. Something's not right with him, and it's not racism. He was on edge the whole time."

"Maybe he's scared of what we were looking for, or what your friend was looking for."

Gabe wrapped a cloth around the pot and served the meal. Already he missed the banana leaf plates. "Say, this is all right. I don't usually like crocodile." He coughed as a slow burn spread down his throat.

"I added some of my special spice blend. It kicks in late but it sticks around for a while."

"I'm not a pepper fan. My sister, now she's the gourmet."

"How old is she?"

"Fifty. Both my brothers are about ten years older than me. My sister was closer in age and she tormented me enough for all three."

"She took a liking to ya, then." Rob stashed his plate by the fire. "What's it like to have a white family? Do ya mind me asking?"

"Oh, it's all right, I suppose." He studied the fire. "I wasn't old enough to understand, really. I had been taught to be careful around the welfare people, and they were always white. Other than that, skin color didn't mean anything much. I just wanted to go home."

He put aside the last of his meal as a butcherbird landed high in a tree. He didn't want to continue the conversation and wouldn't have known what to say if he did. As Rob gathered up the dishes, Gabe decided to stretch his legs.

When he had started this trip, he'd still had hope. Other people had been rescued after months in the wild and Ian could survive almost anything. But his skills were nature based. The message stick, Ian's stubborn sense of right, and the trail of poachers and thieves all pointed to violence. If there weren't any new leads in Katherine, Gabe might have to go home without answers. Without justice.

He pressed his face into the trunk of a tree to block out the bloody sunset. His knees felt weak and his stomach coiled like an echidna under attack. As the stew moved back up his throat, memory squeezed from his heart.

The bus ride from Darwin had been interminable. Andy had been left at the orphanage, and Gabe had worried that his brother would also fall ill and disappear. Everyone said their mom wasn't really sick but by then he wasn't sure what to believe. He only knew that the country outside the window changed utterly during that long day, and he cried silent tears until he threw up.

The smell of fish and brine along the coast made him dizzy. When he realized the social worker meant to leave him with a strange *mperlkere* couple, he begged her to take him back to the boy's home. But he stayed with the people who were older than his mother in a house that smelled of spice and rose water. Even though the woman was gentle, fussing and clucking over him every minute, he was terrified.

His cousin had said the *mperlkere* caught Aborigines and peeled off their skins to make cloaks. For weeks Gabe lay awake at night, straining for the sound of feet padding across the floor. It was months before he understood that the couple wanted him to be their son. Even then some fear tickled behind his ears and it was years before he would go into the potting shed with either parent. The frequency with which his father sharpened the mower blades put him on edge long into adulthood.

Now he felt only the despair that had begun when the welfare swept the brothers past the hills of their home. It had grown and hardened like the lumps men sometimes found in their scrotums, a cancer that ate away every bit of joy. The boy had known he would never go home again. Now the man was never to find his friend.

Gabe crawled away from the tree. His eyes were wide and unblinking even as tears wet the ground. Mucus swung from his nose and he drooled uncontrollably. Gentle hands helped him stand, a strong frame supported his baby steps back to camp. He shivered uncontrollably as blankets heaped over his shoulders and the fire roared.

He tried to find that long-ago uncle who had called him Little Breeze. But Rob was not that man and Gabe could not find that face.

～～～

A champagne cork popped on the hill. Dust kicked up near the fire and the canteen leapt off the hood.

"Christ," Rob shouted, "someone's shooting at us!"

He grabbed the edges of the blanket and pulled Gabe to the ground. Bark exploded and splinters caught in their hair as they wriggled through the trees. Gabe rolled behind a pair of eucalypts joined at the roots. After crawling a little further, Rob sat with his back to a massive trunk. "I think we've got someone's attention," he called.

Leaves rained down as bullets ripped through the branches. Gabe cocked his head. Ian had sometimes taken him along when he practiced shooting, and the sounds told him there were at least two gunman. The attack slowed as the snipers shifted their attention to the Ford. Rob crawled over as the windshield crackled.

"Crikey. Ramie just buffed all the scratches off the bloody glass." He wrapped the blanket around his waist and his yellow shorts disappeared in the gloom. "There's a dry creek bed just to the south where we can hide. Take off your shirt. Anything white will glow like a beacon."

Gabe shoved his shirt under a log then waited as shots ticked off the seconds. After a rapid spurt of gunfire, the men lunged through the trees. They darted side to side, skimming low behind bushes and stumps. A bullet kicked dirt into Gabe's eyes. He continued to run, blind and nearly on all fours, as bushes cut his cheeks. His vision cleared as Rob disappeared like a fish flipping into the sea.

He charged forward as the barrage started again. He fell into the gully, half on Rob and half on a bed of stones. One shooter emptied his rifle in furious strings while the other kept up a measured cadence. The controlled shots came close. Gabe had no doubt of their intention.

Eventually the shooters ran out of ammo or interest. After a long silence, an engine started some distance down the track. Rob poked his head up and watched a pair of headlights bounce away.

[122]

"We have to leave." Gabe's toes and fingers felt as if they'd been sewn to his limbs.

"The sedan can barely handle that track in the daylight. We try it at night, we're sure to lose. Besides, she'll want a little attention before she's roadworthy."

"What if they come back?"

His words were slurred. Rob covered his legs with the blanket then took off his shirt and helped Gabe into it.

"We'll take turns on lookout," he said. "You cozy up there and have a rest. I'll wake you when it's your turn."

Gabe couldn't believe how sleepy he was. He closed his eyes a little and looked for the glow of planets in the sky. The stars were brilliant, like drops of water on his lashes. He remembered that day, the rainbow-sparkle day, the first day he had been called a black bastard.

He had been eight when Jeremy, his best pal and only confidant, invited him to see his new swing set. Jeremy was the only other Aborigine in the same grade and the only black person Gabe had talked to since coming to Townsville. They had met at the beginning of the academic year and after some awkward attempts had become friends.

"You ever been called names?" Gabe asked as they walked home.

"I got lots of names. Stinky, Booger...one time my mom gave me nothing but ten-cent pieces to buy my lunch all week, so everyone called me Quids."

"I mean bad names. 'Cause you're an Aborigine."

"Why? What happened?"

Gabe shrugged and pretended to read a billboard.

"Doesn't matter," Jeremy said. "My mum says there's different ways of doing things. We got our way and the whites got theirs. One's not better than the other but some folks are too scared to say so. Instead they call names like boong or Abo. Just ignore them."

The boys ran the last block and burst through the front gate of Jeremy's house. After they turned the sprinklers to drench the swings, the dew on Gabe's lashes threw haloes around everyone's face.

It *wasn't* like being called Abo or boong, he thought. It was the same *kind* of words but somehow it was different. His back arched so tightly he thought he'd flip from the seat. Higher he strained, clenching the brittle chains. Different, it was different, but why?

And suddenly he knew. *Black* bastard. The words weren't about his race or his culture or any debate pitting civilized against savage. It was about his skin, the simple and sustained fact of his color. His blackness, or his brownness, was the offense, and it lay closer to him than the water shocking his face.

"Hey," Rob whispered, "you're supposed to be sleeping."

The night sky was a round, ripe gourd and Gabe a seed at its middle. He let the stars cover him. He adjusted the blanket and lay the edge over Rob's legs. "Tell me about boong," he said.

Rob was silent for a long time. Then he sighed and peered over the bank. Satisfied the snipers had not returned, he leaned against the rocks.

"Don't know which I hate more, the word or the blokes who say it. First time I heard it used, I was about six. Mum's an old movie buff and we'd just seen some flick where these Yanks coat their faces with greasepaint. I thought it would be fair to paint myself white for Halloween." He laughed and rubbed his scalp.

"Of course, mum wouldn't hear of it. So I said I wanted to be a ghoul. I'm carrying this plastic staff and a tube of face paint through the toy store when this girl shrieks like a galah caught in a windmill. She thought I was a cannibal wanting to spear her and gobble her up!" He peered over the bank again.

"Well, her dad complains to the manager. This fellah cottons on to what's really happening and calms them down. As they're leaving, the mum says, 'Why can't those boongs be kept under lock and key?'"

The butcherbird roosted somewhere to the east. *Sweet pretty creature,* it called. The night did not respond.

"I didn't go out that year," Rob continued. "It seemed like there were more tricks than treats in the world, and I didn't want to go begging lollies from a bunch of lords and ladies. Then when me brother died...."

"It's OK. You don't have to tell me."

"Alice is a small town, hey? I was on the mall when these two fellahs joked about it. To them Mike was just some boong who got beat to death in lockup, nothing less than any Aborigine deserved. I went wild, just lit into them screaming and trying to punch their balls up into their bellies. That was the first real scrape I got into. A kid is no match for a couple of drunk soldiers."

"What did Matty say?"

"Made me swear never to fight again, especially over a drunk's word. She was terrified I'd end up like me brother or that I'd go bad. Lots of kids do, ya know, right at that age. They see no hope in the world and start drinking or huffing petrol." He crossed his arms. "How about you, then? What happened the first time someone called you names?"

"I lost a friend. Jeremy was the only Aborigine I knew but I stopped hanging around with him so much." He shifted deeper under the blanket. "It's hard to explain how I was thinking. It was like I had to prove myself to white people before I could risk having black friends."

"That was a tough time to grow up, mate. Don't be too hard on yourself." Rob tucked the blanket down tight. "Now get some rest. I'll wake you in two hours."

Gabe closed his eyes until they were slits. Jeremy had been as calm as if all the hate in the world could roll by without him blinking. Somehow he had been able to brush off the anger and ugliness, and somehow Gabe hadn't. The gulf between them had been devastating.

And that, he knew, was the real reason he'd drifted from Jeremy. As much as Gabe had tried to prove himself in white society, he felt even more self-conscious around Jeremy's family. He'd rarely spoken unless pressed and laughed only if others had. Jeremy's reaction to the taunts had been just another example of how different Gabe really was from others of his own race.

The stars were too much like his sorrow that day. He rolled onto his side and fell deeply asleep.

20 Lessons

Dana opened his eyes as a rubbish truck ground down the street. He had been awake since much earlier listening to the pigeons rustle under the eaves. He had heard the passing of a woman who sang of love and had felt the hotel shudder as the newspapers were delivered.

He lay with his back arched over a pillow and the soles of his feet pressed against each other. Inhaling deeply, he let his chest open to the morning's birth. Only in the past few years had he noticed any real difficulty stretching. Even then the pain was usually related to some mischief like the previous night's entertainment.

The shaman had smoked the bullets, cleansed the guns, and rubbed a head string with ochre until it was as red as the desert. Throughout the ambush, no other thoughts intruded on his mental picture of the half-caste and the young pup. He visualized their every move as they set up camp and prepared a meal. And when the rifle sights lined up, Dana had felt the pair's vulnerability as surely as the hunter felt the forced silence of prey gone to ground.

Those men knew nothing of hunger or hardship. After their narrow escape, they would leave their quest in the hands of officials who understood less than either of them. Perhaps one day Dana would see them on the streets of Darwin or Alice Springs. He would smile before melting into the crowd, and they would have only the sudden acidic memory of terror coating their tongues.

A clatter outside the door announced the arrival of room service. A kettle of water, packets of black and herbal teas, a plate of fruit and a tumbler of juice sat on a tray outside his door. Dana carried everything onto the balcony to watch the sun pick shadows from the world. One thing comes, a different thing goes.

Katherine was a perfect example of how the sacred life of the desert had changed. Just outside town, a gorge dotted with rock art saw thousands of visitors each month. Once a site for ceremonies, it was now little more than a staging area for the *piranpa's* annual ogle at the spirit world.

Dana enjoyed infiltrating the theme park Katherine had become. The luxuries bought with stolen energy were sweet. All the more sweet, then, to consider how the pup must be crying over his wrecked car. Surely someone would have to coax that half-caste out of the ditch. Both men would have a lot of time to think on their walk back to town. After all, the bullet holes could just as easily have been in them.

<hr>

"She looks like a bandicoot on a burnt ridge." Rob stepped around the Falcon to survey the damage. Bullets had perforated the fenders, the trunk was sprung, and the water jugs had exploded on impact. Every window except the one on the driver's side had shattered and the windshield sagged around a dozen holes.

"Oh, Rob," Gabe said, "I am so sorry. This never would have happened if—"

"Hey, mate! No worries, right? We survived. That's what counts."

"I'll pay for everything, I promise." He looked at the shredded tires and smelled the sweet coolant. "How are we going to get out of here?"

Rob stuck his head under the hood. After some muttering and a few curses, he pulled out a toolbox and handed Gabe a crowbar.

"We work," he said, "and we hope I can wire everything back together."

Two spare tires, one radiator hose and two hours later, the car was nearly ready for a test run. The men debated the wisdom of pouring the last of their water into the radiator. If the car was road worthy, they could drink the water from their canned vegetables until they got to a roadhouse. Otherwise, the move could be deadly.

Rob struck a compromise. They withheld one full canteen and used a gallon of coolant, the water pooled in the remnants of the large jugs, and urine for the car. Gabe felt naughty peeing into the radiator but he was too nervous about the outcome to make a joke.

"Look," he said, "You should drop me at the nearest town. I'll find my own way from there. Things are too dangerous to have you mixed up in this."

"There you're wrong. I'm in this until the end. I knew from the start you weren't playing kiddy games. So the guy who might have hurt Ian is on to us. It's not the greatest news but it proves we're on the right track."

Rob opened the driver's door and brushed glass from the seat. Gabe stood for a moment, considering where this course might lead. When the motor roared to life, his decision was made.

"Move over," he said. "I'll drive."

The fenders shuddered as they clanked along the track and a dozen bullet holes whistled once the men turned onto the highway. The windscreen was frosted with fractures, and Gabe peered through one of the puckers to see the road. But the engine was sound and he pushed on as his thoughts melted into a pipeline above his eyes.

They pulled into the first roadhouse. Rob had the clerk fill the thermos and bought soft-boiled eggs and bread. By the time Gabe had filled the tank, Rob was building their breakfast in the front seat. The bread was soggy from having been frozen and thawed too often and there was no butter to dress the egg. Yet Gabe filled his stomach methodically. Each bite fueled his body, and his body would carry him through this journey.

He studied Rob's profile. The young man had stayed awake all night and the vigil had hung bags under his eyes. A week ago, Gabe had been responsible only for Ian's life...or, really, for reporting his death. People needed the certain knowledge that death had come. That's why funerals were so important. They fed the living, not the dead; they laid a piece of the family's heart to rest. Gabe had come on this journey in part, he realized, to offer Dob and Rosie the peace his own biological family had been denied.

Now he was responsible for seeing Rob home safely, too. Gabe would have to be careful, much more careful than he had been up until this point. He would be responsible for their every action and their every fall. If things turned sour, Gabe would have to put himself between Rob and any harm. No matter what, he wouldn't let Matty lose another son.

⌁⌁⌁

With a steady population of nearly ten thousand, Katherine ruffled and hopped like a lizard on hot sand. Rob wound through the northeast side of town to a single-story rambler on a dirt lot. Two terriers shoved their snouts through a gap near the gate, barking and slobbering until a teenage boy slouched down the walk.

"Who're you?" he asked.

"A friend of Corrine's," Gabe said. "Is Lacy here?"

"Yeah, all right."

He scooped both dogs under one arm and ambled back to the house. Soon a girl about thirteen years old appeared. Her hair was a delicate blond, and she tucked the ends behind her ears as the men followed her to the river. She picked at her nails and glanced back to make sure no one else heard.

"Dad's not here heaps of the time, so my brother's supposed to take care of me," she said. "But he's always out runnin' with his yobbo friends. Real criminal types, yeah?"

"Must not be too nice," Gabe murmured.

"It's all right. I go out when he brings his friends over. Dad doesn't know half of what goes on. Anyway, I was out late when I saw the croc."

"Did you notice what kind of truck it was? The color, maybe?"

"Naw, it was too dark. I was just out for a walk, yeah? Looking for stuff tourists throw out. I've found some nice clothes that way. Like these shorts." She turned up the cuffs with her thumbs. "Guess they can't be bothered to take their stuff back home. Anyway, I smelled this awful stink. All I saw was the croc's head when that guy come up."

"What guy?"

"Some asshole snuck up so quiet, like to scare me out of my shoes! I wasn't doing nothing wrong. All of a sudden it's like Halloween! He was a skinny old bastard, looked like the walking dead." She shrugged. "That's it. I ran and he didn't catch me."

"What did he look like?"

"Old, just old. Had his hair slicked back and his eyes didn't look real. Just like that truck." She kicked the ground. "The truck looked weird, like nothing was there. It just ate up all the light. His eyes were the same, only like they could glow."

"He must have given you a fright."

She shrugged. "He was black, taller than him, not so tall as you. Skinnier than me. Smelled like smoke and something else, like a spice. Even over the stink, I could smell that spice."

Back at the house, Lacy's brother hung over the fence calling her. She squeezed her eyes and went back to picking her nails.

"Thanks, Lacy, that's very helpful. Tell me, what's your favorite dinner?"

"Oh, an egg sandwich with lots of salad."

"I may think of some more questions. Will you be around later?"

"Yeah. That's why he's wanting me home, so he can run off." She brushed back her hair. "I like it better when I have the house to myself. Can think straight without the telly on so loud."

"All right. Thank you again."

Gabe watched her scuff back to the house. She looked everywhere but at her brother until she got to the yard then waved him out the gate. The dogs were set free to resume their stations.

"Come on," Gabe said. "We're going shopping."

<hr>

The spoon stopped before reaching Dana's mouth. The mongrel and his whelp were headed for the shops. The car was a wreck but it had brought them here, past several garages and far from the road to Queensland. They could have only one thing in mind…to talk to that silly girl.

Taking the croc had been difficult. The buyer had demanded a trophy animal at a time when the rivers and billabongs swarmed with tourists. Then the fuel pump went bad, and Dana had paid a mechanic half-blind with grog to patch it up. The girl had wandered behind a trash bin where no girl had any reason to be. If Dana had known she would connect him to that roo shooter, he would have followed her into the night.

Those curs would discover there were worse things than being shot. The shaman knew how a few gentle blows would gather blood into one area and cause gangrene. He knew where to harvest plants that would paralyze the lungs. And the *wirrie,* the sticks he had planted inside the roo shooter's body, had soaked up enough toxins by now to kill.

Those overgrown boys would learn. They would know him not by birth or country but by deed. They would name him with the shake in their bellies and applaud him with the stumble in their steps.

He pushed away his bowl. He would take no more food as he prepared for the lessons.

Gabe loaded a basket with eggs, lettuce, tomatoes, apples, bananas and bread. From the canned foods aisle, he took peas and corn and tinned meats. He even studied the crocodile in the specialty section then put peanut butter and marmalade in the cart instead.

In a clothing store across from the market he picked out trousers, a cotton skirt and shorts for the clerk to wrap. Two shirts and a casual blouse followed, and he threw a package of socks in at the end. He made the clerk swear to let Lacy exchange them if they didn't fit. After dropping off the gifts, Gabe drove back to the main drag.

"Come on, we'll find a hotel for the night. My treat. You can catch up on your sleep while I make some calls."

"Where do you think we should go next?" Rob yawned.

"Darwin. Ian mailed the package from there, and I think we can pick up some information at the port. Smugglers are like any other merchant. They have to ship the product to the client."

Gabe selected the Redwing Arms, a B&B overlooking the river. It was pricey but there wouldn't be any lumpy cots or a noisy pub under the room. After a lunch of garlic sausage and peas, Rob headed upstairs. Gabe found a pay phone up the street and briefed Dob on his discoveries. He mentioned that the truck was being repaired but skipped the accident and the shooting.

"Smuggling a seven-meter carcass out of the country can't be easy," he said.

"You'd be surprised," Dob said. "I've seen things wrapped, rolled, stuffed and baled in the damnedest ways."

He talked about sea urchins and shark fins mined for the Asian market. In his warehouse alone, inspectors had found uncut diamonds in a cod's belly, the fossils of carnivorous kangaroos, even a barrel of koala pelts rolled into a furry swag. The dock master at RBC Shipping, he said, would have leads on smuggling out of Port Darwin.

"You just come back to us, right, Gabe? Find out what you can but don't take risks. We don't want to lose you, too."

After the mutt left, Dana strode up to the pay phone and pulled a single strand of hair from the earpiece. He peered carefully at the ground but found nothing else.

A little, he knew, would be enough.

21 Pelican Man

Officer Rehnquist, a powerful man with salt-and-pepper hair, *tsk-tsked* at the appropriate moments and ended his notes with a flourish. Gabe offered to bring Rob in to give a statement but Rehnquist shook his head.

"We see a few of these cases whenever the temperature tops twenty-four, twenty-five degrees. People go a little mad and pull these pranks. All harmless, except for the property damage, of course."

Gabe's elbows locked into his ribs. Trying to keep his voice level, he spread his hands flat on the counter. "I don't think you fully understand the situation. We've been looking for my friend, a roo shooter who went missing nearly a month ago."

"That long and your friend's probably missing for good. You understand that?"

"Yes. But last week a red truck ran me off the Barkly Highway."

"You fellows sure get around."

"Rob wasn't with me then. Look, I filed a report in Alice Springs. I'm not making this up."

"I've no doubt these events actually happened. But it's difficult to connect the two." He ran his eyes across the paper. "You said the shooting occurred along a track leading from the coast. How did you end up in Katherine?"

"We took the Roper Highway to the Stuart."

"So you passed Mataranka? If you really thought someone was after you, why didn't you file a report there?"

Gabe felt like a sheep whose every burr and cockle was being teased from its fleece. He looked directly in Rehnquist's eyes. "I'm looking for a missing man. I had to talk to someone here about him."

"Okay, I'll pull the other report. Would you mind waiting?"

Gabe withdrew to the benches but didn't sit down. His legs ached and he squeezed the muscles to release some of the tension. As Office Rehnquist punched up the case on a computer, he grunted into the phone now and again. Suddenly Gabe knew Commissioner Charles Dawson was on the other end. Judging by the way Rehnquist looked over the counter, the commissioner had dropped any pretense of warmth.

"Uh-huh," the officer said. "Uh-huh. Right. OK, thanks." He met Gabe back at the counter.

"Mr. Branch, I understand your concern for your friend. Lots of men his age go missing every year. Some really have died and some run off for a new life. We have no evidence of anything suspicious, including your experiences. Now, I can't tell you to go back to Townsville. But we can't recommend that you continue activities that put you at risk." It was his turn to look into Gabe's eyes.

"Go home, Mr. Branch. We'd hate to see something happen to you, too."

Gabe felt cold all over, the same numbness that set in when a dive went on too long at too deep a level. The heat snaking off the pavement didn't touch him and he drove mechanically back to the hotel.

"Bastard," he muttered as he shut off the Ford. "Bloody fucking bastard."

~~~~

"Gabe!"

The voice had Selena's pure tone of joy. Gabe touched the side pocket of his waist bag and felt the opal Rachel had given him. Surely his mind was playing tricks again.

"Ga-a-abe!"

Now a number of voices called over the clatter of a motor. He turned to see a tangerine bus with *Warlbrooken Dance Company* splashed across the side. A half-dozen people leaned from the windows, waving hats and shouting. He walked down the block to the bus and met Selena at the curb.

"What is this?" he asked. "Why are you here?"

"Oh, don't act like a stunned mullet!" she laughed. "I told you we were heading north this week. Only one paved road goes up the middle of the Territory, you know. I'd hoped we'd meet, and here we are!"

She pounced into a full body hug, and he grabbed her to keep them both from falling. "Where's my brother?" she demanded.

"Sleeping. We had a long night."

Selena rolled her eyes. "Here, help me with my luggage. Then we'll wake the mighty tracker for supper."

Soon the trio was back at the hotel pub. Rob was still groggy but a few cups of tea brought him back to normal. Selena waved another dancer to their table. The woman was in her mid-fifties with hair pressed into smooth waves.

"This is Nan," Selena said. "She's semi-retired but she tours with us sometimes. She's a great singer. No matter what we tell her, though, she won't take a salary!"
~~~~

"It's my way of giving back," Nan said. "We load the bus with antibiotics, booster shots and supplies for the remote camps. Besides, it's a good excuse to visit people I haven't seen for a while."

"So you cover this territory pretty thoroughly?" Gabe asked. "Have you seen this man?" He pushed a flier across the table. He had become a single-card dealer hoping for a trump with every round.

"Don't think so. I see a lot of white guys, rugged types, and they blend together. Where's he from?"

"Cairns."

"You're from the coast? I've relatives there. What's your skin?"

"I don't know. I was stolen."

"Oh. Never met anyone who was taken. Tough luck, mate." Her tone was as casual as if she had dropped her napkin. She kissed Selena and headed for the bar.

"She was less than sympathetic," Gabe said. "Not that I'm crying for attention but she acts like she doesn't believe me."

"Lots of people don't," Rob shrugged. "They say it's a conspiracy. You know, like those wankers who say the Holocaust never happened."

"Yes, and I expect men never went to the moon."

After a pause, Selena tried to lighten the mood. She chattered about the long drive, the stops they would make, the outstations they would visit. Although Gabe tried to listen, Nan's words had sounded a hidden depth. He felt the tug of shame like a shark at his toes and was defenseless against its bite.

He had never known his birth mother. He could conjure only a vague impression of an oval face and clear, soft cheeks. In all of his images, her hair was combed back. He had distinct memories of touching its soft loam, of burying his face in her neck and hiding beneath its waves.

His skin mother. The woman who had dreamed his spirit totem, whose color he wore on his hands and face and chest and thighs. If he had stayed with her, he might have learned of Dreaming and of songs. In the life forced upon him, a millimeter of difference had marked the boundaries of *isn't* and *can't*.

On the face of it, the boundary wasn't really there. His color didn't stop him from shopping or riding the bus or doing any of the other things people did every day. Yet it was as tangled as the roots of a strangler fig growing all around him, closing him behind wooden bars.

He had tried to brush off the comments, and the sneers, and the *tsk-tsk* of grocery clerks and women at church and tourists on the beach. But when a teacher asked him to bring in a painting by "his people" for their art lesson, the patina of words and concepts crumbled like a candied shell. He was utterly vulnerable to the *isn't* because he profoundly lacked the *is.*

His world was monochromatic. It reflected the light, returned the spectrum to the sun, allowed nothing to penetrate. And Gabe was *not white.* He was *not of their skin.* A life defined by what it was not could only be animalistic and haunted. Yet clearly he had no idea of what he *was.*

Selena's voice flowed over him. Its warmth was candlelight through an ice sculpture, its touch the eddies that swept the submarine cliffs of the Coral Sea.

"Gabe," Selena laughed, "you look like an emu trying to find food! Did you hear me?"

"Oh. Sorry, no."

"I asked if you'll come watch me dance. I know you won't be able to right away. But after this trip?" She hopped out of her chair. "I'll get our touring schedule. Really, it's a great show. You'll love it!"

As she ran to the director's table, her movements reminded Gabe of rain. In the jungles near his home, storms sometimes blew in from the ocean. Afterward the air was sharp with ozone and filled with the *pat-patter-splat* of water falling from limb to leaf. With his feet cushioned by moss, he could catch the raindrops and taste the canopy. He inhaled deeply, smelling her lavender perfume, and felt alive.

"Tell me about your initiation." His eyes settled on Rob in time to catch the young man's surprise. "If that's allowed."

"No worries. It's just you haven't seemed too interested in those things unless they relate to your friend."

"How long did it take?"

"It's sort of a lifelong process. You get bits and pieces in a series of ceremonies until you learn what every regular bloke needs to learn. Shamans go further and their trials are tougher."

"Here ya go." Selena slapped a copy of the troupe's schedule on the table. "You're talking about clever men, aren't you? I know a lot about that. Heaps more than he does. That's because I know it's true but he thinks it's fake."

"Which is why I'll let the two of you finish this conversation." Rob stood and stretched. "Get me up at first light and we'll figure out what to do next. Meantime, don't you two get into trouble. Unless you want to."

They exchanged a sly brother-and-sister look as Rob left the pub. If Selena weren't so young, Gabe might have thought he was being set up. For now, he was preoccupied enough to let the mystery go unsolved.

"Don't let this guy get to you," she said. "Any fella who uses the *djang* for things like killing is gonna have it blow up in his face."

"Is that part of the Dreaming law?"

"It's karma!" She laughed, the same breathless chime he had first heard under the coolibah tree at her house. "Really, if you do bad stuff it'll catch up to you. Everyone knows that."

"Let's hope it catches up to him before he catches up to me."

Between the dinner rush and the dance troupe, no one paid much attention to an old man at the corner table. He barely moved, nodding over a cup of tea long gone cold. Through narrow eyes, the shaman watched the mutt and the dancer. He felt the energy between them and thought how the half-caste would suffer to see her in peril.

A pity, really. Her soul was so pure, she radiated a lightness that touched everyone around her. But every war had its casualties.

Selena knew about the spiritual beliefs of many tribes. The pub was nearly empty by the time Gabe thought to ask about *djang.*

"*Djang* isn't the same in every place," she said. "Each site has its own level."

"What about places where people have died?"

"Oh, those are powerful. It used to be that a whole camp moved away for a year after a death."

"So people were buried where they died?"

"Not always. But burial grounds are wild. Spirits everywhere, and more spirits to guard them! Don't ever go into a graveyard. Too many ways to get hurt."

"How can you tell which places have more power?"

"You listen from here." She touched his heart. "You can do it. You just have to try."

"Shamanic power has always had a duel nature."

The night had congealed and the pub was nearly empty. Dana sat in the same corner with his back to the wall. The table was far enough away from the stairs and the entrance to feel secluded. Selena perched across from him, facing into the dark corner. There was nothing to distract her from the clever man.

"In the old days, illness was always caused by a spell," he said. "Even healing was a counterattack on the spirit or person who caused the disease."

"My dad died when a blasting sequence at the diamond mine went wrong. That would have been a big curse, right?"

"Oh, no. Accidents are just that. And I've had my fill of those!" He rubbed his knee and winced just the right amount. "Sometimes it's difficult to gather so many years in your life. Your eyes fade, your legs give out...but there I go, taking up your time. The young don't have much use for elders any more."

"That's not true!" She grabbed his hand in both of hers. "Tell me more."

"Oh, how you flatter an old man. Well, anyone can curse someone else, you see. Even modern religions recognize the power of intent. If you have done it in your heart, the Bible says, it is done." He smiled sadly.

"But that knowledge has been lost to the blood of conquest, to black missionary robes and amber beer. Our own sacred colors have been turned against us." He shook his head. "You wouldn't understand. Things were different then. It was a hard time, and long ago."

He remembered the start of his own hard time, the night of his initiation. After the circumcision, one uncle had tended him while the others returned to camp. Instead of caring for his nephew, the uncle had put him in a truck driven by a white couple. Months went by before Dana learned the details of his betrayal. The uncle had sacrificed him to the welfare so his own son could stay on the reserve.

"A hard time," he murmured, "in so many ways."

Selena was on the verge of tears. The innocent were always like that, he knew, so trusting and giving. It was why the world sucked out their entrails.

"You said you are a dancer. If you like, I will tell you a story worthy of your grace."

The pub dissolved into a Dreamtime scene. "Long ago," he said, "the Pelican Men had feathers as white as pipe clay." His voice was so low Selena strained to hear, and only the flutter of his fingers kept her on the conscious side of a trance. As he murmured, her breath deepened. The Dreamtime swallowed them whole.

When the rains came, a flood trapped a group of women on a hill. The Pelican men had a canoe that could rescue only one person at a time. A particular woman, younger and more beautiful than the rest, noticed the way the lead Pelican man looked at her. She knew he wanted to take her away somewhere and rape her.

When at last it was her turn to get in the canoe, she chose instead to jump into the raging water. The rest of the tribe guessed what had happened. They seized the man and stabbed him with their long bills for causing the death of the woman. Then they smeared themselves with ashes to mourn such wasteful deaths, and to this day wear the colors of their grief.

"You, Selena, could be that woman." His voice was gentle, with just enough command in its tone to lift her to the edge of her trance. "Do you see the dance? Can you smell the water, feel the wet sand shift beneath your feet?"

She nodded. For the first time, he returned her caress. A crystal was hidden in his palm. "You're so young but you respect tradition. I'd like to show you something special. Something powerful."

Her eyes lit up. He'd known they would.

Dawn frosted the sky as Rachel snapped awake to hear the chattering whirligigs. Her body felt heavy, as if her spirit had not yet settled fully into her limbs. She had dreamt of Angus' niece. Selena had been a scarlet bird falling, falling, each feather drained of color until she was spun from spider's silk and filled with crumbling dew.

The songwoman gasped. A dingo stood at the back door. It was a male and panted heavily as if having come a far distance. The dog looked toward the horizon then sat facing her. His fur glowed in the firelight, rising in the spectrum from rose to rust to red.

She nodded. The dog ducked his head and was gone. Where he had sat, double crescents marked the dust and the ground was damp with saliva. She touched the spots, now cold, and saw the tracks leading west.

Rachel laid out her ochres and pulled a crystal from a shelf over her bed. She would have to work fast. She hoped it was not already too late.

22 Spirit Walking

The Falcon was packed and ready before dawn. Gabe had bought a plastic windshield as a temporary fix until they could swap the Ford for his truck. They popped it into the frame and cleared the last of the glass from the dash. As they worked, a flock of zebra finches twittered softly. The sound drifted down like manna.

"Seen me hat?" Rob rummaged under the seats. "Huh. Wonder if someone took it."

"Why would they take a hat and leave the camping equipment? Especially that particular hat."

"Maybe they like Vegemite."

"No accounting for taste."

"You can't buy those things, you know." Rob pulled out the choke. "That hat was a promotional gift."

"How many jars did you have to eat to get your gift?"

"Seven big ones. And let me tell you, peeling those labels was no bloody picnic."

Darwin was a few hours away and the men spent most of it in silence. Along the horizon, light grew from a bronze sheen to a brilliant glow. Someone, either Ian or Chance, had told Gabe that a Dreamtime woman patted herself with dirt every morning. She kicked up so much dust that the rays of the sun glowed red. If stories were all he had left of either person....

He held that thought gingerly, like a glass bead on his tongue. Flocks of swifts peeled away from the bushes and flew by the hundreds over the car. Their cries were an instant cut from the roar of speed. As they neared Darwin, Gabe swallowed his thoughts. If he could not have the man, he decided, he would at least have his story.

———

Dana had watched the Falcon cruise through Katherine on its way north. He had waited outside the B&B and tracked their movements through the windows with his binoculars. Just as the plants whispered their secrets to those who would listen, so too did animals impart knowledge.

The way a man walked spoke volumes, as did the flicker of his eyes or the squeeze of fingers on a receiver. Gabe carried his missing friend around his neck and expectation hobbled his legs. His mother's love shored up his spine, and assimilation had left his guts rock hard and festering. If Dana were invisible, this mutt was a scarlet orchid pulsing in the jungle.

And Rob was a cake-and-pony party. His head swiveled from one pretty distraction to the next, his breath idled on pop songs, and his hair was a freewheeling mess. Yet he had stayed awake all night in that trench so the older man could rest. He made a living with bush knowledge even if he didn't understand the call he felt from the earth.

Now they were uncomfortably close to the money trail. Dana could kill them as swiftly as an eagle strikes a rabbit. Instead he would teach them about pain and fear. Particularly about fear.

While the men had been preoccupied with their morning meal, Dana had taken the pup's silly cap. Long strands of the young blood's hair were in the headband, and Dana had lifted the enameled pen Gabe had used at the phone booth. Nothing they would sorely miss, yet personal enough to carry their energy.

Later Dana would pose as Gabe's father. The owner of the B&B would have pity for the story of Gabe's dying niece and would tell the shaman where he had gone. For now he had other chores. He returned to the Fox and Hounds in time to see the mule fumble with his room key.

"Christ!" Kevin bellowed as the shaman appeared beside him. "Fuck all. Why ya sneak up like that all the time? Fucking Christ!"

"I have a job for you. Be sober enough to drive before noon."

"Right, right."

Kevin scratched the latch plate and rattled the handle before finally fitting the key into the lock. Dana waited, not because he had something else to say but because he enjoyed watching the mule jib. Kevin shut the door firmly, yet not so hard the shaman might think he had slammed it in his face.

The funny thing, Dana mused, was that too few drinks didn't bolster his ego enough and too many left him more vulnerable than when he was sober. Of course, most addictions claimed that duality. Food and television and exercise fed one hunger while creating a deeper one for satiation, benediction, emancipation. Feed addiction enough and any man would starve.

It was all deceit, the flashy clothes, fast boats and opulent vacations dangled by a society empty of the divine. The grand things the white men numbered in the good life were jokes more cruel than any Dana could fabricate. The shaman just redirected their bite, and spiced each meal with hidden hopes and forgotten prayers. No lies tasted so sweet as those engorged with the eater's own blood.

Dreams were theirs for the taking, if they chose. Instead they huddled in their stalls to ruminate on past victories. Gabriel was like that, not yet done with the smell of his own sick. He was a man of mixed mind. A divided man was an easy target, and a deserving one. The sorcerer didn't blink as Kevin peeked into the hall.

"Fuck." He nearly retreated then stepped out to use the toilet. Dana tapped the wall, just once, enough to let the mule know he was listening. A minute ticked past, then another, and the ass shuffled and cursed until his urine flowed. The shaman played this game more often as of late. It was a sign of how little time the two had left as a team.

Kevin checked the lock repeatedly before he fell into bed. When the light clicked off, Dana returned to his own room. Today the mule had rattled the knob nearly twice as much as usual.

He smiled.

***

The day was early yet but the streets of Darwin were already filled. At the Wharf Precinct, freighters leveled the sea with anvil hulls. Gabe studied a truck in the middle of the parking lot.

"The vehicle that ran me off the road looked exactly like this one." He checked the grill. "Toyota. Too bad it's not red."

They joined a stream of day trippers walking to the Arcade, a refurbished warehouse with a dozen cafes. Further on lay the industrial wharfs, the gateway to the South Pacific. Somewhere in those containers were artifacts, and someone on the docks was privy to each shipment. Gabe knew just where to start.

***

Selena moaned. Dana heard the feathery scream rise from her dreams and adjusted the hairstring around her torso. This rope was made entirely from the shaman's own hair. With it he could capture the energy of a dead man or make someone sleep as if dead. Any manner of mischief could be worked on the bodies of the enchanted without them waking.

Dana had no such plans for this woman. She was a pawn, a minor player, and would be killed when her usefulness had passed. Meanwhile, he would keep her safely tucked away, even comfortable. He was not a cruel man but he did enforce *Tjukurpa* Laws.

And so he sang her spirit away. The blanket in which she was bound was the confines of the womb, he murmured. She shouldn't be in such a hurry to be born. He passed the crystal over her again and again, soothing the tumble of her soul. And like a baby, she huffed then settled into her lullaby.

Gabe would check back after the shift change for any information the dock master might dig up. For now a meal was in order. The men chose a shady spot in Bicentennial Park where families trailed from one monument to the other.

"Ramie said your truck will be ready this evening," Rob said. "I can drive down and get it while you wait to hear something."

"Maybe. It's a lot of driving and I don't think it'll save us that much time. Might as well enjoy the break."

Rob opened a wad of newsprint holding perhaps a dozen fish fillets and handed Gabe an even larger packet of fries.

"Hungry, are we?" Gabe asked.

"Like you said, enjoy the break."

They ate looking out over the ocean. Sailboats skipped close to shore and a group of kayaks braved the currents. Farther out, red and black freighters pushed back the horizon. The salt air, the vinegary chips and the buzz of tourists was so much like Townsville, right down to the kids flying kites. He reached for another fillet then another until only a handful of chips was left to soak up the grease.

Later Gabe prowled the shops for a couple of new shirts. Anything he bought would turn pink from the dust but he'd feel natty for a few days, at least. The sidewalks were blocked by hillocks of T-shirts and the air simmered with curry, kabobs and stir-fry. He stepped into a shop. For a dizzying moment, the building stretched down the block into infinity.

When his eyes adjusted, he saw a cooler filled with a chorus line of cabbages. To his left the cash register was hidden by a blind of incense. An Indian man with smoke around his eyes hurried to the front. As Gabe pretended to browse, he walked to a counter buried under jars of bark and dried flowers, resins and oils. Statues of the elephant god Ganesh and the many armed Shiva stood among the medicine.

"What can you do to help with the heat?" he asked.

A woman rose from the register and stepped behind the counter. Her smile was as light as the folds of her sari. *What,* Gabe thought, *am I doing?* Herbal teas were fine for a change of pace but this was like asking for a potion.

The woman had already mixed several leaves on a sheet of tissue paper, so he let her finish. He would buy what he had asked for and pitch it out later.

As they trooped to the front, Gabe was startled by another customer. The man was older, also an Aborigine, with skin the same velvet nap as shadows. He was blurry like a watercolor painted too quickly, and Gabe rubbed his eyes.

When he turned away, he could swear the old man was right behind him. He felt the heat rising off the elder's skin and the whisper of breath in his ear. Plunging outside, he was grateful when the sun shook the shade from his back. He turned to look inside but the old man was gone.

<hr>

Dana's spirit floated through the ceiling and back into his body. At first his limbs felt blank and heavy, emptied of all energy. As his heart rate increased, his breath spread his spirit through every cell. Soon he clenched his hands and toes then opened his eyes.

He thought of the shopkeepers who had helped Gabe. The man had been oblivious to any supernatural presence; the woman might have seen him but she covered her concern well. In their chosen homeland, a sterile codex of thou-shalt-nots and holidays that degenerated into booze-ups were poor substitutes for the divine.

Aborigines were the true children of the land. They did the jobs they were hired to do in the age of iron hearts but their souls knew of magic. Dana remembered the day an Aboriginal man named Yancy had approached him in a town along the west coast.

"You doctor, yeah?" His words were breathless, as if he sought something illegal. "Black doctor, you do black medicine? Got hurt running cattle, broke my hip. Now it's pain, pain like burning, all night, all day. You help, yeah?"

They had driven to a shed of corrugated steel. It was well past dinner and groups of men were scattered among the trees. Using feathers to help him see, Dana discovered a blockage in the sacral joint. The energy had stagnated and filled the area with heat and fluids.

The men rubbed the patient with lard and painted his body, particularly around the navel. As Dana began to sing, the group cupped their hands and poured out their energy. They sang songs from the country and of the Dreaming tracks around their home. Dana passed his hands over Yancy's sternum and under his back. He tugged and prodded then extracted a bit of ironwood an inch or so in length.

He showed the splinter to the group before he flung it away. The men sang of rain to close the wound, and the patient lay on a bed of wet eucalypt leaves atop the embers. By morning he moved easily and said he felt young again.

Those most in need often had the least to give. Yancy offered five dollars and a case of tinned meat as payment. When Dana stopped by the pub that evening for a meal, he found Yancy celebrating with an extravagant amount of grog. He saw the shaman and whispered to the group, which burst into laughter. *Haw-haw-haw* went their jaws, *ho-haw-ho.*

Dana flicked a splinter of crystal into the seam of Yancy's hip. For the rest of his life he would suffer the grind of a foreign object in his bones. He had gibbered and begged, dragging himself down the road after Dana's truck. The sorcerer left but not before looting the Dreaming sites of Yancy's tribe.

In his long, long life, Dana had punished many transgressors. The whites were so ignorant that death was often the most expeditious way to deal with them. Gabriel, though, was part Aborigine. Yet he had rejected the magic of his heritage. He was corrupt in body and mind.

A killing would be too quick and the usual punishments too slight. The half-caste had to be broken piece by piece. Fear would be the torment that choked his heart, pain the pressure that twisted his body. Then, after he flinched at every footfall and his mind made him sick with its burdens, then Dana would strike the final blow.

After all, the *karadji* was not only an executioner. He was also a tribe's conscience.

<hr>

After another hour spent fidgeting around the docks, Gabe got the information he needed. It had cost him dearly and had come in seedy packages. First an oily American cloaked in faded tattoos appeared in the shipping office. Later a teenager stumbled in, wrapped in scabs so puffy Gabe thought he might burst if he bumped into anything.

But the two confirmed what the dock master had said: most smugglers dealt animals, drugs or gems; at any given time a dozen small operators might deal artifacts; and two or three looters were in for the long haul.

One of the career thieves was an Aussie called Jim Tinny. Jim drank only Fosters and carried his own supply by the case. The second, Peter Pegswerth, was a Frenchman who ate only British dishes, wore only imported British suits, and presumably had changed his name to suit his Anglophilic tastes. The third was a Pitjantjatjara or Yankunytjatjara. Since he worked through agents, the informants had never met him.

Gabe favored Jim Tinny as a likely suspect. He was Australian and could fit in without drawing attention. The scabby kid said he was blond, which fit Corrine's description of the poacher. Ian could have discovered Tinny's looting, mailed the message stick to Gabe for safekeeping, then tracked the thief elsewhere.

The men agreed to pick up the truck and head directly overland, crossing the Walmanpa-Warlpiri Land Claim where Rob had relatives. On the way to Ramie's, they would tap an art-school friend of his brother for leads. Since Tuffs was currently a roadie for an international religious revival, his current location was vague. Few things about the desert were precise, though, and Gabe was beginning to understand just how small the outback was.

Gabe folded the opal and the dingo tooth into a handkerchief and pressed the bundle deep into his pocket. The charms were warm, almost hot, and pressed into his thigh as if to become one with his flesh.

23 The Bone Pointing

With a jiggle and a twist, Dana popped the lock to Kevin's room. The light beside the table was still lit and the mule's underwear was tangled around his knees. Dana kicked him in the head.

"Fucking Christ!" Anger turned to confusion then fear. Dana said one word, a command the mule dare not ignore.

"Move."

Kevin's jaw snapped shut. As he groped for his clothes, the shaman eyed the thatch of blond and copper hair at the mule's groin. Kevin blushed and turned away. But his underwear had rolled into itself and as he tugged at his shorts, he lost his balance. When he fell against the bed, his buttocks parted to reveal an anus winking in panic.

Through it all, Dana tapped the bureau impatiently. He could barely stand the stench of sweat and pork in the room. There were also other, more fecund odors that indicated the mule had been rutting lately. He pushed the ass into the room where Selena lay enchanted.

"Take a shower," he said. "Rent a car large enough to put her in the back seat. Find a hotel where we've never been. If anyone recognizes you, they are mistaken. Take off her hood and replace it with this blindfold. Every six hours roll her onto her side. If she wakes up, kill her."

"Oh, don't worry." Kevin rubbed his crotch. "I'll take good care of her."

With a speed that caught the mule off balance, Dana shoved him into the bureau. The flint knife parted the knuckle of Kevin's ring finger. The resulting howl would have topped a castrato, and the mule pressed his hand into his stomach. Dana skewered the finger and shoved it under his muzzle.

"This," he said as the meat quivered, "if you touch her, this is your prick. And when I take that, I won't be so quick."

Kevin's only response was an exceptionally loud fart. Tears of shame clouded his eyes but color did not return to his face. As Dana tucked the finger into the rope under the girl's breasts, he was careful not to turn his back. Even a mule in shock could throw a lucky kick. He dropped a wad of bills onto the bed.

"Do as I say. When I'm ready, I'll find you."

He latched the door and went outside. Heat chaffed the earth from above and below, rubbing the buildings and cars into ash. The shaman's mouth was dry. There was no victory in handling the mule and his prey was further down the highway with every minute.

"Let's raise a' offering," said a voice over a loudspeaker.

Rob found a place to park while Gabe surveyed the revival. Hundreds of people milled about, clutching fans and Bibles and soda cans. Children shrilled past, intent on a dozen games that could only be played in motion. The whole thing had a carnival atmosphere but carnival goers were never quite so blissful.

Tents and canopies of midnight blue formed a rough oval. Assistants directed visitors to drop toilets, the first-aid tent, and tables stacked with literature. There was even a portable baptismal pool. At the far end stood the pavilion where the reverend moved among his flock. He wore a pale yellow robe with a scarlet sash any lorikeet would envy, and a wireless mike broadcast his every word.

Like any good Baptist minister, the reverend could improvise a three-hour sermon on any two verses of the old testament or any one of the new. As the men walked to the entrance, they learned the reverend's father's name and his mother's occupation. They heard about his hometown in Mississippi, its population during the 1960s, and what a black man had to do to put shoes on his son's feet. Gabe assumed all this would roll back around to the Bible verses but he didn't yet see the connection.

"Reverend Joe Marchet," Rob whispered. "Sure packs the house, hey?"

Gabe considered himself one of the casual faithful. He avoided fanatics who grasped leaflets as tightly as souls pressed flat in a collection. A traveling revival sounded dangerous but he didn't see anything here to be upset about. The only oddity was the congregation's tendency to be a bit thin, some extremely so.

The woman to his right was the exception. Although her weight wasn't truly unhealthy, next to the others she looked extravagant. She touched Gabe's knee in welcome and her smile awoke a schoolboy's guilt as he counted his unconfessed sins. But her warmth was genuine and he thought this woman wouldn't mind his lapse.

"Do you see your friend?" he whispered to Rob.

"Oh, no. Tuffs will be in the mess tent. It takes all hands to prepare the loaves-and-fishes act."

"What exactly is that?"

"Feed the lost souls in the desert, of course. Plenty from poverty and all. Hope you're hungry 'cause the reverend knows how to barbie!"

The collection plate floated across the last row and the ushers disappeared behind a screen. The reverend mounted the stage, a flatbed parked against the rear wall, and launched another story. This one was about fishing and the best way to fry catfish, and after another twenty minutes swung back around to the same two verses he had read when the men arrived. Eventually he offered a closing prayer and released his flock to the pasture.

"All that talk about spiritual famine and his parish is ready to drop." Gabe kept his voice low. "He puts out a feed for strangers and tells his followers not to indulge?"

"That's what draws a crowd in the bush, mate. Steaks and snakes, a bit of deviled egg, ha-ha, and you've a captive audience. As for his followers, well, they make their choices."

The dining hall was larger than the pavilion. Steam and cooking grease had discolored the stay poles but otherwise the place was spotless.

"These are good." The woman who had welcomed Gabe plunked sausages onto both their plates. "Beef's OK, too. My name's Della."

"Thanks, thanks very much. I'm Gabe." He watched as she speared a hunk of lamb and nestled it beside his sausage.

"Salad's behind you, drinks are in the back. Soda and water, that is. Nothing alcoholic. Here, you'll like this pasta."

"That's more than enough, thanks. I'm actually not too hungry with this heat."

"Oh, just wait until after dark. It'll cool off then we'll put some meat on those bones. For now, have some pineapple."

"I don't think we'll be around later."

"So take it with you." She shrugged. "I think your friend is over here."

Rob waved a chicken breast to guide them through the crowd.

"Rosemary." he said as they approached. "Nothing nicer with chicken than rosemary. Except maybe *altyeye,* the bush banana."

"You ain't never had chicken and waffles, then," Della said. "You two ever get to Texas, you call me. I'll feed you up right." She ate deliberately, clearing every speck of wax beans before advancing to the steak. "Pecan pie's no good. Apple pie's the same. I know the reverend preaches abstinence but the man could use a Southern cook to handle them pies."

"Abstinence," Rob said. "From food?"

"You reject all but what is required for survival. It's a before-and-after thing. Before accepting Christ as your personal savior, you're in the clutches of worldly concerns. Afterward you live modestly, even amidst temptation."

"And where does good apple pie fit into all this?" Gabe asked.

"Honey, ain't nothing more modest than apple pie. Except maybe apple pie wearing hand-whipped cream."

Gabe was the first to notice the Aborigine, a pillar in the milling crowd. He stared at the men from the far edge of the tent. He seemed familiar, unsettlingly so, and when Gabe blinked he materialized at their table.

The world funneled away as he tried to process this impossible feat. In the same moment he recognized the elder from the Indian grocery. And just like before, Gabe felt the shadows converge around the man and pluck at his clothing like rapacious children.

The stranger balanced a bone between the fingers of his left hand. His right hand floated down its length as if gathering something then snapped toward Gabe. He repeated the gesture, faster each time, but he never blinked.

"Honey, ribs are the next table over," Della said.

When Rob looked over, he jumped back so quickly he fell off the bench. Gabe saw only the gentle ivory arc and the dull gloss of its surface. A crystal lashed to the end radiated the same midnight shine as the elder's eyes. When he felt a sting over his heart, he realized he had stopped breathing. He gasped and the man was gone.

"Guess he didn't want no ribs," Della said.

"What...the hell was that?" Gabe struggled to wake from his dream.

"*Karadji* man," Rob said as he got up. "He put a curse on you."

"That's twice in three days! What did I do this time?"

"Let's find out." Rob plunged through the cake line. The man he grabbed, a Jamaican in his early thirties, questioned them with his gaze.

"His hair was loose," Gabe said. "Tied back but not locked."

They searched the crowd and circled the parking area. The *karadji* was gone.

"Sugar, you must've wanted to talk to that man," Della said when they returned. "We don't never move that fast in Texas, and it's hotter here than I ever felt!"

Rob peered at Gabe. "How you feel?"

"Pissed off, that's how I feel. What kind of curse was it?"

"Oh, you know, just a hex."

"Honey," Della said, "ain't nothing just a hex. My cousin lives with a *mambo,* one of the Haitian clergy. I can tell you, cursing ain't no simple thing."

"So, you feel all right?" Rob asked.

"Why do you keep asking me that? Was the curse serious?"

"It was a bone pointing."

"No kidding, Rob. I was there. He pointed a bone. At me, remember?"

"It's a particular kind of curse. Bigger than others." Rob sat and drummed his fingers on the table. "It's sort of a death curse."

"There's no 'sort of' about death."

"Right you are. Well. A bone pointing doesn't always mean you'll die. It just means he'll try to kill you."

"*Mmm, mmm.*" Della fanned Gabe furiously. "You best stand clear of that curse, honey. You don't need that following you around."

"What do I have to do? Bend over the steam trays?" Gabe swallowed his weak laughter. "Sorry. Really, what do I do?"

"Nothing to do, mate. A curse of that level wants another shaman. Even then the cleansing might not work. It's all superstition anyway, right?"

"Is that why you fell off the bench getting out of the way?"

"I was spooked, is all. That guy snuck up in the middle of me cake." Now it was Rob who tried for a laugh but no one smiled.

"What would Angus say?"

"We'll call him when we get to Ramie's. You can talk to him yourself."

"I've got an idea and it's good for right now." Della worked her hand into her bosom and extracted a leather pouch. "The *mambo* gave me this last year. Good for illness, boils, sores and chilblains. No cankers, no corns, no broken bones. The only thing it don't save you from is bad breath, so you'll have to brush you own teeth."

Gabe took the pouch. The embroidery was damp with her sweat. Inside lay a few herbs and a bone.

"If you have a lucky penny or whatnot," she said, "you might put it in there."

"We don't have pennies in Australia."

"I know, sugar, I was sayin' for example. Gracious! You want the bag or not?"

"Yes, please." He tied the cord around his neck. "I feel safer already."

"I put wild mint and the toe of a roadrunner in there. I picked a roadrunner 'cause I might not be able to fly but I sure enough get where I'm going."

"And the mint?"

"For fresh breath!"

On the edge of the Tamari desert, just where the hills bucked from a clay pan, Rachel sat Dreaming. Her breasts were dotted white to symbolize the fullness of a mother's milk. Her belly wore pipe clay stripes to represent health and prosperity. In her hands lay the crystal and pituri smoldered on the coals.

Her mind focused on a single person. Her lips moved, her voice sounded, but she had no conscious knowledge of these actions as she slipped into the ether.

As the congregation gathered for the evening prayer, workers streamed from a canvas neighborhood east of the oval. Tuffs, an Arabic man with powerful forearms and fingers too thick for his rings, wore the peaked cap of the kitchen crew back over his crown.

"Looting's out of hand lately," he said. "They say it's a Pitjantjatjara. I hear he's sold body parts, and that maybe a few of them are fake. You know, modern parts made to look old."

"Pretty gruesome," Rob said.

"This year he's hit the Top End hard. People are spitting mad."

Gabe considered this as they moved down the rows. The man they were after was obviously unbalanced. Who else would trade in dead flesh, and murder besides? The heat in his chest burned cold and platinum bright. He wasn't sure if insanity made a person more dangerous or less.

It hardly mattered. Dob and Rosie needed answers, and so did he.

Dana watched from behind the drink dispenser. The men had looked for a person moving through the crowd. The shaman had been there the whole time, hiding behind stillness and a server's cap. In his dilly bag, a pouch sewn from kangaroo hide, were bits of food the men had handled. With them, he would make charm sticks to torment his enemies. He removed the cap and trotted through the side of the tent.

"Crikey, there he is!"

Rob vaulted over the tables with Gabe close behind. Down the neat aisles of safari huts, dogs barked and a pet galah screamed. They seemed to get nearer to the shaman and twice blocked him between dorm tents. But he was never where they expected. He echoed between the sunshine fabrics, appearing and disappearing until he was only a flicker in the narrow alleys.

"Damn it!"

Gabe gulped air as they circled back to the parking area. Then a red Toyota kicked dust along the makeshift road.

"You take care!" Della called as they sprinted to the car. "I'll pray for you both!"

Good, Gabe thought. They'd need it.

Rob spun the car around and crashed through the scrub. Tree limbs shrieked along the fenders and leaves slapped at them through the windows. When the shaman turned onto a gravel track, both cars roared into high gear. Soon the speedometer read 80, 90, 100 kph and the Ford fishtailed.

"The truck's heavier," Rob yelled. "I can't go any faster on this road."

Gabe grabbed a notepad to record the tags. The pen Chance had given him was gone and he scrambled through the glove box for a spare.

"Shit!" Rob slammed on the brakes.

Gabe had only an instant to see that the Toyota had come to a dead stop. When he threw up his arms, his elbow knocked the plastic windshield from the frame.

"Damn it, damn it, damn it!" Rob plowed gravel as the SUV turned behind an escarpment.

The truck was gone. Only a plume of dust showed the men where to go. As they fell behind, the mist dissipated entirely. Rob stuck to the trail, meandering through acres of acacia shrubs and bumping over rocks.

"I don't like this." Gabe tapped the notebook.

"Neither do I." Rob stopped and looked around. "Uncle Angus always says, when in doubt, get the hell out."

He cut back across the last few loops of the trail. The birds had fled and the buttes were stifled. Only the sound of the motor echoed back to them. The headlights picked the trail from the growing dusk.

"Goddamn it, he's behind us!" Gabe shouted.

His head whipped back as the Toyota smacked the sedan. Rob pulled ahead but the car shook terribly. The rear fender had crumpled into the tire and the stink of hot rubber filled the interior.

The Falcon leapt into a dry creek bed and bulldozed up the other side. Rob steered around a tall escarpment, cursing when the truck smashed them again. The nose of the Ford was shoved into a cliff. They scraped past and gunned up an embankment.

Just as the car began to fishtail again, it reared over the top of the plateau. They landed upright but a large rock finished off the engine. The motor screamed like a turbine as smoke poured behind the firewall.

"This is it," Rob shouted. "Get ready to jump!"

"He's got a gun!"

"He can't shoot both of us. You head for those bushes and I'll go for the rocks. Work your way back to the creek bed. Now!"

He jammed on the brakes and dove into the night. Gabe's door was stuck. Precious moments slipped past as the truck closed the distance. Blinded by smoke, Gabe crawled across the hood and smelled the flesh of his palms burning. He rolled off the car directly in front of the Toyota.

As he pelted toward the mulga, fear cut his hamstrings. He dove into the thicket and scrambled deep into the underbrush. When Gabe stopped to listen, the Ford had died. The Toyota was also silent. Where was the shaman? He peered toward the truck but couldn't see past the glare of the headlights. When he looked the other way, his eyes wouldn't adjust to the darkness. A marching band could walk by and he would never see it.

Damn it, Gabe thought, *I won't sit here like a staked wallaby.* Shielding his eyes, he made out the edge of the embankment they had driven up. If he could sneak around that way, he'd be safe. But the same tangle that had saved him would betray him with a single broken twig.

He stripped off his shirt and tucked it into his waistband. Thanking the fates that he'd gotten a haircut in Darwin, he lay flat and wriggled under the bushes. As he moved, the smell of diesel flooded the scrub. He scrambled up and away as fire swallowed the trees.

The flash sounded like a huge gasp, and Gabe thought of the cod that could suck up a small person with a single gulp. In the next instant, that terror seemed real. He had gone the wrong way. He stepped off the edge of a cliff.

Landing hard on his right hip, he slid over the edge. He threw himself backwards and the burned flesh on his hands ripped as he clawed the ground. A scrawny eucalypt caught under his left knee and three fingers wrapped over the top of the butte. He hung there, frozen in that delicate balance, and tried to remember the course they had driven. Was he hanging from the short embankment or the heady cliff?

Moving gently, he stuffed his free hand inside a crevice and scuffed around for a toehold. A hand grabbed his ankle. Gabe nearly screamed but a shower of dirt shocked him into silence. The shaman was inches away, scanning the plateau for his prey.

After an eternity, Gabe heard the sorcerer move away. Rob guided his feet first to one ledge, then another, and they climbed down together. Sweat raked Gabe's eyes and the tendons in his forearms began to cramp. Each handhold was less secure than the one before, and he felt himself tipping backward into the void.

Then the Toyota came to life. It would take only a minute to drive around the escarpment.

"Jump!" Rob shouted and was gone.

Gabe's whole face squeezed tight as he pushed off. The second he landed, the Toyota raked the butte with its halogens. Rob dragged him behind a boulder as the sorcerer drove to the end of the plateau. He backtracked to within a car's length of the hiding place, playing his spotlight between the rocks before winding off into the bush.

"I landed pretty hard on me ankle," Rob grunted.

The moon was coming up and they had little time to find cover. Gabe hoisted the young man onto his back.

"Hey," Rob protested.

"Shut up."

Gabe trotted around the far side of the butte and into the bush. The burning in his hands had become a tingle, like ice-hot darts, and his grip was slimy with blood. When he found a thick patch of shrubs, he pushed aside the branches. "Crawl under. I'm going back to the car for water."

Rob shook his head. "We can find water. Probably. Besides, it won't take long to hike back."

"What if we get lost?"

"I won't tell Angus you said that." He grabbed Gabe's arm. "It's not worth the risk!"

"What if the Reverend's already gone? Besides, I've got to get the message stick."

"Shit." Rob pulled himself under the bush. "Only get the canteens if you can find them right away. Don't stick around longer than you have to."

The closer Gabe got to the butte, the more he jumped at rats running in the grass. The adrenaline in his system should have let him push the Falcon all the way to Alice. Instead it made him clumsy and twice he nearly fell. By the time he climbed the plateau, the moon bobbed over the trees. Shadows as persistent as eels tangled around his legs.

He watched from the thicket for a time. Finally he crossed to the Ford, now sodden with fluids and stinking of burnt wire. He snagged the canteens from the rear, his bag from the front, and stuffed the notebook in his back pocket. Then he hurried back, stopping occasionally to make sure he wasn't followed.

Before helping Rob stand, Gabe secured the dingo tooth and the opal inside Della's pouch. That shaman didn't know who he was dealing with.

Della stepped from her tent at the edge of the canvas village. She had skipped the evening sermon to pray for the men. In the quiet she heard the red SUV creep back to the road. Its headlights were off and only the flare of brake lights marked its passage.

Her Bible, a leather-bound edition passed down in her family since the Emancipation, warmed her hand. The spine had nearly disintegrated but she didn't have to open the book to know what it said.

A handwritten note on the inscription page read, *To the Reverend Cook with thanks. In the hands of God.* The reverend had been Della's great-great-grandfather, a man with no vestments except those provided by God Himself, a man who had walked from one freed town to another carrying the holy word.

Della searched the sky until she found Jupiter's silver light. The constellations looked different on the underside of the world but she could always find that bright planet. It reminded her of home, the way Texas stood on its own amid a galaxy of other lights. Just like her great-great-grandfather had stood, a lone black man on the dangerous postwar roads. As she now stood, waiting for the men to return.

Dana passed the revival camp without seeing Della. He was back in Katherine before the pub at the Fox and Hounds closed. They had stopped serving drinks long before but patrons lingered for a last game of darts and a final joke. The mule's room was empty; he'd be in some anonymous hotel by now with the living package untouched. The mule was a slave to his lust and he was a coward. Since magic couldn't be fought with fists or feet, he would follow Dana's law.

Before attacking the men, the sorcerer had painted the spirit board and dressed it in hairstring. Now he removed its feathers and headband, and rubbed the ochre from the board into his belly. He wiped the paint off his face but left the symbols on his body. Under a shirt and baggy trousers, his body would assimilate the last bits of the energy he had called on tonight.

He spread a quilt on the floor where the lace curtains had sliced the light from the street lamp into crescents. Pulling his breath into his pelvis, Dana sank into a trance.

At night the outback was an empty theater with only stars to light the stage. Gabe blotted out any thought of the secret play and focused on the path ahead. When the men reached the gravel road, Rob studied the tracks with the flashlight.

"Can you tell which belong to the Toyota?" Gabe asked.

"Yeah. The tire pattern's the same as the ones at Thin Creek Crocs, which also matched the ones at Halfway Downs. Heaps of trucks could have the same type of tire, though."

"So we don't know if this is the right guy."

"Who else is gonna lay a death curse on you?"

"But you can't say for sure. All this time and effort wasted, and you don't know who's following us."

"What the hell is crawling on you?"

Gabe trudged ahead. The burning in his ribs had spread, caging him in his own bones. How long had the shaman followed them? Since Darwin? Since Alice? Since he'd run into those ratbags at the Carrarra pub?

"I'm just tired of chasing phantoms," he snapped. "You're so good at tracking and you can't even tell if we're on the right trail."

"I don't believe you! Your friend is stretched out somewhere in the desert, not even buried. You've got a *karadji* with forty thousand years of magic crawling up your ass and you're going on about...I don't know what you're going on about!"

"Don't stuff around with me! I'm in the middle of this fucking desert trying to find Ian!" He snatched up a rock and hurled it at a shrub. Stalking eyes were everywhere. "I would've been better off going it on my own."

"You don't know the first thing about getting around out here," Rob said. "It's not about having a sturdy car or a good map. When you meet someone, you've got to let them know who you are. What do you think all that dishing around about me second cousin's brother and which uncle married someone's mother is for? We're not holding genealogy class for nothing, I'll tell you that."

"Then what the hell is it for?"

"It's about kin. Who you're related to tells people about yourself. It lets them know, even though you're strangers, that someone somewhere ties you together." He held out his hand. "It lets you know you're not alone."

The shrubs and stones, the clumps of grass were washed the same watercolor blue. Gabe thought of the candy he'd traded for his family and how the ocean never really had shown him that precise sparkling shade. "I'm not like that," he said, and walked away.

"Everyone's got the same worries," Rob called. "It's warped your mind, growing up with your white friends in your white house by the sea. What would you tell your mum if you met her, your *real* mum?"

Gabe didn't think. He couldn't see, or perhaps he shut his eyes for the next few seconds. Either way, he charged with all the force of his rage. Rob twisted around but they landed in a heap. Rolling over and over, the men grappled for position until Rob leapt away. Gabe dragged him down again and straddled his hips. As he pulled back for a roundhouse blow, the flashlight clipped him just hard enough to snap his head back. Gabe froze, panting, then sat down heavily.

"Damn it," he finally said. "Goddamn it. I'm sorry. I—"

"Forget it."

"No, I—"

"I deserved it. I don't understand what you Stolen Generation went through. It's not for me to judge your life." He pushed back his hair. "This is such a crazy kind of thing to be doing anyway. I'm trying my best but I don't know if I'm actually helping."

"Neither do I. About what I'm doing, I mean."

He pulled Rob to his feet. Together they turned down the road.

The tracks of kangaroos divided the creek bed and river red gums grew tall at either bank. The slightest breeze set the leaves clattering. Somehow Gabe didn't mind the staring eyes so much any more. "How's your ankle?" he asked.

"Better. I fractured that bone when I was in high school. Me first and last foray into footy. It gets a little dicey when I've had a jolt but it'll be fine once I ice it down. How's your jaw?"

"Better," Gabe laughed. "I think the swelling will go down with some ice."

"Looks like some big hulk of a guy had something to say."

"Actually, that happened when I jumped off the cliff. It's not as bad as it seems."

"Crikey, don't I credit for doing a little damage?"

"Hardly." Gabe looked into the canopy. "By the way, the house is orange. Butternut rouge, to name it properly. Mum adores the autumn pallet."

"You city folk," Rob said, "are a bit barmy."

25 Silence

Della's leg ached terribly. She didn't often stand this long except during psalms, the reading of the Bible's beautiful prose. She must have waited much more than an hour because the limb gnawed at her like a snake bite.

She rocked to keep away the pain, just like she did during worship. Songs of praise were destined for heaven and standing helped them fly that much faster. Not that God needed any help with His hearing but joyful prayer was more than words and music. Songs were offered with every fiber of a person's being and the body couldn't help but dance.

For now only the hum of the refrigeration truck filled the night. That old geezer was trouble, even without his hexes and bones. And what a pair the other two made! Rob was so handsome and fun, with Gabe more fine than a man his age should be. They were as different as peas and beans.

"Dear Lord," she sighed, "send your angels down."

Cradling her Bible, she continued to wait.

***

Fuck that black bastard! Kevin tipped back the last few ounces of his beer and tapped the glass for another. The server gave him the blank face bartenders reserved for trouble. If the guy knew what was good for him, he would serve fast and piss off faster.

He served all right but he hung around a little too long. He swabbed the bar where only a few drops had spilled, adjusted the glasses on the counter, and emptied the ashtray with every flick of the cigarette.

Probably some poofter hoping Kevin would give him the wink. But he didn't go in for sucking cock. He wasn't above shafting the odd truckie in the ass. Didn't much matter what you fucked so long as you were the fucker. But cum-suckers made him puke.

Finally the man moved off. He was well-built and not as chunky around the middle as a barkeep might be. But he moved too quietly across the wood floor, him and his son both. Kevin swiveled around, leaning against the counter to maintain his balance. Sure enough, the little cunt hovered around the jukebox and pretended not to give him the eye. *I'd fuck him,* Kevin thought, *make him take it like a man.*

He tossed back his last beer and stumbled to the phone. He hoped to talk Rowdy into helping him off the old boong but the number had been disconnected. Kevin would have to wait for Rowdy to resurface or kill the old fuck himself. Even shooting the shaman when his back was turned seemed too risky. He punched the phone.

"Mister."

It was the faggot with his kangaroo eyes and his hands buried in a rag. He rubbed it like he might be coming on to him, each swipe as wriggly as a python. Kevin wanted nothing more than to smash his face into the floor.

"Mister, you want some food? On the house."

For Christ's sake, Kevin thought, *is he asking me out?* Right in front of his queer-bait son. Maybe they liked to tag team the same man. Maybe they liked it if people watched them suck each other. He pushed past and stumbled up the stairs. He needed time to think, time to quiet the flashing lights inside his head.

Fuck that black bastard! He jammed the key into the lock. They hadn't even raided any sites lately. Since the rock carvings, it had been nothing but errands. Drive here and fetch these charm stick. Drive there and hide that woman.

And the directions...the fucking directions! As if Kevin hadn't grabbed a woman before, as if he couldn't figure out when to kill someone! He slammed the door. It bounced out of the frame and caught the back of his heel. He slammed it again then stood panting in the cramped room.

The woman moaned. Kevin stared as if he hadn't put her there himself, as if he hadn't removed her hood and tied the blindfold tight. The felt was still damp from her drool. He bunched the cloth under his nose then licked the wet spot. He could smell only the bitter herbs Dana burned when he did his bush-baby act.

She moaned again. Her sharp inhalation was his single note of joy. If she woke up...his hands itched to fold her delicate neck in two. He would crush her with his body and cum against her thrashing thighs. But her breath receded beneath the blankets. The tip of his ring finger poked over the ropes, more pale than a grub and already stinking.

He slammed the door on his way out. He couldn't think straight with a boong in the room. At least the faggots were white. He stomped back down to the bar.

When he passed the back room, he heard the wife yammering. She had started when he'd signed in and by now was nearly hysterical. Granted he hadn't showered yet, his shirt was a bull's-eye of blood, and a pair of underwear was tied over his hand with a sock. But this was the outback, for Chris' sake. A man had a right to look a little grubby.

He brought in a six-pack from the truck. Alcohol finally muffled the throb in his hand. He sank deeper over the stool, mentally wandering through the sites they had looted and the hotels they had visited. A weak spot was in there somewhere. He just had to find it.

━━━━━━━

"You're up late," Rob said as Della caught them both in a bear hug. "We've had a bit of a hike. Are there any leftovers?"

She laughed and led them to her tent. At the entrance, two folding Adirondack chairs flanked a matching table. Citronella candles scented the air and a pitcher of water sweated heavily. Gabe got Rob settled and took the canvas seat Della offered.

"Tuffs is waiting for you," she said. "That truck went by some time ago, so I knew you'd need help. You can sleep in his tent tonight or he can drive you right out. We're breaking camp in the morning, so you can always hop on the bus. Tell me what you need."

"Ice for his ankle and some for my knee," Gabe said. "You wouldn't happen to have a satellite phone?"

"The only communicating we do out here is with God. It's not always convenient but you have to let Him take care of things." She smiled. "Of course, you also have to know when to do it yourself."

She moved off as Gabe rolled a glass against his forehead. The night was absolutely still, one of those frozen times the desert served up when he could least handle it. Not a breath of wind rustled the tents. The crickets had finished their symphony and even the dingoes had gone to ground.

On a similar night years ago, a camper had pulled in beside Gabe and Ian. The driver was old enough to be their father and chattered like a drunken parrot. When he ran shy of stories, Ralph shared various trinkets he had stored in the van. First was a tiny gemstone he had found in the Flinder's Ranges. Then came a coconut head from his trip to Fiji. Eventually he produced a didgeridoo, a musical instrument made from a hollow branch.

"Can you blow this?" He offered the instrument to Gabe.

"Ah, no. I never learned how."

Ian also declined. Obviously not one to disappoint, Ralph took a ragged breath and coaxed a drone from the tube. With another breath he mimicked the howl of a dingo.

Then the desert dropped away. Night stripped every rock, tree and hill from beyond the fire's light. No rats would rustle through their gear later, no clouds would cover the sky. If Gabe wandered too far, he would float into that void and be lost forever.

When the didgeridoo sounded again, he nearly dove under the Land Rover. The drone called something out of the silence, a presence as strong as that of the men. Then Ralph, wheezing with the effort, put the instrument aside. For once Gabe was relieved to hear nothing at all.

The next day, Ian had called Ralph a clown without a circus. He also said the didgeridoo had probably made a bush spirit very happy. Gabe had a hard enough time reconciling himself to a single divine ruler, so an army of otherworldly beings wasn't appealing. He didn't much care what had happened. He just never wanted to repeat the experience.

Yet there he was in the wilderness again, hearing that terrible silence and dreading the arrival of some invisible thing. Would the hum of the refrigeration unit mimic the didgeridoo? Would the prayers sent up from this camp attract spirits hungry for worship? He squeezed the pouch around his neck.

Damn, he thought. All that nonsense about curses and ghosts was ridiculous. He had to stay focused.

"Ya reckon we're still chasing Jim Tinny?" Rob asked.

"Hardly seems likely." Gabe shook his head. "I just can't figure how this guy works. If he ran me off the road then he was on to me long before I had the first clue about him. He could have killed me any time. Why stuff around like this? Why risk getting caught?"

"Ah, mate, that's your problem. You're thinking like a Twenty-first Century bloke with your nose stuck in a law book and your hopes hung on a jail cell. The shaman plays by the old rules. I reckon he was trying to scare you off before."

"And now?"

"Like I said. A bone pointing is a different kind of curse."

"Well, I'll be damned if I'm playing his games. I'll just be damned."

"No, honey, don't you say that, not even in jest."

Della had returned with towels, ice and Tuffs. In the flickering light, she looked like a dark moon.

"The sooner we get back on the road, the faster we can find that bastard." Gabe ducked at her frown. "Sorry. I don't usually swear."

"Honey, if any man deserves a name calling, it's that fellow you all chased outta here tonight. Just use something a little more G-rated or you'll turn out like him one day." After she fixed ice packs for both men, Tuffs led them to an ancient motorbike outfitted with a sidecar.

"You're joking." Gabe sniffed at the machine's aura of oil and leather. "I'm not riding in that thing. Besides, Rob's ankle is hurt. He should use the sidecar."

"Rob's twenty kilos lighter," Tuffs said. "He rides behind."

Gabe folded his legs into the compartment. There was no seatbelt but he supposed it didn't matter. In an accident, his head would pop right off his neck. At least the seat had a fair amount of stuffing. Della handed him a sack.

"Apples, crackers and biscuits. They ain't buttermilk but they're fair. I'll pray for you and your friend." She looked steadily at Gabe then seemed to come to a decision.

"Leaning," she sang, "leaning, leaning on the everlasting arms..."

Her voice was a scatter of doves that hovered over the men as they circled around to the road. Her smile came from her heart, the words blazed from her soul. She was far out of sight before Gabe realized his hand was still in the air.

The moon had disappeared. The track was lit only by a headlight that banged against the handlebars. Ghost gums rushed up to the road, their branches a caterwaul of scratches. Eyes watched from a ditch. A fox, probably, but Gabe didn't look too closely.

Beyond the roar of the engine lay an abandoned hall and a black marquee. He had never traveled into the void before, and the headlight created bits of the stage as they moved. He was terrified they would plunge off the tiny set and equally terrified that Tuffs might stop. Once that silence closed in, only dawn could break it. He hunkered down and urged the sun to rise.

～～～

Rachel floated above Selena's body. The young woman's energy, normally effervescent, was flat. She lived but her spirit was far away. The songwoman rose again, searching, searching.

26 Skin Name

The world took on a fish-belly glow as the motorbike turned onto the Stuart Highway. The shadows streamed from Gabe's clothes like saline. A kookaburra cackled and Rob pointed out a pair of brumbies, feral horses as small and rugged as the hills.

They hit Tennant Creek in the middle of the breakfast rush. Truckers, always the first to rise, warmed up their diesels while the last of summer's tourists threaded between the trailers. The men wore shorts hemmed high on the thigh while the women preferred straw hats with rainbow scarves. They hurried into the roadhouse, eager for their morning mug, as truckers wandered out. Only the shift change at a factory was more efficient.

Tuffs waved and pulled back onto the highway. Gabe's head rang with fatigue and the squawk of cockatoos hammered the back of his neck. When Ramie rushed from the garage, his gangly legs nearly sent him sprawling.

"Rob, have you heard?" Ramie's tic fluttered wildly. "It's Selena? She's gone missing."

The next twenty minutes were a blur of voices and phone calls. Nan, Selena's roommate at the Katherine hotel, said they had both stayed out late. When Nan returned to the room, she thought Selena was in bed and left the light off so as not to disturb her. Not until after breakfast did she realize the lump on the other bed was Selena's luggage heaped under the blankets.

When the police arrived, the ache in Gabe's chest burst like a bloated carcass. Acid flowed into his arteries and spread through every cell. This was the shaman's work, all of it, and it was Gabe's fault. The sorcerer had made that clear by leaving the enameled pen on the table where he had charmed Selena.

Gabe answered the officers as best he could but nothing he said was of much help. They would investigate the wreck site and interview the revival workers. None of their efforts would lead to Rob's sister. Gabe would head out after her right now if only he knew where to go.

His only hope was to solve the puzzle about Ian. Everything came back to the message stick, an eight-inch artifact Ian had salvaged from the shaman's haul. Gabe's journey until now had been a sort of crash-course in the world he had lost so long ago. Had he learned enough to start thinking like the sorcerer? He hoped so. It was Selena's only hope.

"Listen, Ramie, can I use your computer?" Gabe asked. "And we could both use a little sleep."

After settling Gabe in front of the wall of electronics, Ramie fidgeted near the doorway then disappeared on another walk. Breakfast was the last thing on anyone's mind but the men forced themselves to eat Della's biscuits.

"If we can find a pattern to the thefts," Gabe said, "perhaps we can guess where this shaman will show up next."

"I can make a few calls while you surf the net," Rob said. "Tuffs said this fellow hit the Top End hard this year. Knowing where he's been is half of knowing where he'll go."

"He seems to go wherever I go. He bloody well knew who I was and where to find me the whole time. Until yesterday, I never even saw him."

The ache in his ribs doubled as he realized he was wrong. His vision in Darwin had been of the same man with the same dark energies snapping off him. Had a flash of light really shot from the crystal or had his memory embellished the bone pointing?

"Will you check with Angus about all this?" he asked.

"Yeah. Let me sniff around a little first, see if I can come up with something more to tell him."

They turned to their work, oblivious to the shadows creeping along their sundial paths.

～～～～～

Dana drove to a secluded spot in the bush. Using the food Gabe and Rob had handled, he would prepare *ngathungi*, charm sticks. With them he could drain the men of their life energy.

No one believed such things anymore. But a lack of faith didn't necessarily mean a lack of results. Energy resonated at specific frequencies. If a man, a clever man, had the right training, he could channel energy in a specific direction.

Nearly all religions understood this flow and managed its use through taboos. Christianity forbad the vain oath because the name of any god was sacred. Their Bible said that in the beginning was the Word, and the Word walked across the face of the dark to create the world. The *Tjukurpa* said the same thing. The ancestors had walked a formless earth and sung out the names of everything in the universe.

Modern Christians scoffed at their own roots. Others remembered, and that knowledge made them strong. He laid a kangaroo hide on the ground then rubbed the fat of a monitor lizard into his skin until he shone. Coal, ochre and pipe clay layered his body, each symbol a piece of Kulpunya's Dreaming.

He removed the spirit board from its pouch. Greeting it as his brother, he painted the board as if it, too, were alive and dressed it with a headband and feathers. Here he sang the making of Kulpunya by the Mulga-seed men as ghosts gathered close.

After cutting two sticks from a tree, he tied the food onto the narrow ends. Then he coated the bundles with spinifex resin and set the *ngathungi* aside to cool. Only another medicine man could undo their effect, and then only if the clever man were clever enough.

He thought of the mutt who had no Dreaming, the boy who demanded the privileges of a man. He thought of how offensive Gabe's very existence was to the *Tjukurpa*. "Let breath leave your body," he sang. "Your day had already disappeared in the Western sky."

He was done. The shadows were hidden beneath the rocks and trees and grasses, and the world bristled. Dana would follow the men and pick his time with leisure. As he waited, he whispered the death song so softly only Gabe's spirit could hear the words.

～～～

Gabe ignored articles about vandalism and focused on damage done for profit. In the desert, spinifex clumps that represented the pubic hairs of a Dreamtime ancestor had been dug up. Along the coast of Western Australia, a cache of shells had been stolen. Rock carvings near Alice Springs had been chiseled from a cliff and carted away.

Loss was not limited to theft or spite. Letters, reports and speeches protested the destruction by developers. He began to see that each disruption was a hole in the web of spiritual energy. The Dreamtime was an organic force that connected people and place. Wounding one spot spread illness and death into the world.

He found dozens of recent cases that were unsolved and hundreds that stretched back decades. Every state, island and coral atoll had been hit. Any number of men could have perpetuated the crimes. Gabe was only interested in one.

He logged off and gathered the papers together. He understood the enormity of the loss now. But his awareness came from the logical sympathy of an outsider. The devastation was nothing compared to the theft of a family.

He watched Rob for a few minutes, calculating the odds that they would both come through this unscathed. He didn't like the tally.

Rachel rose up and up, feeling for Selena in the ether. She cast her own light into the world, the songs rang true in her heart. Yet she felt nothing from the girl, nothing but the draft of magic around every vibration that might belong to her.

The songwoman dove into the earth where the dead went to rest.

Rob's hours of phone work had tracked down the keepers of looted sites in the north. A woman responsible for a conkleberry increase site had bitterly described a theft from four years ago. A man had wept at the destruction of an initiation cave, and a teenager had sworn that his grandfather had died because the energy had been drained from a Kimberly area site six months before.

His scattered notes told the stories: *Blood sacrifice. Lizard Dreaming. Bushberry Woman.* Every one was a scrap of heritage scavenged by dogs. Rob shook his head. "I haven't made much effort to attend ceremonies in the past few years," he said. "Suddenly my absence seems selfish."

"The world's changed, Rob," Gabe said. "You can't expect to work in Tennant Creek and run home for every event."

"I remember the year after Mike died. Angus took me up to Anzac Hill, an overlook point, nearly every week. He'd have me name the Dreaming sites visible from the hill. *'Anthwerrke,'* I'd say, our word for Emily Gap. Angus would tell how the Caterpillars spread out across the flats from there. *Ntaripe,* Heavitree Gap, was where the wild dogs fought." He searched Ramie's wall until he found Mike's picture.

"I remember all those stories. I can hear Angus' voice right now. When we had named the whole region, we walked back home. Those days, Matty watched for me whenever I left the house. It was years before I realized how scared she must have been. If Mike could be snatched away, she probably thought the whole world might shatter. She never stopped me from going out but she was always at the window, counting my steps to the door."

Gabe knew what it was like to lose a friend, someone close enough to have been a brother. But he had no words to soothe his own loss, let alone that of another. He fixed fresh ice packs and handed one to Rob.

"Some bloke's been busy," the young man said as he sifted through the printouts.

"More than one, no doubt. I found so much material I'm not sure where to begin."

"I do. I've got a name." Rob plucked a piece of paper from the desk.

"Dana Pukatja. You think that's the Aborigine? The shaman?"

"No. Well, yes and no. It's the name he uses but it's not a skin name." He caught Gabe's questioning look. "Each tribe has a kinship system, ways to tell who's related and how they should treat each other."

"They aren't necessarily blood ties, right?"

"Right. People are divided into groups, and only certain groups can marry people from other groups. Otherwise you might marry your sister."

"Like incest but not biological?"

"Spot on, matie. Each group gets a skin name. If you know someone's skin name, you know how you're related to that person. If you're not part of that system, you can at least tell what tribe they're from." He pulled a map from the drawer. "See, Pukatja is a settlement near Uluru. Maybe the shaman was born there. But it's not a skin name, so we can't tell what clan he's from. And that makes him harder to find."

"Tuffs said he was Pitjantjatjara. How would anyone know?"

"Look at his age. When you've been around that long, *somebody* knows you."

Gabe considered the scrap of paper. Until now, the elder had seemed a dream created by heat and exhaustion. Putting a name to the face gave him blood and breath and bone. "Have you called Angus yet?" he asked.

"I saved that call for last. I thought you'd want to talk with him yourself."

27 Possum Dreaming

The wind imported the red talc called bull dust into the suburbs of Alice Springs. The soft ash sifted onto lawns and gardens filled with kangaroo-paw flowers. Once inside, it drifted in the currents of fans and air-conditioning, restless even in the shadows.

Angus could smell the dust. Each breath painted images in his mind, memories from his sighted life and the more vivid ones he imagined after darkness had come. Always the dust brought him these visions, and always he closed his eyes to see them more clearly.

He had not touched his ochres all day. Nor had he moved from the back porch where the sweet tang of the bottlebrush was heavy enough to veil his skin. Tiny stingless bees explored his ears, and twice crested pigeons soothed him with their wavering calls. Angus would rouse himself when the thought or vision he awaited finally conjured. Until then he might sit for days, rising only to return to his bed at night.

Today Angus thought about Rob. He remembered the frightening, exciting time when his nephew had become a man. The boy had been swept away from his mother, smothered under blankets, cradled by his uncles, cut and cared for then taught the songs of men. He had returned not as a mature version of the boy who'd left but as a man who'd risen from the death of the child.

Selena had undergone her own ceremony, of course, run by women at the onset of her menses. Angus had felt as proud as Matty but those events were outside the realm of men. Rob's initiation had been the last ceremony Angus had attended with his brother before the mine blew out his life.

The phone rang and soon Matty brought the receiver outside. Rob's voice was starched with fatigue. In the darkness, Angus saw the trail of thefts described by his nephew. The bees began to swarm.

"So what do ya think, Uncle? Does this Dana Pukatja sound familiar?"

"Too much so. He's older than me, older maybe than anyone understands. I ran into him once along the Plenty Highway."

"Was he a crook back then?"

"There was talk of looting but it was just talk. He dropped out of sight for about ten years. When he returned, it was only to move in white society. We hardly knew he was around unless someone spotted him on the street. He never stayed in one place for long but no one who met him ever forgot his face."

"So he's not everyone's favorite mate."

"Depends. Some are attracted to his power. He fools many people and not just the whites." Bees weighted his lips as he spoke. "Possum. This shaman is like a shattered mirror. He can reflect many things but you won't know which is true."

"I'll be careful, Uncle. Hang on, Gabe wants to talk with ya." There was rustling as the phone switched hands.

"Do you still have the dingo tooth?" Angus asked.

"Yes. It's in a pouch with a stone Rachel gave me. That's sort of what I wanted to ask you." He hesitated. "The cursing...the bone pointing...what does it mean? Rob told me what it *means* but what do you think of those things?"

"What do you think of it?"

"Not much, I suppose. You have to believe in those things for them to work, right? I'll only get sick if I think I will. Right?"

"You won't get sick, Gabe."

"Will he kill me?"

The pigeons arrived for a final visit. The smell of grapes drifted from the kitchen where a concerned neighbor was fixing them lunch. "We all die," he said. "It's only important how we live."

"Right. Any idea where I can find this Dana?"

"Go where there's power. The things he steals are material forms of *djang.* He takes the energy and sells the remains. His need for power is his weakness."

"All right. Thanks, Angus. For everything."

The elder broke the connection then went inside. Matty picked up her sandwich and put it down a dozen times. Each time Angus heard the plate shift, and each time he knew she had not taken a bite.

"Well?" she finally asked. "When is he coming home?"

"They know who they're looking for now. They'll be done soon."

"My daughter is missing because of this foolishness. Why can't Gabe do this alone?"

"Rob is a man."

"Man enough to deal with the likes of a murderer? What if something happens to my children?" Her voice broke. "Why does it have to be them?"

Angus found her arm. Her muscles were rigid and her heart boiled. She hugged him, her husband's brother, her children's uncle. They rocked together as bees flew into the window.

Today, Angus knew, he would begin a new bark painting. Red would stand for blood and the ghosts would be white. He would paint a possum in its nest with the ancestors gathered near. It would be his Dreaming to bring Rob home again.

Selena would be taken care of by the prayers of women.

Gabe dug through his waist pack. Since the previous night on the escarpment, he had worn the pack and Della's medicine bag continuously. Before he had treated only his wallet with such care. But money, the license that proved his identity, and the credit cards that proclaimed his merit could all be replaced.

He unwrapped the message stick. The artifact was less of an enigma now. He knew its origin and its function, and he could guess at the events that had brought it into his possession. Its iron core held something more, though, something Ian hadn't meant.

He fixed his gaze on the splintered end. The stick felt warmer there, as if an aura leaked from the crack. The gap grew and he looked deeper. The flakes of ochre were the scales of a snake, the bark peeled from a tree. He saw red and yellow, earth and sun, ochre and charcoal. The misty forms of spirits flitted at the edge of his sight.

Then Gabe looked around. The world was suddenly in focus, as if a camera crew had flooded the area with light. His veins flushed cool and the ache in his heart fizzled. He stood abruptly.

"Rob, you and Ramie should take this information to the police," he said. "I've had enough run-ins with them that they won't believe me. Ramie lives here year-round. If he vouches for you they'll be more open to what you say."

"Do you really think showing them these printout will make a difference?" Rob asked. "Not many blokes understand this stuff."

"It's a long shot but we've got to take it. Otherwise we're on our own again. And with Selena missing, I'd rather have them for us than against us."

Rob nodded and shuffled the papers into a stack. Ramie had switched the pumps to automatic earlier that day so they set off immediately, walking arm in arm down the street. When they turned the corner, Gabe grabbed a copy of the printouts from behind the computer.

He had a good thirty minutes to clear some distance between himself and Tennant Creek. If his hunch panned out, he didn't want Rob within a hundred clicks. He couldn't bear to see the young man hurt. And neither could Matty.

Ramie had done a fine job with the Land Rover. The SUV had been patched up, pounded out, and tuned to symphonic pitch. New tires were on the front and the spare parts had been restocked. Gabe pushed the truck past its top speed. The vehicle shook from the wheels to the roof but he slowed little as he turned onto a gravel track.

His effort was for the living and the dead cried in his head.

⌇⌇⌇

Gabe kept an eye on the time. Nearly an hour had gone by since he'd sent Rob on that little diversion. Although he would have made better time taking the highway to McLaren Creek before turning off into the bush, that path made it easier for Rob to catch up with him. Instead, he drove twenty clicks south then took a spur that hooked up with a track through the Murchison Ranges.

The track followed the footprint of the mountains, and corkscrewed around boulders and stones. More and more often as he drove, Gabe cut corners. Half of him felt the shaman's presence like the slippery ocean on his back. The other half of him wondered if this was all a waste of time. A covey of spinifex pigeons burst from the grass and skimmed past the windshield. A single feather, chestnut with a black bar near the tip, caught in the wiper blade.

Gabe jammed on the brakes. The feather winked in the breeze and the downy puff at its base moved like the ripples in a billabong. He tied it in the fringe of Della's bag. He might find Ian on this trip, and his stomach dreaded what the corpse might prove. But he had to find Selena before she also stepped into the spirit world.

A buzz echoed off the ranges. Gabe peered down the track and saw a dust cloud rise from a tiny figure. A man on a motorbike wove along the track, turning the curves faster than the SUV could clatter overland. Gabe swore and gunned the motor anyway.

Within minutes Rob pulled alongside. Gabe continued driving, never taking his eyes from the road. Rob flipped open his visor and yelled something; Gabe rolled up his window and bounced into the bush. The bike pulled in front, curving and dipping no matter where the truck turned, and gradually they both stopped. Gabe locked the doors.

"Go home!" he yelled through the glass.

"Let me in!"

"Go home! It's too dangerous out here."

"Aw, come on, mate. I helped you all this time and now I can't go to the party? Let me in!"

Gabe cracked the window. "Matty needs you," he said. *"Angus* needs you. Go home!"

Rob looked at him for a long time. The weak smile he had offered disappeared and his eyes moved into some deep part of his mind. Gabe felt the shift as cleanly as heat radiating from a campfire.

"Selena needs me," Rob said. "She's my *sister."*

They stared at each other through the slim opening. Gabe knew he could back away right now and Rob would not follow; the slope of the young man's shoulders showed him that. He would watch the truck disappear, as helpless as the boy had been when the bus hauled Gabe away from the Darwin orphanage. He could guarantee the young man's safety by leaving him here. But at what price to Rob?

"Fuck," he said, and unlocked the passenger's door.

<hr>

"Cunt. Fucking cunt!"

Kevin had found the weak spot. Bev was the one person who tied all the links together. She located the sites through her job, picked up the artifacts, passed them through Port Darwin, and laundered everyone's cut through Dana's accounts. She could drain his money with a simple transfer.

Even though she was a boozy hag with more miles than an outback taxi, Kevin had planned to woo her until she cashed out. But she was soppy for the old Abo. A quickie wasn't enough to turn her against him, so Kevin let his fists do the talking. He backhanded her and the end table splintered under her weight.

"You bastard!" she screamed. "When I tell Dana about this, he'll kill you!"

A single step closed the distance. Her neck was so small he had to stretch her head back to fit both hands around her throat. He squeezed and squeezed, lifted her up, shook her now and again. The scab on his stump burst and blood trickled down her spine. She clawed and kicked, growing weaker. Then there was nothing and the purple swell of her tongue was the only sign that she once had lived.

He threw the body against the wall and scoured the apartment for cash. Her purse had twenty dollars and her jewelry was shit. He found a bankbook with the PIN written on the back. The money, some eight hundred and change, would keep the young boong hidden until Dana coughed up more cash.

By then Rowdy was sure to turn up. When the old man dropped the ransom, Kevin would play a game of his own, one he called Kill the Boong. If the old bastard refused to pay, Kevin would turn him in for kidnapping. And rape. And murder.

He tugged at his shorts as he considered all the pleasurable things he had yet to do. He might not end up with any cash but without Bev to pass along information, neither would Dana. No matter what happened, the old fuck was fucked.

He locked the door behind him and trotted down the stairs. His thirst was powerful but today he felt in control. He could wait a little while, make small withdrawals from multiple ATMs then celebrate at a pub across town. No need to hurry.

He remembered how the girl looked tied up on the bed and the round firmness of her breasts. Since he had given up a finger, she could pay him back with her own flesh. He turned the radio on full volume and belted the lyrics to whatever rock song came on next.

28 Little White Boy

"So, what made you run off like a robber's dog?" Rob asked. "Do you have a destination in mind or do you just not care for me company?"

Gabe pointed to the printouts on the floor. "Angus said to go where the power is. Some of these sites have more power than others. One looting looks like any other until you divide the sites *by djang.*"

"Now you sound like Selena." His smile never made it to his lips.

"There's a pattern." Gabe handed him stacks of articles bound by rubber bands. "These sites aren't used because things have been built on or around them. Their energy is depleted. Then come sites that still hold *djang* but not that much." He touched the third pile.

"These are the heavy hitters. Graveyards, the Tree of Life, the Dreaming tracks of major creators."

"One man isn't responsible for all those thefts."

"Right. Remove the ones where only obvious artifacts were taken, the work of someone who didn't know junk from *djang.* Reject sites missing only things that were easy to steal." He winnowed a small collection from the pile. "These are left."

Rob scanned the articles. The only sound was the grumble of the motor.

"Crikey, I think you've got it. Where do we go now?" He shook his head as Gabe tapped the first two articles. "You sure about this?"

Gabe nodded. His jaw was tight and the smile was forged across his face. He had never been more sure about anything.

* * *

"Pull over," Gabe said. "Let's take a break."

"Don't really need one, do ya?" Rob's eyes remained fixed on the road.

The track had deteriorated badly in the past hour. Gabe knew they were unlikely to reach their destination before dark even without extra stops. But neither man had slept in nearly forty-eight hours and their last meal had been a scanty breakfast with a side of fear.

"We won't find anything in the dark," Gabe said. "Even if we did, trying to backtrack at night so we can notify the police might leave us stranded."

"I have to think of Selena." His face froze at her name but he continued driving.

"I'm worried about Selena, too. But you're not thinking straight. We can help her best by taking a break. *Now.*"

Rob let off the gas and stopped in the middle of the track. He blinked once then again, and faced the older man.

"They didn't believe me." His voice was nearly a sob. "The police took the printouts but they didn't think it could help. I could see it in their eyes. They thought I was some hysterical relative drawing puzzles in the sand. They...they *pitied* me!"

Gabe hesitated for only a moment. He put his hand on the young man's shoulder as he collapsed. As he held Rob tight, he remembered how strong Andy's arms had felt in those long-ago years.

***

Rachel finally found Selena moving toward the light. The girl stopped. They hovered together, linked by song.

***

The sun squandered its last moments in colors as bright as clown fish. The trees, staghorn coral grown large, glowed with ghostly phosphorescence. Galahs flooded the sky just as they had at Halfway Downs. But none of them touched down and the birds stirred the watery air.

After eating, Rob had set off among the trees to find a cockatoo feather. When they found Selena, he'd said, she would know her brother had kept her safe by using the feather. Gabe had thought it best to stick together and escorted him into the woods.

As they walked back, a pair of honeyeaters parted the sky. The air tasted of leaf mold and talons, and the shrieks of the galahs sifted through the canopy. Gabe thought suddenly of Annie and Bret, of the life they had built despite isolation and drought. Clearly Bret had known something about the looting but Gabe didn't think he was a killer. Before starting this trip, Gabe might have sold artifacts himself if it meant supporting his family.

His own family. At his age, he didn't figure children would ever be in the picture. But he could still marry, he could still enjoy a second lifetime of beach weekends and evenings in. He thought about the final meal he had shared with Chance. After their picnic, they had gathered the cones of the she-oak like keepsakes of their day.

He would have to call her soon. That was it, he decided. He would call her from the next roadhouse. Just to say hello, to see how she was doing. For a moment, he thought everything would turn out right.

Gabe. The voice was in his ear. He whipped around to see the trunks rising like headstones.

"Mosquitoes are bad, hey?" Rob waved a cloud from his face.

"Did you hear that? Someone called my name."

The voice called again.

"There! Just now!"

"I heard...something." Rob peered around.

"Someone's here. I heard him as clearly as if he were standing next to me."

Rob's eyes widened. Watching the canopy, he dragged Gabe through the woods. "Stay away from the trunks. And watch your feet. A pile of leaves, a mound of dirt, anything that could cover a snare."

Gabriel!

"Jesus! Don't you hear that?"

"I do now. He's throwing his voice. He could be anywhere. Just get the hell out of these trees!"

As they trotted through the gloom, branches groaned to their right. Was there wind in the canopy or had the shaman moved along the branch? Deadwood cracked under Gabe's feet and he trembled to know he was breaking the forest's bones.

"Look up! Look around!" Rob hissed. "It's you he's after!"

Look up, look out, watch the ground...it was all too much. He stumbled and Rob was gone. Some instinct made him squat and he heard...nothing. Not the *pock-pock-pock* of Rob's sneakers nor the evening call of the butcherbird.

Boy!

The voice was the crack of bamboo. Gabe lunged through the trees. Hopping over a log, he cursed; he might have tripped a snare hidden on the other side. He slipped off a rock and cursed again. The branches to his left shook wildly. He veered right and saw filament a second before it dug under his jaw. When he landed, a rock wedged between his ribs and bound him with pain.

Little white boy, the voice called, intimate and ghostly. *Why play games you don't understand? Go home to your mama, white boy.*

His breath was gone. Claws scraped bark and the vapor of crushed leaves drifted past. He had to make a break for the truck but which way? Light lingered in the canopy but he saw no silhouette, no movement or glint of metal to reveal his stalker.

Then he saw the faintest red arc in the sky. It was the dust rising from the Dreamtime woman's bath, the last of sunset's show. He would run toward her, toward the truck that lay southwest of the trees.

He rolled to his knees. Footsteps circled on the left and scratching came from the right. Could a shaman move so quickly? Or was it the burly white man whose sneer had taunted him during the wreck? The steps resolved into the *plock-plock* of sneakers.

"He'll find you!" Rob's voice was muffled and odd. Gabe had a vision of him snared by branches, his mouth filled with shadows.

"Follow me!" Gabe hoped he could see. But he hoped more to draw the danger away from the young man.

"He'll find you!" Rob's voice was loud enough for Gabe to have been face to face, yet he still couldn't see anything. The *plock-plock, plock-plock* continued without drawing closer.

Look up, look down. Night had crushed the thin red band. He had to find Rob and risk loosing the escape route. Or was this another trick? The air held the sedentary scent of bark and a chill wriggled between the hairs on his arms. The smell was wrong, he knew. Alarms shrieked in his mind and he didn't know why, he didn't know where to run or if the voice was really that of his friend....

His breath blew out in a mighty push as Rob's words became clear. *He's behind you!* Gabe whirled to see the sorcerer with those luminous eyes swarming down a trunk with his nails going *scritch-scratch-scritch* and his mouth a translucent grin.

Materializing from the dark, Rob charged straight at the shaman. Gabe cut off the young man and hauled him toward the truck, in the direction he hoped led to the truck. They ran without thought of traps or snares, ducking parasols of leaves and leaping wide logs. Gabe had trained for this all those years in high school and pulled ahead as they reached the road. He slammed into the hood and rolled over to the driver's side.

Blood was everywhere. Blood was cool on the vinyl and sprayed in long streamers across the windshield. A lump of fur sagged across the passenger's seat.

"Christ!" Rob flung it away and swore again as he sat in the blood.

Gabe fired the engine and gunned down the track. When he wiped at the glass, the blood smeared in lurid waves. "What was that, anyway?" he asked.

"Possum." He held up his missing cap, sodden with the creature's life. He folded the hat as if to put it away then threw it out the window.

"What does it mean? Why would he steal something of yours then give it back?"

"It means," Rob said roughly, "he plans to kill me, too."

Dana cursed as the taillights faded. He cursed the mongrel's luck at running toward the road instead of deeper into the bush and he cursed the single misstep that had cost him his prey. He'd hoped to draw blood tonight, one of many wounds to come.

With his back against a tree, the shaman crouched alone in the dark. A series of ropes and lassoes had carried him through the canopy until one snared his hand. The bones at his wrist were broken and the last two fingers had nearly been pulled off. After using a clump of fur from his dilly bag to close the wound, he leaned back to look at the sky.

In the countless years the world had already spent, his people had named every star. The Pitjantjatjara understood the intricate pattern of this and that, they knew that one was affected by the other as surely as breath affected the body. No tree stood that did not feel the rain, no rock tumbled that did not know its own weight. The work Dana had begun could not be left undone.

He stared into the void between the stars. As his eyes adjusted, faint stars came into focus. He eased his line of sight away from their brilliance, up into the dark and deep into himself. He felt the sturdy strut of each bone, the gelatinous cushions that floated within the joints. When he could trace the path of blood through his veins, he probed for the outermost reach of the pain.

The nerves in his arm fired all the way up to his neck before the sensation turned icy. He pushed the frost across the shoulder and past the elbow. Eventually it compressed into a white-hot pinhead that he lifted outside his body.

Still deep in the void of his own body, Dana snapped the wrist back into place. His eyes guided his feet through the woods but his mind remained focused on the star that burned inches from his skin.

"What the hell just happened?" Gabe peered into the mirrors to see if they were being followed.

"That was a fine display of the *karadji's* power. It's like I told Collin. A little suggestion, a clever way of doing things and a lifetime of practice. Nice party trick, hey?"

"Except it was intended to be our wake."

"Not necessarily." Rob's voice grew steady, as if explaining the details could bring everything back into balance. "The *karadji* aren't policemen but they're not just executioners, either. They're worse."

"Death seems like the ultimate punishment to me. It's not like you'll have a repeat offender. Besides, he's the criminal."

"You have to look at this a different way. *Karadji* work with *djang,* so they have this...sanctity, a special energy around them. In a way you *are* a criminal, at least to him. He called you boy, right?"

"White boy. Little white boy, to be precise."

"Some people believe the Stolen Generation can never return to their country because they've lost too much. They missed all the ceremonies that make them adults and they're too old to learn it the proper way." He leaned back. "They believe it's a violation of law not to know your Dreaming."

"I had no choice!"

"Choice or circumstance has nothing to do with it, mate. Law is all that matters."

"Is that what you believe?"

"No. And if you're going to be angry, would you mind hitting someone else?" Rob gave him a tired smile.

Gabe wasn't in a joking mood. Instead his guts hardened into a block of compressed lightning. With that mass anchoring his spine, nothing could bowl him over.

They crawled down the track until the moon went back to bed. Gabe was so exhausted he had visions of the shaman clinging to the roof. Twice shadows falling on the hood turned into the sorcerer, and the ghost was a spiky man-beast with pointed teeth. Rob was probably worse off, having eaten little at dinner. He appeared to be in a trance and stared out the side window as if the darkness were a billabong into which his mind might dive.

Gabe touched his arm. "Can you drive? I want to pull off the track but it's too dark to pick a path safely. I'll walk ahead with a flashlight. All you have to do is follow me."

Rob moved over as Gabe circled the SUV. Satisfied that no demons or shamans clung to the sides, he struck off into the bush.

Walking at the outer reach of the headlights, he picked their way past fire-hardened acacia stumps that could puncture the tires and pits of soft bull dust that would bog the vehicle. From the ground stared the eyes of foxes and rats, and once he heard the rough hiss of an owl. So long as it wasn't the cannibal woman or the shaman, those kinds of night frights were just fine.

Angus had told him a similar story. That had been only a week ago but Gabe struggled to recall the details as if a decade had passed. There used to be a cannibal, an old woman who traveled with two dogs for companions. She snatched people of all ages, children and teens and seniors like herself. Her appetite was so voracious and her dogs such fierce protectors all the clans trembled to know she was near.

Then two brothers, heroes with a litany of exploits to their credit, heard about the woman. The brothers killed the dingoes with boomerangs and chased the woman from the country. When the red dog bled out its life, a vein of red ochre ran into the ground and where the yellow dog died, yellow ochre formed.

Gabe wondered if Angus knew any stories about how to defeat a shaman. Somehow he didn't think he'd have the opportunity to ask.

When he judged they were about a quarter mile off the track, Gabe waved for Rob to shut down the engine. They rolled out the swags in the rear and took turns sleeping. Rob didn't argue when Gabe took first watch but neither did he fall asleep right away. The whites of his eyes floated like pale coins on the depths of his face.

Although Gabe could see nearly a hundred meters in every direction, some stray worry jingled at the back of his mind. He was missing something important, something that might compromise their safety. Suddenly he grabbed the flashlight off the seat.

"Rob, I'm going to lock you in. I'll be back in half an hour."

"Where the hell do you think you're going?"

"Back to the road. I've got to erase the tire tracks where we turned off."

Rob cursed then apologized. Angus, he claimed, would have said something right off. "With all the time he's spent teaching me, I haven't learned much if I missed something that basic."

The young man looked utterly miserable. "At least let me drive you halfway," he said.

"Too risky. If the shaman's near, he'll hear the motor. Besides, if he gets one of us, the other can keep going."

Gabe waited for him to lock the doors then followed their trail back to the road. He cut branches from a shrub and swept the tracks from around the road, just as Rob said the shaman had done at the sites he'd looted. As he hiked back, Gabe kept the image of the Dreamtime brothers in his head.

Come *karadji* or cannibals, he was ready to fight.

29 Karadji

The shaman hadn't bothered to follow the men. He knew the precise locations of every site he'd raided within a hundred kilometers. The pair wouldn't get far tonight and it wasn't difficult to guess where they'd appear next. The closest sites were a Cockatiel Dreaming place to the west, a truffle increase site to the south, and a burial ground to the east.

Dana would wait for them at the graveyard. Even though the cockatiel area was closer, its Dreaming was less important. Besides, the burial ground now held a modern corpse, that of the roo shooter. Gabe couldn't possibly have figured that out by any clues but he might have had help. Magical help.

Dana smirked. He'd like to see the songman or songwoman who tried to stand against him. An owl whispered in the night. The flight was so soft, Dana heard only the squeal of a mouse as its back was broken. The bird watched the sorcerer, its claws deep in flesh, as the prey spasmed. With a snap of wings, it disappeared.

Dana nodded. Dawn was near and the time for hunting almost over. He'd been so close. But the young blood's love for the half-breed had been stronger than Dana anticipated. Possum would have to be eliminated first. Then the shaman could take his time with Gabriel.

He had learned this lesson before. He had been younger, so much younger, cruising the lonely west coast. In Monkey Mia, an enterprising young man willing to trade on the color of his skin found that business was brisk. Fathers and daughters, newlyweds and retirees exchanged dollars for charm sticks that were hardly more than twigs tied with string.

One year a customer confronted him. He was a hulking fellow, probably a former athlete, with muscle gone to fat. The onlookers, once so ready to lap at Dana's ankles for a sweet crumb of *djang,* went on guard. To have the crowd turn against him...*him!* A shaman with access to universal energies!...was too much. Sneers were pitched like horseshoes across their chins. *I wasn't falling for it,* their feet said as left squared off with right. But they *had* fallen for it!

Dana smiled. It was his brightest, most obsequious smile and showed a kilometer of his gums. His eyebrows shot as high as Uluru and his eyes blazed. The man took the tiniest step back.

"Satisfaction is guaranteed," the sorcerer said. "Allow me to refund your money."

He peeled bills off a wad so thick he could barely hold it in one hand. As the man walked away, the shaman marked him with a single word.

Grieve.

The curse carried over the breeze and dropped through the crown of the man's head. He whirled around but Dana had already hiked past the pier into the red dunes.

At a colonial-era grave strung with barbed wire, the sorcerer called Kulpunya. He sat where he could watch the man's child, a delicate creature about six years old, as she harvested shells from a lonely stretch of tide line.

The sorcerer cleared a patch of sand to represent the beach. Below this he drew wavy lines for the ocean. A piece of driftwood became a doll and a twist of dried grass its hair. The toy kangaroo the girl had left at the picnic table was tied to its waist.

"Come to me," Dana sang. "I am calling you, come to me. Look up, here I am."

He turned the fetish toward the wavy lines. "Come to me," he sang. "I am calling you, come to me."

After some hesitation, the girl walked into the ocean. "I can't see you." Her voice carried across the water, across the red lines at his feet.

"Look up, here I am. Come to me."

The water deepened around the pier. She waded up to her knees then to her waist. Her bucket began to float. When the doll was half submerged in the sand, the girl cried out. In a flash Dana knew she'd stepped on a scorpion fish. The venom coursed up her leg, sending fire and a deadly promise to her heart.

"Mummy! Mummy!" she cried.

"Look up," Dana sang. "Here I am, come to me."

And the child limped forward even as poison burned through her bones. She was up to her neck then her chin, and her nose turned up for air. But she wouldn't swim, not so long as the doll plowed the dirt. The grass spread out across the sand and disappeared into the dune.

A park ranger hauling buckets of fish looked up as the girl's hair disappeared. The woman squinted, puzzling out what she had seen. Then she dropped the buckets and pounded down the pier. Despite Dana's pressure on the doll, the girl was pulled out and rushed to town for antivenin. The father stared at Dana, panic flooding his eyes, until the truck rounded the curve.

Anger blew around the shaman like dust. It wasn't enough that the girl had *almost* drown, that she would *almost* die. She had been, they would say, confused by the venom. She swam, they would say, in the wrong direction. The huckster black fella would be a joke, another complaint the *pi_ranpa* could lodge against a world that did not serve their greed.

If only he had waited until the parents were sleeping, he could have walked her all the way to the shipping channel. What a lovely mermaid she would have been, washed ashore with bloated cheeks and seaweed braided into her hair.

Dana had forgotten that lesson, and had paid a heavy price. He would not make the same mistake again. He would strike isolated prey whose only defense was flight. And Gabriel had no wings.

—⁓—⁓—⁓—

Tom frowned as he jiggled the lock. Their blood-soaked customer hadn't returned after leaving the night before. When Rita found blood smeared on the doorknob, she insisted they check his room. Zack hovered in the hall, silent and nearly invisible. When the lock remained frozen, Tom jimmied the latch with a screwdriver.

"Holy Christ," he said.

Zack glimpsed a body on the bed.

"Get your mother," Tom said. "And call the police. Go!"

—⁓—⁓—⁓—

Desperately hot. It wasn't even midmorning and already Gabe was mummified in the cling of his clothes. Sweat ran like fat beetles over his scalp and pattered onto his thighs. Soon his flesh would erode like the jagged hills, exposing tissue as pink as the rock.

The men had set off at first light. Gabe's sleep had been deep and dreamless, more like a death dive into an ocean trench than repose. He assumed Rob had experienced the same because both men sat as if entranced by the landscape. Gabe scanned the area constantly but the flick of his eyes across the mirrors and out the windows barely registered in his brain.

After a while, he wondered if they had driven anywhere at all. Everything looked the same, everything smelled the same. The hills might as well have been the center of a carousel the men rode round and round. He shook his head. He had to stay alert.

They arrived in the general area of the first site and spent a half hour identifying the actual spot. A lizard ancestor had eaten desert truffles on the other side of the ranges then vomited them on this side. The apricot-sized pitted stones that were said to be the fossilized truffles had been carted away.

Gabe had selected the site for its high level of *djang*. The desert truffle had been an important food source, and the youngest offered a surprising amount of fresh water. The rocks would have been unremarkable to the casual traveler and would only appeal to a collector with a taste for the unique. The kind of collector to whom Dana catered.

The work had been tedious rather than heavy, and it must have taken hours to gather the hundreds of stones. Although the looting had been recent, few clues remained. Rob dug up a mound of beer tabs from a small area that could have been where they'd parked.

"It's not the best clue in the world," Gabe said as they got back into the truck, "but we'll tell the police anyway. If they can link one of these sites to an intercepted shipment or a specific buyer, maybe it'll help track down the shaman."

Rob nodded. Both men knew they were grasping at ghosts. Their efforts felt like self-imposed busywork and the weight of their helplessness showed on the young man's face. If Gabe hadn't formulated a plan, he might be as frail as Rob.

But he was already seeing results. The shaman had been on his trail since the beginning, of that he was convinced. Dana had kept the upper hand by using the *karadji's* tricks, stalking unseen behind his victim and moving in when least expected. His tactics were meant to cause panic and confusion, and until now had worked.

When he had ditched Rob, Gabe had wanted it to appear that he was still searching for clues. His real purpose, though, was to draw the shaman into the open. The ambush in the trees had been exactly the kind of thing he craved.

Now they would travel back over the Stuart Highway and past McLaren Creek. If Dana didn't appear there, Gabe would visit other sites until he showed. Until then, he had to stay ready. He thought of the rifle Dob had packed. For the first time, he missed its comfort.

"Rain's coming." Rob pushed his hand out the window.

Gabe turned his face to the wind. There was a tinge of something cool under the breeze. With luck the shower would be just enough to cool things down without turning the track into a pasty muck. To their right a thicket of grevillea shrubs blazed with golden flowers. Rob stared.

"That's Selena's totem," he said. "It's called *irrwerlenge.*"

"Irrwerlenge," Gabe repeated. "Would it be all right to pick some? I mean, as a way to focus our thoughts on her?"

"Yeah. That's exactly the kind of thing she'd want us to do."

They pulled over and walked into the thicket. The flower tops grew around their heads and the air was giddy with pollen. As they broke the stems free, nectar showered their faces and hands. They licked it from their fingers, tasting honey and sweat in the same instant.

Gabe whirled at the sound of feet but it was the rain, as sudden as swallows at dusk. The chill made them gasp and Gabe drank the sweet, sweet drops from his lips. He helped Rob gather flowers, piling the blossoms in the front of his shirt. When water ran under his waistband, his testicles contracted and his body hair reared in delight.

Rob found a rock with a wide depression at its center. After he cleared the red water from the bowl, they stacked the flowers in the basin. As rain filled the bowl, they sucked the dripping blossoms. Honey ran down their chins and pollen clumped on their gums. The rain continued, diluting the nectar, but they drank until the taste was only that of water and stone.

Gabe wasn't sure but as Rob wiped his face, he saw a few tears. Even though he was thirsty soon after, he hesitated to drink from the canteen. The nectar was still on his tongue and nothing would taste the same.

———

A small fire, just enough to burn herbs, blazed beside a kangaroo hide. Dana spread out the tools of his magic, and beside those, tools for killing. First was the flint knife he had shaped as Tjamu had taught him so long ago. Then he set out the rifle, the same .22 that had brought the roo shooter to his knees. Finally came the *wirrie.*

The sticks had soaked in the roo shooter's corpse, gathering toxins as the body rotted. They were dry now but Gabriel's blood would wash out some of the bacteria. His final hours would be excruciating as his own blood putrefied in his veins.

Dana would be there for every moment. He would stand over the mutt and drag him into the sun. His skin would crack and peel back like ragged cloth, his eyes would shrink in their sockets. And just before septicemia blanked out the half-caste's mind, Dana would punch him in the stomach. When he gasped, Dana would throw the hairs of *iltilpa,* the itchy grub, into his mouth. He would choke to death, yet the swelling would disappear before any coroner could determine the true cause of death.

"Let breath leave your body," he sang. "Your day has already disappeared in the Western sky."

30 Cannibal Song

The men hiked along a dry riverbed where red gums slicked the banks with shade. When they found a pile of driftwood, Gabe started a fire. The canned meat was precooked but they both needed a hot meal and strong tea.

"We'll hear any vehicle long before it arrives," he said. "I doubt even a clever man can make a motor run quiet."

He leaned into the smoke. It smelled of mint and camphor, and when it touched his flesh, he relaxed. "Better eat up. We don't know what we'll find at this burial ground."

"Burial grounds are scary places," Rob said.

"So you do believe in *djang.*"

"I know there's something out there. I never really thought it was something you could call on, like Selena claims. Maybe I'm not as sensitive as others. But Angus always said a bloke shouldn't go walking in a place like that alone."

"I promised Matty I'd see you home safe. I'll get you out of there if I have to fight those spirit warriors myself."

<hr>

By the time Kevin returned to Marbella, his cock fought his zipper like a Tasmanian devil caught in a bag. He pictured the girl naked and bound, her cries muffled behind a gag, her breasts flopping free. He would fuck her tits, finger her cunt and tear her ass.

She would pay for his blood, for the money Bev refused him, for his humiliation when the faggot bartender offered to suck him off. He would keep her for days like that, giving her cum to drink and feeding her his backhand. Eventually, Kevin would fuck her to death.

The thought nearly made him blow in his shorts. He turned the corner gingerly and raised his hips off the seat to reduce the friction in his pants. The street was lit up like Christmas, strung with red and blue strobes from at least three patrol cars. The devil retreated to its burrow as Kevin cruised past the hotel. Fuck! They'd found her. They'd fucking found her!

He pulled behind a pump at the petrol station. Any minute he expected a cop to shove a gun in his face. The boong probably wasn't even in there now.

He hadn't left anything more than some clothes behind, so at least they couldn't tag him with his own license. But without the girl, Dana couldn't be lured into the trap.

He pumped gas as he considered his options. He might blackmail the old man by threatening to go to the police. He could say Dana cut off his finger as a threat to keep quiet, that he was only in it for the money, never for hurting someone. Still, losing the girl made everything a mess. The more Kevin considered his options, the deeper the devil sank into its tunnel.

It's all because of that fag, he thought. If the poofter and his fruity son hadn't minced around so much, the plan would have gone off easy. He wanted to charge into the pub and break that faggot's head wide open. Then he'd fuck his wife, without a gag so the cum-sucker could hear her scream as he died. And he'd use that queer-bait son of his like a punching bag until his pretty face wasn't pretty any more.

There were too many cops around. He'd have to wait for things to cool off a bit. Christ, how he hated to wait. He'd take that out of their hides, too.

Or, he thought as Zack crossed the parking lot, he could do something about it right now.

~~~~~

Thirty miles from Gabe and Rob's lunch site, the rain clouds stalled. The water funneled down the trunks of eucalypt trees and ants floated in pink slicks. Where runnels formed along the hills, creeks swelled in long-dry beds. Soon a river tumbled to life.

Far downstream the rain was over but the water was yet to come.

~~~~~

Zack flung himself onto the corner bench. He was angry and more than a little confused. He had told the police about finding the woman, the beautiful Aborigine suspended in twilight. He reported Kevin's behavior, his phone call, the way he had arrived without his usual companion. He described the rock carvings and the logs, ducking his head when Tom frowned because he had snooped through a guest's possessions.

Then Tom had squeezed his shoulder like he did when he complimented Zack for a job well done. The teen couldn't quite place his expression. But there was pride there, and the strength of two men sharing a burden, and Zack knew something had changed between them.

He hoped the woman woke up. He had tried to tell the police about the old Aborigine, the one who stole magic from the country. He was responsible for the woman's condition, Zack was sure of it. The officers asked if he knew what drug had been used but he shook his head. How could he tell men who relied on the hard fact of a bullet to enforce the law that the woman had been enchanted? Then they wouldn't believe anything he said.

He wished he'd known what to do for her. He had helped untangle her bonds, and had nearly thrown up when he realized Kevin's finger was tucked into the rope like scat left to mark a territory. As Rita had pressed cool towels against the woman's face, she had not moved or sighed or moaned. The body lived but the spirit was far away.

Would she be a point among the stars tonight, he wondered, or would she haunt the hotel if she returned to find her body missing? With such worries tumbling through his mind, Zack didn't see Kevin step from behind the post office.

———

A single bullet dropped Rob to his knees. The billy crashed into the fire and steam rolled up from the sand. Gabe dragged the young man, who groaned and stumbled weakly, across the riverbed. Too late he saw the flash of metal. He had run from an echo and was headed right toward the shaman.

Their combined weight pivoted on his weak knee. The tendons strained as he pushed, desperate to find cover, desperate to put himself between Rob and the shaman. He felt the next shot before he heard it, felt it slam into the young man's belly. Rob collapsed as Gabe floundered through the sand.

———

Among the broken cliffs of the Stokes Range, Reverend Joe Marchet was winding up his sermon on Lot's daughters when Della fainted. Tuffs cradled her head as people rushed to help.

"Leave her be," the reverend said. "This child has something to discuss with the angels."

———

Gabe heard a rumble and looked up, expecting to see the crimson truck plowing through the sand. Instead the ground was molten like the glow of a comet. He blinked and smelled ash and the pinprick of water. He blinked again and the flow touched his feet.

He lunged for the bank as water dug the ground from under his heels. Hauling Rob by his belt, he grabbed at roots as the water surged past his knees. Then a rampart of sludge and foam ripped them from the edge of safety.

———

Dana threw the rifle into the water. He had no further need for it and he didn't want it turned against him. Neither shot on the young blood had been clean but the combination had knocked him out of the game.

He tucked one of the *wirrie* into the bandage around his wrist. The splint would be just strong enough to punch the stick into Gabe's flesh. He struck straight out into the bush. Kulpunya was with him and the dog's breath was hot in Dana's chest.

———

Zack felt a blow to his stomach, hard enough to knock every inch of wind from his lungs but oddly without pain. The stench of sweat and beer and blood, of yeast and semen and socks clogged his mouth as he struggled against pinscher hands and banded arms.

His foot connected with a shin; there was a curse like a cap gun in his ear and a blow to his chin. The world dimmed as he was dragged beyond the outskirts of Marbella, across the railroad tracks and into the bush.

His feet found the ground. He almost didn't recognize Kevin. His face was deadly pale and as waxy as if he were melting. But his eyes were that same glazed jelly, like gumdrops sliced open and stuffed in the sockets.

Zack struggled but the chest was a wall and the arms were pythons. He squeezed his ribs together and twisted around, nearly breaking free, and got a punch in the nose. Blood poured down his throat and the air turned saline.

The bands sprang open and he landed on the tracks. They had come to the curve where the rail line headed back toward Darwin. They weren't too far from town but no one was likely to hear if he yelled. He scrambled to his knees and a foot in the middle of his back shoved him down again.

A hand fumbled with the button on his pants. He grabbed his waistband as the jeans were tugged down then clawed at the arm choking off his breath. The gravel pinched his penis as Kevin's full weight crushed down. Fingers spread his buttocks wide, the rush of air felt so rude, and Zack's mind was a galloping horse with panic rimming its eyes.

Then Kevin was inside. Zack writhed like the calves his father had branded, he bawled like the young bulls when they were castrated, and his universe was swallowed by a burning pain.

———

Gabe hugged the young man as mud clogged his ears. When the current pushed him to the surface, he sucked in bubbling water and flipped over a submerged log. Then his feet touched bottom. His sneakers had come off somewhere in the torrent, and he pushed against the pebbled sand. Choking on silt and water, he touched the opposite bank as a second surge moved down the channel.

The water lifted them higher up the bank. Gabe hauled himself half out of the river but the current had Rob too tightly. He hung over the water, his shoulders aching as if his arms might be pulled from their sockets. Rob's body rippled with the torrent. He looked dead. With the last of his strength, Gabe dragged the young man from the water.

Blood welled from Rob's shoulder and side. His skin was so light he looked like another man and his hair lay in streamers over his face. Gabe turned his socks inside out and packed them into the wounds. Using his shirt and a gentle touch, he cleared the grit leaking from Rob's eyes and nose and mouth.

Not until he was done did he realize he was humming. He sang the cannibal song, softly, softly, just as Andy had sung for him. He stopped. No birds called and even the river seemed calm. The shaman was near.

━━━∼━∼━━━

Somewhere, dimly registered between the slits of Zack's eyes, was a light. The palms of his hands picked up a vibration in the rail. The train was coming and the tracks sang of its speed, of the stiletto way it sliced the kidneys from the desert. Zack knew that it would not stop, and he knew as Kevin pushed his head onto the rail that he meant to kill him, to come inside him and leave him broken for his parents to find.

As he struggled anew, unaware that his groans and cries mingled with Kevin's grunting and braying, he felt a warm trickle down his neck. Somehow the drool was more offensive, more dirty than the battering from behind. He pushed up with a mighty wail, hovering on all fours while Kevin punched and fucked.

The train roared, illuminating the pair with a halogen brighter than the sun, and their shadows danced a crazy twisting jig. There was another scream, another voice. The train itself shrieked and Zack's arms trembled near breaking. He bucked weakly, not enough he knew as his elbows collapsed and he ditched face-first into the rail. He heard the line singing, singing, and a rain had broken over them, had slicked the ties, and he smelled the gravel and the wet-iron flavor of dust and knew he was going to die.

Then there was no weight. Zack thought the train had struck him and he was already dead. He rolled down the incline as a scream ripped through the train's chant. He flinched at the grasp of hands but it was his mother, her eyes burning, and they held each other while the rain washed away blood and mud and cum. As the last car whipped by they saw Kevin kicking in the scrub, his

[193]

leg gone from slipping on the tracks, and Zack knew his mother had no remorse for pushing him to his death.

He covered himself from her eyes. He pulled up his pants and took her arm. Her murmurs and questions and gentle touches were different, would always be different. From then on Zack would support her and care for her and take away the burden of this terrible day.

As the rain became a gentle mist, they left Kevin to die in the desert alone.

31 Blood

Gabe's first thought was to move upstream and find a shallow place to cross to the Land Rover. When the shaman tried to stop him, they would fight until the end. Drawing Dana out was a small advantage, to be sure, but it was the only card Gabe had left.

He abandoned the plan almost as quickly as it formed. It would lead the sorcerer right to Rob. Dana had to be drawn away from this spot, and quickly. The wounds didn't appear to be bleeding anymore but Rob's breath was shallow and his skin a bruised gray. Gabe checked the belts strapped over each wound then crawled from the river.

He paused. The *mambo's* bag was warm to the touch, and the scent of mint strong in the air. Gabe dug the opal from the pouch and tucked the bag in Rob's hand. When he slipped the stone between his cheek and gum, mint oil coated his tongue.

Gabe slithered from the trees. The sorcerer had always been eight steps ahead. He'd known where they would go, whom they would meet, and what they would find. It pissed him off nearly as much as it scared him. Dana had stayed ahead because Gabe had been predictable. They had been perfect fools, manipulated by their—by *Gabe's*—need for truth.

He had one chance to fix it, or destroy everything.

Exhausted, Matty slumped on the couch and stared out the window. Somewhere beyond the suburbs lay the Mt. Gillen ranges, a ridge formed when the wild dog had defended the Arrernte territory from the Dreamtime intruder. She pulled her rosary from her pocket. She had circled the beads dozens of times already for her daughter. She began another round, this one for the man who held her children in his hands.

"Hail Mary," she prayed, and held Gabe's long face in her mind.

The plain heaved with heat. Corkwoods writhed from islands of spinifex and Flinders grass while figs fringed a nearby butte. The rise would give Gabe a better chance to spot the shaman. By crawling on his belly, he might make it out of the trees undetected. As he crawled, the flesh on his elbows split and his swollen knee found every rock. The bandages on his hands fell off, and his palms oozed blood and fluid. When he crossed a bull ant nest, the insects swarmed under his pant legs and up his arms. Their half-inch mandibles pierced his back and the tender skin of his armpits.

Each bite was a fierce as a staple gun. A dozen became a hundred, and still they swarmed. When they crawled into his hair, he rolled over and wriggled in the dust. Most of the tormentors were dislodged and soon the others fell away. Gabe noticed their absence as little as he'd noticed the pain.

Snaking from stump to bush, he paused behind an acacia tree. Then he heard a click like two stones or a hammer falling on an empty chamber. He ran, heedless of who might see, and dove into the wild figs. Under the heat was the peculiar chill that warned of another storm. He had to get Rob out of there before guns or currents killed them both.

The wind picked up as he worked his way up the slope. Only a few small boulders offered cover. The rocks looked as if they had deliberately assembled there, and Gabe pictured them rolling under cover of night across the lonesome bush. In his mouth, the opal was as slick as his thoughts.

The stones were watching, he knew that now. They studied him, Gabriel Branch, the boy who had breathed the ocean so deeply because the dust was no longer his to smell. They would know of his actions at this moment, of his life from this day forward or of his death under the desert sun.

He touched a boulder. It was surprisingly cool, like the thigh of a woman. Yet the energy that shot into his palm belonged to an ancient being, one so old that gender had ceased to be an issue. For a blazing moment he saw the Dreamtime hero crouched there. He smelled the smoke as the warrior straightened spears over the fire. The songs were thick and he understood every word.

Then Andy's voice, urgent and young, cried, *"Alaye!* Look out!" The shaman rose from the rocks like a pillar of fog. The landscape behind him flickered beneath his skin but the knife was undeniably real. Gabe shielded his neck as the blade moved in a wide arc.

The flint slashed his forearm as something hit his thigh. He stumbled backward up the hill. A thin stake had been driven almost entirely into his leg. The shaman took solid form as Gabe grasped the stick and pulled. Anger fractured his scream. He did not blink, the scream was his first attack, yet the shaman was gone.

Gabe whirled completely around holding the hot, hot stake as his weapon. There was only a flash of crystal shrapnel then nothing. The boulders hid no body. The hill betrayed no passage with broken stems or scattered seeds. There was only the wind and the ghosts whose whispers brushed the down on his ears.

※ ～～～～ ※

Dana lay in a shallow wash not twenty feet from Gabe. He was by no means hidden, at least not the way a white man might expect. The body paint broke up his outline so his exposed arm looked like a branch. The feathers and leaves in his headdress became a plant while his flesh merged with the earth. The mutt wouldn't see Dana unless he stepped on him.

He fitted the second *wirrie* into his splint. Like a death adder, Dana waited to strike.

※ ～～～～ ※

Gabe's arm bled steadily and he had only a strip from his pants to tie over the wound. He tore a second strip from the other leg and wrapped it around his right hand. When the shaman attacked again, Gabe would try to disarm him by grabbing the blade. The strip would protect his hand somewhat.

Although the hole in his leg welled only a bit, the muscles were oddly numb. The smell of putrid meat clung to the stick. He threw it away and immediately regretted his haste. If the shaman had soaked it in poison, his only chance would be for a lab to analyze the substance.

Behind him one rock struck another. There was nothing to see but a puff of dust. He was high enough to look into the grass on the plain, which left only a skinny mulga as a hiding place. The shaman would have to be a world-class ball player to throw a stone that far. It sure as hell hadn't leapfrogged over there by itself but deciphering the trick wouldn't get Gabe out of this jam.

Riding the cool breeze was the smell of smoke and death, of eucalypt and pus. Gabe started to turn when something smashed the back of his head. As he stumbled forward, the shaman lopped up the slope, club in hand. With his vision still blurry at the edges, Gabe sprinted after him.

Just as he was about to tackle the sorcerer, Dana flung himself under an overhang. Both men scrambled on all fours until the rock squeezed down. Dana flopped flat and rolled deeper into the crevice. Gabe's hand shot out and grabbed an arm.

The flesh was stiff and cold, and as Gabe scrambled backward, dragging his prize from the cave, his body told his brain something was wrong. When the blazing sun fell on him again, he saw that he held an old tree limb.

He crouched there, strangled by frustration and fear, until he heard a footstep. He threw out his arm to grab for the knife but he never really saw the

[197]

shaman. The wind left him as a second stick punched into his belly. He looked around but he was totally alone.

The second stake had pierced at an angle and lay embedded under the flesh of his abdomen. The entry hole was a puckered point with hardly any blood but Gabe could see and feel the ridge of wood riding his diaphragm.

He fell backward. Some deeper part of him floated free while the thin shell of his logic made his hands move. He had to pull the stick out before it punctured an organ. Even though the stake was buried in flesh, the stink nearly made him vomit.

With fingers made clumsy by tremors, he backed the stick through the wound.

———

Dana worked his way down the slope, never once taking his eyes off his prey. Then he stopped. A dingo had come and sat atop the ledge watching the battle. The dog was only a few meters from Gabriel and its fur flashed red in the sun.

Kulpunya had come to watch his triumph. The dog's eyes snapped and drool gathered on its lips.

Dana licked his own lips. Victory was his.

———

Gabe limped up the slope. No need to disguise his position; the shaman knew where he was, had always known. A rifle, he now understood, was far too impersonal to use against him. The sorcerer had eliminated Rob the way ranchers shot dingoes and roos. Ian had died the same way. Gabe could taste that certainty in the back of his throat, and he spat to keep the bitterness from tainting the opal.

The faintest sound like the rustle of boar hairs came to him. He turned to find the shaman nearly on top of him. Gabe knew to watch his other hand and ducked when the knife again sliced at his face. Caught off balance, he crabbed sideways along the crest.

Then the ground disappeared. For a moment he was suspended, as light as a bird on the wing. Then he landed and plowed headfirst through shale that slashed his legs and chest and lips. He dropped off a second cliff, thankful to be in the dust, and the iron-red dirt clogged his wounds.

He scrambled into a field of pituri. The wide, fleshy leaves closed over his body and trumpet-shaped flowers pattered his face as he wriggled deeper among the plants.

———

Dana paused at the second ledge. The mutt had disappeared into the scrub. No matter; the shaman would track his blood trail as easily as signs on a highway.

The pituri ruffled in the breeze. He spotted one place where the plants moved more than the others. The rain would come soon, falling on the field as if Dana had used the pituri for the rainmaking ceremony. Surely that was a good sign.

With the dingo not far behind, the shaman climbed off the ledge and picked up the trail.

Papery wildflowers grew between the plants and the air had the sweet bite of a weaver ant nest. The profusion of life was boggling. Was this another illusion? What if Gabe was actually lying in the open? Panic sliced his bladder. His throat convulsed, and the opal slipped down into his stomach.

His hand closed around a rock. Not six inches away stood a spinifex pigeon. *I can see your totem animal,* Selena's voice whispered. *It's a bird of some sort.* The pigeon cocked its head, and a second later Gabe heard footsteps.

They were soft, those steps, and the plants barely rustled as the shaman searched. Gabe eyed the bird. The creatures had an ugly habit of fleeing at the last possible moment, exploding underfoot with an awful whirring and clapping of wings. Gabe might hide there even if the shaman passed very near. Too near, though, and the bird would applaud his death.

He gripped the stone. As blood seeped through the cut on his arm Gabe saw the red tides in Townsville, the slick of coral spawn on the moonlit sea. He blinked and took a deep breath.

The air froze in his belly. He heard something. No, he realized. He heard *nothing,* the silence of ocean depths where life was crushed by expectation. The shaman was near. Gabe could feel the desert watching his approach.

The wind died. Gabe glimpsed movement and the plants behind him whispered. As he twisted to look over his shoulder, a twig snapped meters from his head. Footsteps ran past, as loud as sneakers on a sidewalk. The pituri didn't move. He heard a call, neither animal nor human, and the smell of burnt herbs floated among the flowers.

The shaman was nowhere and everywhere, as sly as a shark and twice as dangerous. *God damn it!* Gabe thought. *Damn these games, these fucking games!* He clenched the rock and nearly stood. To do what? To run? To try to capture someone who had tracked him across thousands of miles, through cities and jungle and bush land?

The sounds stopped. The pituri stirred faintly like the rise of hair on a dog's back. Gabe looked straight ahead, his eyes unfocused, and noticed that the pigeon was still with him.

Patience, he thought. Patience separates the hunter from the prey. Running would exhaust him and a foolhardy attack would get him killed. He pushed all thoughts of Rob and Selena and Matty from his mind. To defeat the shaman, he had to use the shaman's clever tricks.

He waited. And in the silence of each breath, he watched.

The bird froze then hunkered down. Its wings cracked the air as Gabe exploded from the earth.

The rock clipped the shaman under the jaw as a bright heat circled Gabe's torso. The knife was deep in his side and the shaman wrenched it toward his kidney. Gabe twisted into the knife, winding his whole body into a back swing. The rock smashed the sorcerer's temple.

***

Dana heard the dingo's howl, the triumph of a wild dog routing an intruder. The shaman had made a grave mistake. Kulpunya had not come. The dog had not been for him.

His heart sank even as his eyes rolled back in his head. He had been wrong about the *djang,* as ignorant as a novice with no songs in his heart. The spirit board, its feathers soaked in his blood, clattered to the ground. He heard another howl, one of shame and defeat, and knew his entire life had been nullified. He had failed the *Tjukurpa* law and there was not a moment left in which he could make amends.

***

The sorcerer crumpled and Gabe fell to his knees. Convulsions shook Dana as blood warmed Gabe's legs. He threw the knife into the bush but the shaman was already dead.

32 Brothers

The hospital in Tennant Creek was small but efficient. The staff flickered from room to room, phantoms in white against the white walls. Whenever one floated across the mural in the lobby, Gabe felt dizzy.

Or maybe he was groggy from blood loss. He had been stitched up in three places, pumped full of plasma, rigged to an IV for antibiotics, and handed painkillers the size of scones. Despite the doctors' insistence, Gabe refused all drugs except local anesthetics. The police interview had been too important to postpone. Besides, Matty would arrive any minute.

Gabe's attempt to ditch Rob had saved both the men's lives. After hearing about the articles, Commissioner Dawson had pulled some strings at the Aboriginal Heritage Registry. The keepers of dozens of looted sites had been asked to inspect their areas for additional activity. After Gabe had dragged Rob back to the Land Rover, he'd passed out. The keeper of the graveyard found the pair half-dead and encased in a sun-baked clay of blood and dirt.

Gabe had revived well enough to give the hospital Matty's number. He then proceeded to be a difficult patient, screaming like a galah when they tried to give him painkillers and pestering the staff for Rob's status. He was dizzy and his head wobbled like one of Rachel's whirligigs but he wouldn't rest until he had talked to Matty.

Rob was wheeled out of surgery. Other than some loss of movement in his shoulder, he was expected to be fine. As the young man's heart sang the hour along, no thoughts rambled through Gabe's mind. There was only the weight of Selena's absence, of Rob's coming pain. Somehow, he knew, he would have to explain.

***

Time passed as it does for the ill, the defeated and the triumphant, in a gilded world. The heart monitor beeped a hundred times, a thousand, but for Gabe it was all the same suspended moment until Rob stirred.

He told Rob what had happened, little of which the young man seemed to comprehend. He kept saying he had dreamed of Selena, a nightmare, really, and squeezed his eyes to keep the words from seeping in. Even when Matty arrived he cried out against his visions.

Angus touched Gabe's arm. "The shaman?" he asked.

"He's dead. I...I killed him."

For the first time it hit him. He'd taken a life, killed with brute force and a blank mind. Telling the officer had been easy, with the detached authority of reports and badges to keep his thoughts in order. Now, seeing his words reflected in Angus' eyes, the deed was visceral.

"They called it self-defense," he whispered.

"Remember that, Gabe. And remember the bush is your mother."

"Mrs. Kamare?"

Commissioner Dawson stood in the doorway. Gabe didn't know whether to welcome his assistance, belated though it was, or shake him until his teeth fell out.

"A woman matching your daughter's description was airlifted to Darwin," he said. "We should have a photo faxed down in a few minutes. There's no signs of trauma but she's non-responsive. She's in a coma."

Matty swooned and the men helped her into a chair. Gabe smelled the commissioner's cologne, the starch in his uniform, and the kerosene odor of his freshly polished buttons. What did he know of the law, the universal laws that allowed one person to steal another's soul or a group to steal the future of a whole race?

His anger flared like the wildfires that burned so hot the trees exploded. Then it was gone. He watched as Charley's hands supported a grieving mother, as his eyes searched for some comfort he might offer.

The commissioner had done what he could within the limits of his world. He was helpless as the mending of body and soul was taken over by doctors and councilors and family and friends. His intimacy with life and death, corruption and justice was not an easy knowing and this event would add its weight to his brow.

Dawson's way used to be Gabe's. He also used to follow the rules of man, rules created in a foreign land and transplanted to red soils. When an officer brought the fax, he knew there was more to be done.

***

Dawson arranged for Matty to be airlifted to Darwin. No one was in any condition to drive and flying was the quickest way north. Gabe finally gave in to the pain and took a pill before they boarded. The drone of the engines was a lullaby that swept him through the night.

They arrived in the small hours of the morning. Under the fluorescent lights Selena's features were totemic, chiseled and cold. Matty's tears rained a tender shower as she touched her daughter's cheek. They sat and talked to her, and heaped up their love around her body.

Red is sacred, Rachel's voice whispered. The color of blood and land.

Gabe thought of the opal in his belly. Its candy-apple colors were Selena's laughter and its sparkle her life. He felt a hitch, nothing more than a hiccup, really, and the opal was in his mouth. When he moved to wipe it clean, Matty stopped him.

"All the body's fluids are sacred," she said.

Gabe nodded. He pressed the opal against that cold, cold forehead then against Selena's heart. The stone grew cool then hot, and he moved it to her belly. Eventually her features softened and her skin darkened.

Matty's hand covered his. As their sweat and hopes and tears mingled, they held the opal to her crown. There was a single intake of breath, a long exhalation, and the young woman opened her eyes.

"See?" she whispered. "You just had to try."

<hr>

The house in Alice Springs was full once more. Both children were home, Ramie was camped out in the back yard, and Gabe bunked with Angus. Tidiness was a distant dream but Matty seemed happy with the trade. What mother wouldn't be?

"What did your girlfriend say?" Selena winked as they gathered for lunch.

"Manners!" Matty fussed.

"It's OK. I think Selena has the right to ask a few questions after what she went through." Gabe passed a pitcher of water around the table. "Chance is my *former* girlfriend and she's going back to Jamaica for a time. I might visit over the holidays. At any rate, she's doing well."

"As are you," Matty said. "Before you seemed...I don't know. Lost. I suppose that's what had me worried. You seemed so desperate."

"But we came back alive," Rob said around his sandwich. "And I've a great story to tell my customers! Since that article came out, the phone hasn't stopped ringing. Between the garage and keeping my schedule up to date, poor Ramie's worn thin!"

"Might ask for a raise?" Ramie nodded. "Get that surveillance system I've been wanting for the station."

They finished the meal and left Gabe to pack. The coroner had released Ian's body, so he would escort the remains back to Cairns. They were lucky to have found him, along with the shaman's body, thanks to a dog trained to find disaster victims. Hopefully the McCabes would find closure with the funeral.

He wondered how the row house would feel when he got home. Even in his memory it seemed empty, desiccated by the salt air and flattened by ocean breezes. His family drew him back but the place, he knew, would be different. He stood in front of the bay window and gazed at the ranges peeking over the neighbor's roof.

"I didn't mean to say you're responsible for any of this," Matty said. "Rob makes his own decisions."

"I know, Matty. I'm glad he came back to you."

"And I'm glad you found your friend. His parents will thank you, as well. It's better to bury a child than to go on not knowing." She pressed her lips into a smile. "What I meant to say earlier...you're different now. You've found your friend but you seem to have found something more."

"I haven't found it yet. But at least now I'm looking."

After loading everything in the truck, including a cooler stuffed with Matty's ready-made meals, Gabe hesitated. Angus caught him in a long hug.

"You'll come back to us," he said. "Next month, yes?"

"Yes. My mother and uncle might already be dead but I can probably find Andy." He wiped away tears before they could fall.

"Do I get a kiss?" Selena laughed as he stuttered. "Don't worry. I don't mean anything by it. You're such a tease!"

Then it was Rob's turn. Gabe held him gently, mindful of his wounds.

"We're like the two Dreamtime brothers," Rob said, sniffing against his own tears. "We went all around our country and had a big adventure. When you come back, we'll do it again."

"Something a little less dangerous," Matty said.

Gabe smiled. Then there was nothing more to say, just a flutter of good-byes like the flush of pigeons. As he backed down the driveway, he looked once more at the people on the lawn. They held him with their eyes and their energy flowed into his heart. No matter what the outcome of his search, Gabe knew he had an Aboriginal family after all.

Thank you for reading

The Family Made of Dust

Please support this book by leaving a review on your favorite site.

Please enjoy this free sample from
Laine Cunningham's second novel,

A sensual noir thriller
Recipient of one arts grant.
Supported by two arts residency programs.

CHAPTER 1

THE DAY MARGO DIED was like any other. Being only nineteen years old, she thought no more of death than any other student attending the fall semester's classes at her small West Virginia college. Instead she hustled every morning through Wheeling's dark streets to the bakery in the historic district. For a few hours she mixed eggs and flour and water then made pastries for the early rush. Later she drove a few miles up the mountain to West Liberty State College where she vacillated between music composition and statistics. The afternoon released her to studying and chores before hungry commuters pulled her from bed again.

Her apartment was part of a house that had been subdivided into four separate units. Although the sink was cracked and the tub a distressing shade of yellow, the kitchen window overlooked a bend in the Ohio River. The pleasure boats that lingered during these still-warm days were too noisy for her liking. In winter, though, she perched on the counter for hours watching barges thrum past. As the chill crept through the glass she thought that her brother was like the speed boats, hyped up on drugs and constantly turning back to founder in the turbulence of his wake. How a big brother could have grown to prefer the company of methheads and crack addicts was a problem neither the rules of mathematics nor the cadence of music could solve or soothe.

When her father, a vibrant soul who had swept his daughter into dizzying rumbas every Saturday, succumbed to Alzheimer's, Margo realized that having people in her life didn't always mean she was in theirs. Perhaps that was why she didn't mind her elderly neighbor stopping by several times a week. He disguised his loneliness by borrowing sugar or passing along magazines he'd just finished. She always made time for him even if it equaled only a few of those minutes lost with her own family, seeing in him some reflection of what her father might have become and a bit of what her brother wouldn't live long enough to be. So when the knock came that Friday evening at 5:45, or perhaps it was already a quarter past six, she didn't check the peephole to see who was there.

QUINN LAWRENCE STOOD ON THE LANDING. If anyone had seen him enter the building, they might have noticed the trim of his waist or how his shoulders had been broadened by weight training. They might have noticed his crown of salt-and-pepper hair or the cologne that eddied in faint sandalwood and citrus trails around him. If they had seen him stop at Margo's door, they might even have thought he was her father. But no one had seen him. He held the knob ever so lightly to feel it turn. The moment the latch was fully retracted, he shoved the door hard. He heard the tiny cry as he pushed inside.

"Margo," he panted, "I need your help. It's my daughter. She's threatening to kill herself. You have to call her! You have to talk her out of it! Where's your phone?"

As he looked around, he closed the door behind him and slid the bolt quietly into place. He'd met the young woman at the bakery months ago, and had spoken perhaps a dozen times whenever business brought him back to Wheeling. Right now, he knew, she was trying to remember if she'd mentioned where she lived. Fear was rapidly gaining the upper hand. He had to keep her off balance.

"But I don't know your daughter," she stammered as he led her to the phone.

"You're her age and you're both in college. She'll relate to you. Please!"

He looked into her eyes. In that moment, he allowed her beauty—an overwhelming, staggering beauty so incandescent that light streamed from her skin, her fingers, every strand of her hair—to touch him. Tears filled his eyes. Just as he'd planned, Margo read those tears as a father's concern for his daughter. "I'll pay for the call," he said. "I know it's long-distance."

She waved off his concern and punched in the numbers he recited. Months of planning had culminated in this moment. Quinn breathed in the scent of her hairspray, the pale of her skin, the kaleidoscope of her apartment. Then he whipped her into a headlock that prevented anything more than a muffled scream. She struggled more vigorously than a woman her size normally could but he knocked her feet out from under her. After a quick loop of duct tape hooked her wrists, he buckled a ball gag into her mouth, bound her ankles, and pulled short lengths of rope from his pocket.

There was no need to hurry. He never hurried, not even when adrenaline sent blood rushing through his ears like a lake that had burst its dam. Somewhere under the roar his heart kept time and wound the movements of his hands and legs as surely as cogs. He counted the turns of each bond, the loops of each knot, the tugs and half-tugs that tightened every strand. He was careful to apply the ropes in a way that was visually pleasing. He would mark her with bruises later, eventually marking her heavily, and he wanted the imprint left by the ropes to enhance the artistry of his work. Above it all would be her face, pristine and unmarked, glowing with the radiance achieved only at the moment of death.

She accepted his hands quietly, perhaps hoping he would spare her life. He smoothed her hair back and swept away tears with his thumb. Her sepia hair had been cut into jagged layers, her ears were pierced only once, and her body was almost adolescent in structure. But her eyes were the dun of an autumn moon. With them, she saw the light of this world as surely as did he. Therein lay her true beauty. Quinn constantly sifted the crowds for them, women who paused to admire the buds on an avenue's trees or who turned their heads to smell the oranges piled outside a corner market. Only women who treasured the beauty of the world became his. Only they received his gift.

He retrieved his gym bag from the landing. With the steady confidence of experience, he installed a telescoping chin-up bar in the archway to the kitchen. Margo would hang there later allowing him access to every inch of her flesh. First, though, he cleared the dinette table of placemats and plants then unpacked his instruments. Canes of varying lengths and diameters, light clubs of wood and beef bones, even a scrap of rabbit fur filled the table. The canes were an assortment of birch branches, fiberglass rods and walking sticks wrapped with handles of silk. Margo's silks, including the cord that would end her life, were navy. When the equipment had served its purpose, it would be burned. Although destroying the equipment ensured that nothing traced back to him forensically, he did it for the women. He made every one of the tools himself. The rods were sized to one frame, the clubs weighted for a precise impact. Using them on someone else would cheapen the experience.

Hunting in West Virginia's Northern Panhandle region gave Quinn the chance to find women he would never meet in his old-money Philadelphia neighborhood. Since Wheeling's tourists and transplants wanted culture with their mountain lifestyle, the region's many arts fairs, music festivals and historic events made hunting easy. He used these different venues for his initial approach. If the woman was young, he produced pictures of children he claimed as his own even though he'd bought the snapshots from a photographer's studio in Boston. Slightly older women were approached as associates while women his own age were treated with the casual ease his generation had championed in the era of free love.

All were dosed with charm; all sensed his absolute adoration. Women, he knew, were works of art. Their shapes were pleasing to the eye, their voices soothed the newborn, and their flesh was a soft rapture. But few let light permeate their souls. That was how Quinn chose his partners...that's what he called them, these women to whom he ministered—partners. Margo was his most recent, younger than average but still deserving of his gift. Dawn would touch the mountain's peaks before she received that climax. Tonight would be the last night of her life, and it would be exquisite.

PRIYA CONLIN-KUMAR LOOKED OUT THE WINDOW at the mountain ridges stalking the hotel. The last few days like the days preceding all her transfers had been a rush of paperwork, garbled orders and a dearth of information.

Although she'd been with the FBI for nearly fifteen years, she'd never really learned how to manipulate the bureaucracy. She was also far from what people expected in a special agent. Barely five-four with a single thick braid that fell past her ribcage, she often took people off guard when they saw her shield. Add to that a mix of Indian and American heritages, a honey-brown face and dark lotus eyes, and she knew exactly why her duties had taken on a new dimension after 9/11. While a small percentage of the population could tell South Asians from Hispanic and Arabic people, paranoia couldn't sort curry from Creole.

Priya had known the FBI was preparing to rotate her assignment again and had been mentally preparing to leave the few friends she'd found during her two brief years in Chicago. Although every police department from small cities to major metropolitan areas now hosted an agent tasked with homeland security, she hadn't expected to be rotated to West Virginia. Although Wheeling's digs included the FBI's fingerprinting lab, the place was more of an outpost than a field office. Priya's assignment to investigate potential money laundering through North Carolina's national banking institutions promised to be as dusty as the boxes of papers she'd have to study.

Before her transfer had officially come through, the body of an Ohio resident had been dumped just inside West Virginia's state line. The victim was one of dozens who'd gone missing from in and around the Panhandle in recent years. While the number of missing persons was higher than average, until corpses started to surface, the police hadn't been able to open any murder investigations. The break they'd been waiting for had finally come. Although the body was badly decomposed, the woman had been identified as a thirty-two-year-old history buff who gave tours at a museum in nearby St. Clairsville,

Ohio. When a college student was found beaten and strangled in her own apartment two days later, the Bureau was asked to investigate whether Wheeling had a serial killer.

Priya had been hustled off with only a few hours' notice. Now, after the sun had dropped behind the ridge and brought a premature dusk, she looked over the tumble of houses and highways that was her new home. Nothing, it seemed, ran in a straight line. There were only funhouse slopes, spasmodic roads and the constant press of trees bearing down, always down. Only the Ohio River, visible as a strip of waxy skin, had any sense of purpose. As the light continued to fade, a thick fog billowed down the slopes like the milk churned in the Hindu creation story.

The universe, it claimed, had once been a vast ocean of milk. Then a gigantic *Naga,* or serpent, had wrapped itself around a mountain. As the snake spun and the mountain turned, the cosmos had become a churn. The milk separated into the different parts of the material world including a poisonous blue haze. The god Shiva swallowed the mist to save the newborn creation. Shiva wasn't on the Alleghenies and Priya didn't see any giant snakes, yet the fog grew as if whipped by a churn. Great waves of mist boiled around the restaurant across from the hotel. Cars honked as the mist clotted around the stoplights and street lamps snapped on. A rumble grew as a poisonous blue haze rose toward Priya's floor.

She couldn't help but step back. When she did, the mist disappeared. The soft scent of cream gave way to the hotel's bland odor. Only the slow traffic on the street hinted that the mist had been real, and the cars picked up speed so quickly Priya doubted they had ever slowed. *Jet lag,* she thought, even though she knew the explanation was poor. The flight hadn't been long enough to make her miss a meal let alone much sleep. She shook off the odd vision. Her supervisor was waiting to brief her. Since he'd been working the bank case for so long, he would keep that on his desk for now and let her ramp up on the murders. She would attend the task force meeting the next morning, so she hoped her boss could tip her off about any political landmines that might be scattered around town.

She rummaged through her overnight bag hoping her clothes weren't too wrinkled. The moving company even now was packing her household, so it would be a week or two before her things caught up with her. With sudden transfers inherent to her job, she viewed the Bureau like an oversexed boyfriend—it always came on at the worst time and if it finished first, there wasn't much to do except sigh and roll over. At least with the Bureau she didn't have to shower afterward. Occasionally she tumbled with bad guys but most arrests were handled by local officials. The FBI just offered support—manpower, labs and specialists, the occasional profiler. They rarely got their hands dirty and focused much of their time on financial fraud and other crimes heavy with paperwork.

Assignments like these killings had drawn her to law enforcement. Violence had been Priya's companion since before her birth. Her mother had been gang-raped during her parent's second honeymoon in India. The daughter conceived that night had been an eternal reminder of one terrible hour. Although Priya never sought any logical explanation for that type of behavior, she'd heard plenty of theories. She didn't buy a speck of the feminist prattle that claimed all men would rape given the opportunity.

Nor did she swing to the misogynistic opposite and think that domineering women turned their sons into monsters. Sadistic killers had been around long before Jack the Ripper. People frightened by mutilated victims conjured up vampires, werewolves and witches, allowing the real monsters to slide away under the chaos. Profiling had taught her that these ghouls were horribly human. She supposed she could have become angry and blamed the world for the acts of a few barbaric men. But she hadn't, in part due to her mother's straightforward attitude.

That hadn't stopped Priya from turning those feelings inside, though. Her zeal for taking down sexual predators at times felt as frantic as if she'd integrated some blue haze, some poisonous corruption, during her own creation. She knew it wasn't true, of course. Yet deep inside her was a throb as faint and threatening as an enemy drum sounding across the battlefield.

You've just finished reading the first chapter from

BELOVED

A sensual noir thriller

About the Author

After Laine Cunningham's first novel won two national awards, she enjoyed a ten-year relationship with a leading literary agent. Jack Scovil of Scovil Galen Ghosh worked with Norman Mailer's literary estate and Carl Sagan, Morris West, and Arthur C. Clark. He represented two additional novels from Laine before his death in 2012.

Laine's latest is *The Tipping Time,* the first in a five-book historical soft fantasy, which follows a Puritan woman's coming of age. Her struggle against the oppressive social structure reveals how wealth, power and politics influenced even groups founded on religious beliefs. This work was supported by a six-week residency at The Rensing Center and is represented by a new agent.

All Laine's novels interweave social, cultural, historical, political and spiritual movements that have occurred within different groups and at different time periods. These elements are intended to engage modern readers in discussions of how similar forces have changed or are changing the contemporary world...and what might lie in our own future.

The end result hopefully engages not just debate but action. When individuals recognize how large issues build over time from multiple small steps, many of which were taken up by individuals just like them, they recognize that everyone can foment change through their choices and their decisions.

Laine's second novel, *Beloved,* blends in the Hindu mythology that helps the main character face her past. She is the product of a gang-rape that occurred when her parents renewed their wedding vows in India; the storyline unfortunately resonated with the horrific gang-rapes that made headline news after the novel was released. This work was supported by a residency at the Vermont Studio Center and was shortlisted for three national awards.

Laine's third novel is *Reparation.* Aidan Little Boy, a Lakota Sioux man, must stop the leader of a Native American-style peyote church before he enacts the largest mass murder ever to take place on US soil. *Reparation* has been compared to Terence Malick's *The New World* for its integration of historic facts with a contemporary plot. The work was shortlisted for three national awards.

Laine's tenure in publishing spans twenty years and encompasses ghostwriting and pitching for other authors. That expansive experience fuels her efforts to reverse engineer the publishing industry. Her first step is *Writing While Female or Black or Gay: Diverse Voices in Publishing.* The book is available in print and electronic editions.

Visit the author's website at:
www.LaineCunningham.com

Visit the author's Patreon page at:
www.Patreon.com/LaineCunningham